Once Chosen

BOOKS BY BLAKE PIERCE

ADELE SHARP MYSTERY SERIES

LEFT TO DIE (Book #1)

LEFT TO RUN (Book #2)

LEFT TO HIDE (Book #3)

THE AU PAIR SERIES

ALMOST GONE (Book#1)

ALMOST LOST (Book #2)

ALMOST DEAD (Book #3)

ZOE PRIME MYSTERY SERIES

FACE OF DEATH (Book#1)

FACE OF MURDER (Book #2)

FACE OF FEAR (Book #3)

A JESSIE HUNT PSYCHOLOGICAL SUSPENSE SERIES

THE PERFECT WIFE (Book #1)

THE PERFECT BLOCK (Book #2)

THE PERFECT HOUSE (Book #3)

THE PERFECT SMILE (Book #4)

THE PERFECT LIE (Book #5)

THE PERFECT LOOK (Book #6)

THE PERFECT AFFAIR (Book #7)

CHLOE FINE PSYCHOLOGICAL SUSPENSE SERIES

NEXT DOOR (Book #1)

A NEIGHBOR'S LIE (Book #2)

CUL DE SAC (Book #3)

SILENT NEIGHBOR (Book #4)
HOMECOMING (Book #5)
TINTED WINDOWS (Book #6)

KATE WISE MYSTERY SERIES

IF SHE KNEW (Book #1)
IF SHE SAW (Book #2)
IF SHE RAN (Book #3)
IF SHE HID (Book #4)
IF SHE FLED (Book #5)
IF SHE FEARED (Book #6)
IF SHE HEARD (Book #7)

THE MAKING OF RILEY PAIGE SERIES

WATCHING (Book #1)
WAITING (Book #2)
LURING (Book #3)
TAKING (Book #4)
STALKING (Book #5)
KILLING (Book #6)

RILEY PAIGE MYSTERY SERIES

ONCE GONE (Book #1)
ONCE TAKEN (Book #2)
ONCE CRAVED (Book #3)
ONCE LURED (Book #4)
ONCE HUNTED (Book #5)
ONCE PINED (Book #6)
ONCE FORSAKEN (Book #7)
ONCE COLD (Book #8)
ONCE STALKED (Book #9)
ONCE LOST (Book #10)
ONCE BURIED (Book #11)
ONCE BOUND (Book #12)
ONCE TRAPPED (Book #13)

ONCE DORMANT (Book #14)
ONCE SHUNNED (Book #15)
ONCE MISSED (Book #16)
ONCE CHOSEN (Book #17)

MACKENZIE WHITE MYSTERY SERIES
BEFORE HE KILLS (Book #1)
BEFORE HE SEES (Book #2)
BEFORE HE COVETS (Book #3)
BEFORE HE TAKES (Book #4)
BEFORE HE NEEDS (Book #5)
BEFORE HE FEELS (Book #6)
BEFORE HE SINS (Book #7)
BEFORE HE HUNTS (Book #8)
BEFORE HE PREYS (Book #9)
BEFORE HE LONGS (Book #10)
BEFORE HE LAPSES (Book #11)
BEFORE HE ENVIES (Book #12)
BEFORE HE STALKS (Book #13)
BEFORE HE HARMS (Book #14)

AVERY BLACK MYSTERY SERIES
CAUSE TO KILL (Book #1)
CAUSE TO RUN (Book #2)
CAUSE TO HIDE (Book #3)
CAUSE TO FEAR (Book #4)
CAUSE TO SAVE (Book #5)
CAUSE TO DREAD (Book #6)

KERI LOCKE MYSTERY SERIES
A TRACE OF DEATH (Book #1)
A TRACE OF MUDER (Book #2)
A TRACE OF VICE (Book #3)
A TRACE OF CRIME (Book #4)
A TRACE OF HOPE (Book #5)

Once Chosen

(A Riley Paige Mystery—Book 17)

Blake Pierce

Blake Pierce

Blake Pierce is the USA Today bestselling author of the RILEY PAGE mystery series, which includes seventeen books. Blake Pierce is also the author of the MACKENZIE WHITE mystery series, comprising thirteen books (and counting); of the AVERY BLACK mystery series, comprising six books; of the KERI LOCKE mystery series, comprising five books; of the MAKING OF RILEY PAIGE mystery series, comprising six books; of the KATE WISE mystery series, comprising seven books; of the CHLOE FINE psychological suspense mystery, comprising six books; of the JESSE HUNT psychological suspense thriller series, comprising seven books (and counting); of the AU PAIR psychological suspense thriller series, comprising two books (and counting); of the ZOE PRIME mystery series, comprising two books (and counting); and of the new ADELE SHARP mystery series.

ONCE GONE (a Riley Paige Mystery—Book #1), BEFORE HE KILLS (A Mackenzie White Mystery—Book 1), CAUSE TO KILL (An Avery Black Mystery—Book 1), A TRACE OF DEATH (A Keri Locke Mystery—Book 1), and WATCHING (The Making of Riley Paige—Book 1) are each available as a free download on Amazon!

An avid reader and lifelong fan of the mystery and thriller genres, Blake loves to hear from you, so please feel free to visit www.blakepierceauthor.com to learn more and stay in touch.

Table of Contents

Prologue

Sheriff Emory Wightman held the big flashlight steady while two of his cops continued digging into the soft earth. The long, narrow hole was getting pretty deep now.

Officer Tyrone Baldry paused and climbed out of the excavation. Leaning on his shovel, he wiped his forehead with his dirty sleeve.

"Hey, Sheriff," Baldry said, "care to take over for one of us for a little while?"

"We could use a little breather," Officer Newt Holland echoed, still scraping at the earth at the bottom of the pit.

Wightman scoffed. "Somebody's got to hold the light."

Both of the cops grunted sarcastically.

But indeed, the little clearing in the woods had grown dark while they worked. Wightman considered stopping everything until they could bring in proper lighting. But if there was anything in this grave-shaped hole, he wanted to know it now.

There had been nothing at all here the last time.

He felt a flash of déjà vu as he glanced into the surrounding darkness. It had been on a cool fall night just like this, almost a year ago. They'd come out here on a sinister tip, looking for a missing person—a young woman named Allison Hillis, who had vanished a few nights earlier on Halloween. An anonymous note had directed them to dig here, where freshly turned earth had looked like it might actually be a grave. But when they had removed all the soft dirt, they had found nothing.

Now, nearly a year later, the woman was still missing, and no body had ever been found. A newly delivered note had led them here again. And again, loose earth had made it appear that something—or someone—could be buried in this place.

And again, this was beginning to seem like a cruel hoax, dragging the police out here for the same fool's errand.

I'd like to get my hands on that prankster.

Maybe I'd even press charges.

Staring down into the pit, Baldry asked, "How much deeper do you want us to go?"

That's a good question, Wightman thought.

How deep did they need to dig before they could feel confident that this late-night errand was an act of futility? That it was again based on a prank.

"Just keep digging," Wightman replied. "I guess it's getting tight down there. You can take it in turns."

Holland started shoveling again, while Baldry just stood on the edge of the hole. Glancing into the surrounding darkness, Baldry said with a smirk, "Sheriff, I hope you're keeping an eye out for the Goatman."

Wightman growled under his breath.

It wasn't a very funny joke, given how those anonymous messages had mentioned the old legend, both then and now. The vicious Goatman was just a regional tale, of course, but when Wightman had been a kid, it had seemed scary enough to keep him awake nights.

He was about to call an end to the digging when he heard a shaky voice from within the excavation.

"Sheriff," Holland said. "Bring the light closer."

Wightman and Baldry leaned over the edge of the hole.

Holland was brushing loose dirt aside with his hand, uncovering something.

Baldry's voice sounded frightened now.

"Oh, Jesus. I've got a really bad feeling about this."

Wightman held his hand out to shine the light directly where Holland was working.

"It looks like black cloth," Holland said.

As Holland cleared more dirt away, they could see white paint on the black background—white stripes that looked like ribs. The cloth was part of a Halloween costume.

The missing woman had been wearing exactly that sort of costume when she'd disappeared last year on Halloween—a skeleton costume, black with white bones painted on it.

"Oh, no," Holland said. "Oh, Christ, no."

He kept scraping the dirt away with his hands. He hesitated when he uncovered the skull mask.

"Lift it," Wightman said, knowing all too well what they'd find behind it.

Holland lifted the mask, then let out a cry as he scrambled backward away from the sight.

It was another skull—a real one. Desiccated flesh clung to the bones, and there were mangy tufts of raggedy hair on the scalp.

The truth flooded over Sheriff Wightman like a tidal wave.

Allison Hillis was no longer a missing person.

She was a dead one.

Baldry retreated away from the edge of the hole, whimpering with horror.

Wightman stared down at the skull with his mouth hanging open.

"What do we do now, Sheriff?" Holland asked in a hushed voice.

For a moment, Wightman had no idea what to say.

What does this mean? he wondered.

Why had the anonymous tipster led them here on some pointless errand last year, only to bring them out here again to find an actual corpse?

And why had Allison Hillis been murdered to begin with?

Wightman remembered what the cryptic note had said in cut-out letters...

THE GOATMAN IS STILL HUNGRY

Whatever else it might mean, Wightman felt sure of one thing.

This was obviously a murder, and there are going to be more.

Holland repeated his question. "What do we do now?"

Wightman took a long, deep breath.

"We're going to call the FBI," he said.

Chapter One

Rounding up her daughters for breakfast seemed to be an impossible task for Riley this morning. After arguing over who was taking too long in the bathroom, April and Jilly kept popping in and out of each other's room to chatter about nothing in particular. When they finally came downstairs, they even started playing games in the family room until Riley dragged them out.

Have I got more than two girls? she almost wondered.

"Come on, let's eat," Riley kept saying. "You're going to miss the bus to school. And I'm not going to drive you this morning."

Finally she managed to herd both girls into the kitchen, where their Guatemalan housekeeper, Gabriela, had a delicious breakfast ready as usual. As soon as they sat down at the table, Jilly asked a question.

"Mom, can I have forty dollars?"

"What do you need it for, honey?" Riley asked.

"I need to rent a zombie costume," Jilly said.

For a moment Riley wondered, *Zombie costume?*

Then she remembered—Halloween was just a couple of days off.

"You don't *need* a zombie costume," Riley said.

Sixteen-year-old April poked her younger sister and said gleefully, "I *told* you she wouldn't let you have it."

A whine rose in Jilly's voice as she said, "But I need a costume to go trick-or-treating!"

"You're too old to go trick-or-treating," Riley said.

"I'm fourteen!" Jilly said.

"Exactly what I mean," Riley said, taking a bite of her breakfast.

"This isn't fair," Jilly said. "I've never been trick-or-treating in my life. I'll definitely be too old *next* year. This will be my last chance."

Riley felt a pang of surprised sympathy. "You've *never* been trick-or-treating?"

Jilly shrugged and said plaintively, "When would I have had the chance to do anything like that?"

April added, "You know she's telling the truth, Mom."

Indeed, Riley was sure of it. It had just never occurred to her before.

Jilly had only recently become part of the family. Last October Jilly had still been in a social services home in Phoenix, and before that she had spent her childhood in the care of an abusive father. Riley had finalized her adoption in July and gotten her settled into a more normal life, but she knew that Jilly had missed out on a lot of ordinary activities—including trick-or-treating, apparently.

She asked Jilly, "Who will you go trick-or-treating with?"

Jilly shrugged again. "I dunno. Can't I go by myself?"

Riley shuddered a little at the very idea.

"Absolutely not," she said. "It can be dangerous for kids to go trick-or-treating on their own. You need to go with somebody older. Maybe April will take you."

April's eyes widened with alarm.

"I'm not taking Jilly anywhere!" she said. "I've got a party to go to!"

"What party?" Riley asked.

"At Scarlet Gray's house," April said. "I'm sure I told you about it."

"And I'm sure you didn't," Riley said. "Anyway, you're not going to any party. You're still grounded."

April rolled her eyes. "God, am I going to be grounded for the rest of my life?"

"Just until Thanksgiving," Riley said. "That's what we agreed to."

"Oh, that's just great," April said, poking at her breakfast with her fork. "I'm grounded *and* I have to go out with my kid sister trick-or-treating. It doesn't even make sense."

"It doesn't have to make sense," Riley said sternly. "I make the rules here."

Riley glimpsed Gabriela nodding at her with sage approval. The stout, no-nonsense housekeeper had taught her to say "I make the rules" once when Riley had gotten too wishy-washy with the kids. Gabriela often seemed to be as much a parent to April and Jilly as Riley herself could ever be, and Riley was deeply grateful to have her around.

"All right," Riley told Jilly, "you can have the money for your zombie costume. But we'll still have to work out the details before you go anywhere."

Jilly seemed to be perfectly happy now, and April seemed to be perfectly miserable. But at least the matter was settled. As they finished their breakfasts in silence, Riley found herself thinking that Thanksgiving was coming up fairly soon and her strong-minded older daughter would no longer be grounded.

What April had done was deadly serious. When Riley had bought a pistol for April to train with during the summer, she'd felt confident that her older daughter would handle the weapon responsibly.

But it had turned out that Riley's confidence was misplaced. Not only had April failed to make sure the gun wasn't loaded after bringing it home from the firing range, she'd dropped the weapon while trying to put it away in Riley's bedroom. Riley could still hear the accidental gunshot echoing through the house. And she'd only recently repaired the holes the bullet had made in two walls.

We were lucky nobody got hurt—or killed, Riley thought. That grateful refrain had been running through her mind every day since then.

She wondered if she should have grounded April for longer—all the way through Christmas and New Year's, maybe. But it was too late to change her mind now. She had to be consistent. Gabriela had helped her learn that lesson too.

Riley watched through the window as the girls finally left the house and headed for their bus stop. She found herself thinking about how much she hated Halloween. She wasn't sure exactly why.

Maybe she was troubled by the idea of kids going around pretending to be monsters. After years of working as a BAU agent, Riley had long since learned that the world was much too full of genuine monsters as it was. It struck her as kind of perverse to go inventing make-believe monsters just for fun.

Of course, kids also dressed up as more positive characters on Halloween—superheroes, for instance. But Riley didn't like that either. As far as she was concerned, the world needed *real* heroes, not phony ones in capes and tights. More than that, there should be more people who could be heroic about the little things in life.

Like getting their kids off to school, Riley thought with a smile as April and Jilly rounded a corner and disappeared from sight.

The truth was, being a crime fighter never struck Riley as an especially heroic activity. The everyday tasks of being a parent often seemed much more formidable than ridding the world of actual human monsters. Those villains could often be caught, their rampages put to an end. The job of parenting went on and on, requiring an unflagging effort.

Not that I'm much of a hero at parenting.

But at least she'd managed to navigate her kids through breakfast, out of the house, and on their way to school this morning. With no immediate assignment at BAU, she'd taken the day off.

And she had some special plans.

She smiled at the thought of it...

A rendezvous.

It seemed odd to think of it that way, particularly considering who she was going to meet for lunch. But an important relationship in her life had taken an unexpected turn recently. And now...

We're dating, I guess.

She was glad to have the rest of the morning to get herself ready.

When she went to her bedroom, she picked up her cell phone from the nightstand and saw that she'd received a voicemail message.

When she played the message, she heard a familiar gruff, husky voice.

"Hey, Agent Paige. Van Roff here. Call me."

She felt a sharp tingle of anticipation and worry. From the sound of the caller's tone, he didn't have good news.

The question was, did Riley want to hear what he had to say right now?

She sat down on her bed looking at the cell phone, trying to decide whether to call him back or not.

Van Roff was a technical analyst in the Seattle FBI field office. Riley had worked with the brilliant, overweight computer geek in the past, sometimes on less than legitimate tasks. She'd learned that Van was willing to bend and even break the rules on her behalf from time to time, especially if the problem at hand interested him.

Now was one of those times.

Riley sighed as she remembered how her then-partner Jenn Roston had disappeared during the last case they'd worked on together, leaving behind a cryptic note that hadn't explained anything at all:

Riley,
I'm sorry.
Jenn

It had come as a terrible shock, and it had gotten Riley into trouble with her boss, Brent Meredith, who rightly suspected that Riley knew more about Jenn's disappearance than she was willing to say.

Jenn had confided to Riley that she had been raised by a sinister foster parent who called herself "Aunt Cora," and who trained children under her care to become master criminals in her own criminal organization.

Jenn had escaped Aunt Cora's clutches long enough to become a brilliant and promising young BAU agent. Riley had been the only person whom Jenn had told about her sinister past. Riley also knew that Jenn still heard from Aunt Cora from time to time, and that the diabolical woman kept trying to draw Jenn back under her control.

After the case was solved, Riley had received a package containing Jenn's badge and gun and another cryptic note:

I tried.

Riley had known right then that Jenn had fallen back into Aunt Cora's dark world. Riley had dutifully delivered Jenn's badge and the weapon to Brent Meredith, who had already received a letter of resignation from her.

As far as Meredith was concerned, Jenn's relationship with the BAU was over. He had no interest in finding out where she'd gone or why. He didn't care if he ever heard her name again.

But Riley couldn't help hoping maybe she could reach Jenn somehow—maybe even help her get away from Aunt Cora for good.

Certain that Van Roff would find this puzzle interesting enough to attract his considerable skills, Riley had turned to him for help.

And now he was responding.

I'd better find out what he's got to say, she thought.

She punched in Van Roff's number, and he picked up immediately.

"I wish I had better news for you, Agent Paige," Van said.

"Have you been able to find out anything at all?" Riley asked.

"Not a thing," Van said. "You mentioned that maybe I could find something in her personnel records—something about that foster home where she'd grown up."

Riley nodded and said, "Jenn told me there was something about that in her records. The foster home closed up long ago, but even so I thought maybe any information at all about it would give you a clue—"

Van interrupted her, "Agent Paige, there aren't any *records.* Somebody hacked into the FBI files and deleted Roston's personnel files. It's like she never worked for the FBI at all."

Riley felt light-headed with shock.

Van continued, "Somebody doesn't want anybody to know what happened to her. And whoever that 'somebody' is, they've got great hacking skills. Zapping away FBI records is quite a feat."

"What about that address I gave you?"

Riley meant the return address on the package that had contained the gun and the badge—an address in Dallas, Texas.

"Phony," Van said. "There's no such place. And I used every trick in the book to find out if she might still be in Dallas. I can't find her there or anywhere else. It's like she's disappeared off the face of the earth."

Riley felt thoroughly defeated now.

"OK," she said. "Thanks, Van."

"Don't mention it."

Then something else occurred to Riley.

"Van, I've told you a few things about Jenn that nobody else is supposed to know. I hope you'll—"

Van interrupted in an incongruously cheerful voice.

"Well, it's so nice of you to call, Agent Paige. I really appreciate it. I like staying in touch, keeping tabs on each other."

Riley smiled a little. She knew this was Van Roff's way of saying this whole conversation had never taken place as far as he was concerned. She could always trust Van to keep a secret.

"Goodbye, Van," she said. "And thanks again."

She ended the call and slouched miserably on the edge of her bed. She remembered something Van had said just now.

"Somebody doesn't want anybody to know what happened to her."

Riley had a hunch that that "somebody" was Jenn herself. Jenn didn't want to be found. And if Van Roff couldn't find her, nobody else possibly could.

She's gone, Riley thought. *Jenn's really gone.*

Riley struggled for a moment with feelings of sadness, anger, and betrayal.

There's nothing I can do about it, she told herself. *Jenn made her own choice. It's not up to me.*

Meanwhile, Riley did have something pleasant to look forward to. She got up from the bed and went to her closet to find something nice to wear for her lunch date. As she looked through her clothes, she smiled at the irony of wanting to look her best today.

How odd, she thought.

Here she was, trying to impress a guy who already knew her better than almost anyone ever had.

Chapter Two

They had ordered their sandwiches, and now Riley sat quietly, looking across the table at her partner.

Bill gazed back at her.

She smiled, and he smiled back.

Neither of them said anything, but it didn't seem to matter.

At least we're not uncomfortable, she thought.

In fact, things seemed very comfortable between them right now.

They were seated in a cozy, private booth in Hannigan's Public House. After years and years of grabbing something to eat on the run, eating in grubby cafés and fast food joints, or ordering pizza in motel rooms, this was quite a change for the two of them—or at least the two of them together. She couldn't remember their ever having lunch together in a place like this.

Certainly not when we weren't working on a case.

She was pleased that Bill had chosen Hannigan's for their...

Date, she reminded herself. *We're actually on a date.*

In fact, this seemed almost quaintly like a traditional date. Bill had even picked her up at home and driven her here. She was also pleased to see that, like herself, he had gone to some effort to look nice. He was wearing a stylish button-front cardigan, and his still-thick dark hair was flawlessly combed.

A handsome man, she thought.

Bill had never been a golden boy like her ex-husband, Ryan. He had never been smooth and pleasant-looking like her ex-boyfriend Blaine. His features were those of a man who had lived a hard life, but he also had the look of a man who had accomplished things.

Riley knew that life had left its mark on her too. Her own dark hair, like his, showed touches of gray. Shadows around her eyes, like his, reflected ugly encounters over the years. Although men in general seemed attracted to her, she knew that most of them had no idea what Special Agent Riley Paige was actually like.

Finally, Bill reached across the table and took her hand.

He asked, "Riley, is this going to work?"

Riley laughed just a little.

"I don't know, Bill," she said. "I'm not even sure what 'this' is. Are you?"

Bill laughed as well.

"Well, I've got some ideas, but I can't say I know where 'this' is going."

"Me neither," Riley said.

They fell silent again. Riley knew only one thing for sure. "This" was something romantic—a change in both of their lives, from being best friends to something more than friends.

Riley remembered the sweet, warm moment when "this" had started. It had been a couple of weeks ago, just after they'd finished their last case. They'd been sitting together in Riley's hotel room, and both of them had felt troubled and sad. Riley was bitter and hurt about Jenn's unexplained disappearance. Bill was frightened that Riley had almost been killed by a psychopathic madman.

It hadn't been the first time either Riley or Bill had narrowly escaped death, of course. In fact, it probably hadn't even been the hundredth time. But this time, Bill had seemed to be taking it especially hard.

Finally he had told her exactly why.

"I don't think I could stand to ever lose you. I don't think I could live without you."

Then, without saying another word, they had kissed.

After that, they'd quietly held each other for a while without saying a word.

That was really all there had been to it—a single kiss and a long, silent embrace. They'd both been too battered up from their final struggle with the killer to take things any further.

Riley's smile broadened at the memory.

She saw that Bill's smile widened as well.

Is he remembering that moment too?

She wouldn't be the least bit surprised. Like an old married couple, they often found themselves thinking the same things and finishing each other's sentences.

She and Bill had worked together as partners for years. They had rescued each other from monsters, helped each other through terrible times, and even survived her one clumsy drunken pass at him back when he'd still been married.

They had also seen each other through divorces and, in his case, the almost complete loss of contact with his boys when his ex-wife moved away and remarried. He knew a lot about her off and on struggles with Ryan, her divorce, and even her recent affair with Blaine.

They just hadn't seen much of each other since finishing that case. They hadn't had a chance to talk things out.

Bill had visited Riley at home a couple of times, and they'd talked on the phone a little. They hadn't mentioned that kiss to each other, but of course Riley had been thinking about it the whole time, and she knew perfectly well that Bill had too.

And now here they were, on their first real date.

And like all first dates, it was fraught with all kinds of possibilities and uncertainties.

Finally Bill shook his head. "Riley, we've got some things we really need to work out."

Riley realized she was holding her breath, unsure what to expect next.

"I care about you very much," Bill said. "I know you feel the same way about me. And I guess it's... only natural that our relationship would... you know..."

Riley squeezed his hand and chuckled.

"Evolve?" she said.

Bill chuckled as well.

"Yeah, evolve. It's natural, and it's... wonderful. And I don't want it to stop."

"I feel the same way," Riley said.

Bill shrugged and shifted in his seat.

"But I worry about... things," he said. "I mean, what will this mean to us as partners?"

Riley sighed. "I wish I knew. Of course the FBI doesn't have any hard and fast rules against... well, fraternization."

"I know," Bill said. "But that doesn't mean it's going to be easy. I can think of one guy who'll want to make it as hard for us as possible."

Riley nodded. She knew exactly who Bill meant. Rules or no rules, Special Agent in Charge Carl Walder didn't approve of agents having romantic relationships while working together. In fact, Walder was pretty much disapproving of anything agents did unless it made Walder look good.

Worse, Walder harbored a violent dislike for Riley. He'd suspended and even fired her more than once. If Riley and Bill got openly involved, Walder would doubtless find all kinds of new ways to make their lives miserable. At the very least by refusing to let them work together, but possibly even relocating one of them to some distant field office.

Bill squinted thoughtfully for a moment.

He said, "I also worry about—well, stepping into your life, I guess, and bringing all my baggage with me. I mean, you've got a family, and I've got..."

Bill shook his head sadly.

"Well, you know what I've got," he said. "Too much of nothing. For one thing, I've been through a nasty divorce."

"So have I," Riley said.

"Yeah, but your ex-spouse didn't take your kids away."

With a deep pang of sympathy, Riley squeezed his hand again.

"I know," she said. "I'm sorry."

Bill's voice thickened a little.

"But you—well, you've got a family. Do you want me to be part of it?"

Riley was about to say of course she did, but Bill interrupted.

"Please, don't answer that question without really thinking about it."

Riley nodded sadly.

It really was a good question, and it reminded Riley of how rich and loving her home life really was. She had two daughters and a live-in housekeeper who was much, much more than just an employee.

Is there room for anybody else? she wondered.

She'd tried to make room for two different men, and it hadn't worked out well. When her ex-husband, Ryan, had come around pleading for another chance with her, she'd let him move in for a while. He'd let her and the girls down, of course, which had left her feeling stupid for expecting anything else from him. The last time he'd come back, she'd sent him away quite firmly.

At first, everything had seemed to go smoothly with Blaine Hildreth, the charming restaurateur Riley had been involved with. He was a single parent with one daughter April's age. At one point Blaine had even planned to expand his own house so they could all move in together.

But the dangers of Riley's life had finally proven to be more than Blaine could deal with.

Even though she couldn't really blame him, Riley was still stinging inwardly from his final rejection. It had left her feeling bitter and disappointed. She'd found herself wondering—would there ever be a man in her life she could fully trust and depend on?

But at this moment, that seemed like a stupid question.

She was looking at that very man right now.

She and Bill had had their quarrels and disagreements and ups and downs. But in the end, they'd always been able to trust each other with their very lives.

What more could I want from a relationship? she wondered.

Maybe that was exactly the problem.

She stammered, trying to find words for what she wanted to say.

"Bill, I . . . I feel like you know me better than anybody else ever has. Better than Ryan, even. You've seen me at my worst as well as at my best. You've pulled me out of the depths of . . . well, drunkenness, despair, self-pity, failure . . ."

Bill shook his head. "Well, you've gotten me through worse than that."

Riley shuddered a little. She knew all too well what Bill was talking about.

And she remembered vividly the text message Bill had sent her when she'd been working on a case last spring . . .

Been sitting here with a gun in my mouth.

Jenn had covered for Riley's absence so she could rush to Bill's apartment in Quantico. If she hadn't gotten there to help him, she still didn't know what might have happened.

But she wouldn't have had it any other way. Their friendship had been built as much on awful moments like those as on the good ones.

Riley paused for a moment.

Then she said, "I guess what I'm thinking is . . . maybe we're already a perfect couple. Maybe we've been a perfect couple all these years. God knows I feel a lot closer to you than I ever did to Ryan."

"And I feel closer to you than I ever did to Maggie," Bill said.

Riley took a deep breath and said, "So maybe ... we shouldn't go changing things between us. Maybe we should leave things just the way they are."

Bill smiled a bit sadly.

He said, "Riley, things have changed between us already. They've changed whether we want them to or not."

Riley knew exactly what he meant.

That kiss.

It had changed everything between them.

Just then, the server appeared with their sandwiches.

And Riley's cell phone rang

She thought about ignoring the call until she saw that it was from her boss, team leader Brent Meredith.

When she took the call, Meredith got right to the point as usual.

"Are you ready to take on another case, Agent Paige?"

Riley smiled at the question. Saying "no" to Brent Meredith wasn't really an option.

"I'm ready," she said.

"Good. Then come to my office immediately."

Meredith ended the call without another word.

Bill said, "I take it that was Meredith being his usual talkative self."

Riley laughed and said, "Yeah, he does ramble on sometimes. Anyway, I guess we're needed—and right away, as usual. Sorry about lunch."

"We can eat on the way," Bill said. "Nothing unusual about that."

Bill waved to the server to ask him to bag up their sandwiches and bring the check.

He said, "How many times do you think we've been called away from lunch?"

Riley chuckled and said, "I guess some things never change."

Bill paid the check, and they took their lunch with them as they headed out to his car.

Chapter Three

As they walked into the BAU building, Bill kept thinking about Riley's words when their attempt at a date had come to such an abrupt end.

"I guess some things never change."

Bill too found it almost comical the way a phone call had interrupted their conversation ... just as it had so many times before.

They had hastily packed up their meal and scrambled into the car ... just as they had so many times before.

Now they were hurrying through a familiar hallway on their way to Meredith's office. Today was all too typical of the unpredictability he and Riley had lived with for many years.

And yet, he knew that the kiss they'd shared a couple of weeks ago had changed everything between them. He was aware that Riley knew that too. He really wished they'd had more time to talk things through. Sooner or later, they were going to have to come to terms with those changes.

Sooner would be better.

But now was obviously not the time. They had said almost nothing to each other during the drive here. They'd been busy eating the sandwiches they'd taken out from the restaurant, but Bill also sensed that Riley's mind was already on the case that was coming up.

Mine should be too, he thought.

He wondered—was this the way things were always going to be? Would their work together always matter more than anything else that might happen between them?

As they walked into Meredith's office, the daunting division chief with black, angular features looked up from his desk. His expression was stern as he remarked, "I hadn't expected to see you, Agent Jeffreys."

Bill's eyes widened with surprise. He saw that Riley was startled as well.

Bill stammered as he and Riley sat down in front of Meredith's desk, "Well—Agent Paige said that... you'd called about a new case and I just assumed..."

Meredith shrugged. "Yeah, I've got a new case for *her.* I hadn't asked for you. In fact, you won't be needed for this one. Agent Paige will be working with a different partner."

Bill felt a surge of alarm.

What's going on here? he wondered.

Had Meredith already figured out that something was going on between him and Riley, before they'd even clarified it themselves? He couldn't imagine how, but Meredith had an almost uncanny way of knowing what was going on with agents under his authority.

Is he going to split us up? Bill wondered.

"I'm just trying to break in a new agent," Meredith explained. "A rookie. I figured it would be a good experience for her to work with Agent Paige, at least this time around."

A new agent? Bill thought

He was relieved that the arrangement didn't sound permanent, but he also felt a new anxiety kick in. Their work with their last two rookies had turned out badly. He couldn't bear to even think about Lucy Vargas, who had won their admiration but had died in a terrible shootout. The most recent new recruit, Jenn Roston, had brought other problems along with her.

Bill couldn't deny that Jenn had been a brilliant and promising young agent, but she hadn't even settled in completely when her complicated past had apparently caught up with her. Worse, Bill was well aware that Riley knew some secrets about Jenn's past that she hadn't felt free to tell him—secrets that had led to Jenn's mysterious disappearance a couple of weeks ago.

He'd been trying to convince himself that whatever secrets Riley and Jenn had shared weren't any of his business. But he couldn't quite do it. He remembered how, just a little while ago, both he and Riley admitted they felt closer to each other than they ever had to each other's spouses. There was nothing unusual about that, really. It was the way things were supposed to be between partners.

But Jenn had bonded considerably more with Riley than she had with him, leaving him feeling excluded—and even somewhat bitter. For almost two decades, Bill and Riley had kept few secrets, and had seldom if ever lied to each other outright. Which was why Bill hadn't liked Riley harboring secrets about Jenn.

Was the same thing going to happen again with a new young recruit?

I hope not, he thought. Things were complicated enough between him and Riley as it was.

Meredith glanced at his watch. "I called for her to join us. She should be here any minute now. Her name is Ann Marie Esmer, and she's as green as they come. She just got out of the academy, and she's never worked on an active case."

Riley tilted her head curiously.

"You mean she's never worked in law enforcement at all?" Riley said.

"That's right," Meredith said.

"Then how did she get into the academy in the first place?" Riley asked.

Meredith steepled his fingers, swiveled slightly in his chair, and smiled.

"The same way you did, Agent Paige. She solved a case as a civilian, fresh out of college. The FBI took notice, and the requirement for prior law enforcement work was waived for her. Like you, she did well in the summer intern program, and then at the academy. So we're giving her a chance in the BAU. I'm told she has a lot of promise."

Bill felt a tingle of curiosity. He knew that Riley had been recruited by her mentor, Jake Crivaro, after solving a spate of serial killings at the college where she'd been a student. Like the new agent, Riley had excelled in the intern program and at the academy.

Is this kid going to be a young version of Riley? he wondered.

He wasn't sure he liked the idea. He was somewhat dismayed at the idea of Riley working with another partner at all, but especially with such a green one.

Meredith leaned back in his chair.

"I've got my reasons for sending the kid out on this case," he said. "For one thing, it shouldn't be too challenging for her. A woman disappeared in Winneway, Maryland, about a year ago. Her body was finally found last night. The sheriff thinks the killer is going to strike again, so he wants our help."

Bill squinted skeptically and asked, "Has the sheriff got anything more than a hunch about this?"

Riley added, "Why does he think the killer is going to go serial?"

Meredith said, "It's got something to do with a couple of anonymous messages the police received. I'm hazy on the details, but it sounds to me like the cops there are the victims of some sort of prank, nothing the BAU is needed for, certainly not a serial. You'll probably go there and turn right around and come back again. But at least it will give the kid a chance to put her toe in the water."

Bill found himself bristling with resentment in spite of himself.

Keep it to yourself, he thought. He knew it was never a good idea to contradict Meredith's orders. Even so, he blurted, "Sir, I can't say I'm happy to be sidelined on this case."

Meredith leaned across the desk and peered at him sternly.

"Agent Jeffreys, what part of what I just said didn't you understand?"

Bill cringed at what was surely coming next.

Why couldn't I just keep my mouth shut?

Meredith growled, "I don't think this is a real case, Agent Jeffreys. I sure as hell don't think it's a serial killer, just some dumb prank. Sending you would be overkill. Besides, I think it would be best for this kid to work with another woman one on one. That's final."

"I understand, sir," Bill said.

"Do you?" Meredith said. He glanced back and forth between Riley and Bill and knitted his brow and drummed his fingers on his desk.

He said, "I've got an odd feeling something's going on here."

Bill felt his face flush. He glanced and saw that Riley, too, was blushing.

Once again, Meredith's instincts were proving to be uncanny. He clearly sensed that something had changed between Bill and Riley—although surely he hadn't figured out exactly what that something was.

"Is there something the two of you aren't telling me?" Meredith said.

"No, sir," Riley murmured.

"Everything's fine, sir," Bill added meekly.

As soon as the words were out, Bill thought, *Did Riley and I just lie to Brent Meredith?*

In fact, they had, and Bill knew it. Not only had they lied, but they'd lied badly, with faces glowing like traffic lights.

Meredith's suspicions must be rising by the second.

Bill glanced at Riley and could tell they were both thinking the same thing.

Should we just tell him?

Riley shook her head slightly. Bill silently agreed.

At last, Meredith leaned back in his chair.

He said, "Jeffreys, if you're all that anxious to be involved, just hang around the building today. If there turns out to be anything to this case, you'll be able to do some research."

Bill felt stung.

Research?

Meredith surely knew how he was making Bill feel by offering him a lowly support task.

He's sure not happy with Riley and me, Bill thought.

Meredith glanced at his watch and said, "Well, young Agent Esmer ought to be here any minute. I hear she's prompt, I guess we'll find out. Agent Paige, I want you to take our new agent and drive a company car over to Winneway as soon as she gets here. It's just about an hour away. My guess is you'll get to the bottom of this prank and get back here tomorrow morning. Leave the murder itself to the local cops. It's not our job."

Just then the office door opened, and a young woman stepped inside.

"I hope I'm not late," she said.

From his first glimpse of Agent Ann Marie Esmer, Bill had the feeling that Riley and the girl probably weren't going to be a good mix—even for just a day's work debunking some sort of prank. He couldn't help feel just a bit relieved.

At least I don't have to worry about a competing partner, he thought.

Chapter Four

Riley kept glancing at her new partner as she pulled onto the interstate to drive away from Quantico. Somehow, she couldn't quite believe that Ann Marie Esmer was really an FBI recruit.

At the moment, the young woman was on her cell phone talking to the county sheriff over in Maryland, telling him that she and Riley were on their way, and she was making arrangements for them to meet him. Ann Marie was jotting down notes as she talked.

Her voice, ultra-polite and ultra-cheerful, sounded to Riley like some kind of high-end receptionist, or maybe a voiceover artist on a TV commercial. She was good-looking—actually remarkably pretty, with sparkling blue eyes and blond hair pulled back and arranged so perfectly that it must have been styled at a beauty shop.

Ann Marie had shown up at Meredith's office properly prepared with a go-bag, as had both Riley and Bill. She'd obviously understood the need to be ready to pick up and go at the slightest notice. She was also dressed sensibly enough, in a simple slack suit with practical shoes. Even so, the clothes looked new and expensive, and she was wearing a patterned scarf with colors that seemed to be coordinated with her hair and skin tone.

She ended the call and said to Riley in her pleasant, chirping voice, "Sheriff Wightman is super glad we're on our way. He wants to meet us at the crime scene when we arrive in Winneway. The county medical examiner is there right now examining the body."

Ann Marie tapped her pencil against her notepad and added, "I've got the directions written down. Don't worry, we won't get lost. I'm great with directions! I'll get us there even if GPS doesn't."

I don't doubt it, Riley thought.

This girl seemed to be nothing if not efficient and alert.

Then Ann Marie said, "Wow. I still can't believe it. I feel like pinching myself to see if I'm awake. I mean, here I am on my first case after weeks of pushing papers around at Quantico, and I'm partnering with Special Agent Riley Paige!"

She let out a musical laugh and added, "If only the guys at the academy could see me now. People there talk about you all the time at the academy, you know. We studied your cases a lot. I hope you don't mind my saying so but . . . Agent Paige, you are *so* brilliant! Everybody knows it, too."

Riley knew she ought to feel flattered. Instead, she felt vaguely uneasy.

She said to Ann Marie, "So how are things back at the academy?"

"Well, pretty exciting for a kid like me. But boring to you, I'm sure."

Ann Marie then began to chatter about her session at the academy—not so much about the curriculum or her studies, but stories and gossip about her fellow cadets, including accounts of her dating life during that time.

She was right about one thing, Riley thought, stifling a sigh. *It's boring to me.*

Riley found it strange to hear FBI Academy life described in such social terms. Ann Marie had obviously had a great time there and had made all kinds of friends. Riley's own experience many years back hadn't been nearly so . . .

Well, cozy.

Like Ann Marie, Riley had been admitted to the FBI honors program and then to the academy partly on the basis of a strong recommendation from a respected agent. That meant each of them had already demonstrated unusual skills, but it also meant that they had been placed over other qualified applicants. Even worse, Riley had been pulled out of both programs to help her mentor with critical cases. When she'd returned to her classes, she had felt isolated and even disliked. She only had one close friend during her academy days—her roommate, Frankie Dow.

So it struck Riley as odd that this girl's experience there had been so different from her own.

People find her likeable, I guess.

Riley wasn't feeling exactly the same way about her new partner, though she had to admit that probably wasn't all Ann Marie's fault. It wasn't just the girl's hyper-cheerful personality that rubbed her the wrong way. The truth was, Riley felt more than a little blindsided by this arrangement. She couldn't help thinking that partnering with anyone except Bill never worked out well. Their most recent junior partners hadn't gone on to the great FBI careers they'd seemed destined for.

Riley had grown really fond of Lucy Vargas, and that had ended badly. Her death had actually driven Bill to the brink of suicide.

Jenn Roston had been harder to get used to, but Riley and Jenn had come to trust each other with some pretty dark personal secrets.

Riley realized that she still wasn't used to Jenn being gone.

Before long, she knew she'd turn around and expect to see Jenn instead of Ann Marie—expect Jenn's strong, African-American features instead of this young woman's pale, perfect complexion; expect Jenn's confident, no-nonsense voice instead of all this birdlike chatter.

Riley stifled a sigh as Ann Marie continued to spout academy gossip.

This isn't going to be easy, she thought.

She remembered something Meredith had said.

"My guess is you'll get to the bottom of this prank and drive back here tomorrow morning."

Riley certainly hoped so.

Although today would be better.

She also hoped this partnership was going to be a one-time thing.

As Riley drove over the Woodrow Wilson Memorial Bridge across the Potomac into Maryland, she felt as though the short trip was turning out to be a lot longer than it really should be. Ann Marie had stopped chattering, but she'd turned the car radio to a station that played pop music that was much too upbeat and silly for Riley's taste. She was actually glad when the GPS system occasionally interrupted the sound with updates on their route.

Meanwhile, Riley's thoughts kept wandering back to the meeting with Meredith. She cringed as she remembered how Meredith had glowered at her and Bill.

"Is there something the two of you aren't telling me?" he'd asked.

Of course, Meredith had been right to be suspicious. After all, his summons had interrupted her first real date with Bill—a development that Meredith had every right to feel curious about.

And then we lied to him.

Both of us.

She shuddered to think of what the consequences of those lies might eventually be. Worse, she felt guilty toward Meredith. He'd been an intelligent, fair, and respectful superior for years.

We should have told him the truth, Riley thought.

But what was the truth, exactly?

That was the real problem. She didn't know what they could have told Meredith. They hadn't had time to sort it all out themselves.

Riley and Bill still didn't know which way things were going in their relationship. When they had a better idea, maybe they could sit down with Meredith and put the record straight. She hoped Meredith would be sympathetic, and perhaps even happy for them.

After about an hour on the road, they drove on into Winneway, an expensive, history-conscious town. Riley found it incongruous to see that some of the big, handsome homes dating back to Colonial times were now flanked by swimming pools. Riley always found herself ill at ease in such affluent surroundings. People she'd encountered in settings like that tended to treat FBI more like servants than like the professionals they had to be.

Finally the GPS informed them that they had arrived at Ironwood Park, a vast expanse of well-groomed grass spotted with wooded areas. Colorful autumn leaves made the scene especially pleasant.

Riley turned onto a curving road that led into the park. Soon they came upon a group of parked vehicles—a couple of police cars, a county sheriff's car, and a medical examiner's van.

"This must be the place!" Ann Marie chirped cheerfully.

Riley winced at Ann Marie's lighthearted tone. She felt like warning the girl that they were about to walk into a deadly serious situation—a crime scene with the body of a murder victim still present.

But Riley thought better of saying anything.

Just let it be a surprise, she thought, suppressing a wry smile.

She knew that Ann Marie had seen cadavers during her training at the academy, but only in clinical, forensic settings. Seeing a corpse at a crime scene was a whole different experience—one that Riley felt pretty sure this apparent social butterfly wasn't ready for. If the rookie couldn't handle it, Riley would be perfectly happy to send her back to Quantico right away.

They got out of the car and headed toward a wooded patch that was surrounded by barriers and police tape. Riley was pleased to see that a tent-like structure had been set up among the trees, obviously to protect the crime site. A couple of cops stood sentinel just outside the tent.

The cops here know what they're doing, she thought.

Riley and Ann Marie held up their badges for the sentinels to see, then ducked under the tape and stepped inside the tent. The interior was lit by a couple of standing lights, and it was occupied by several men, a large hole with a pile of dirt on one side, and a covered corpse stretched out on the ground.

Riley introduced herself and her junior agent to county sheriff Emory Wightman and chief medical examiner Mark Tyler, who had been waiting for them to arrive. The sheriff was a solid-looking man in his forties, although a pot belly indicated that he wasn't really keeping in shape. The thin and wiry medical examiner appeared a bit older. Both men looked slightly uneasy for a moment, then Wightman finally asked, "I guess you want to inspect the body."

"It's not a pretty sight," Tyler commented.

Wightman added, "I guess agents like you have seen plenty of—"

"Of course," Riley interrupted him.

She suspected that the sheriff's reluctance was because the agents were both women, but even if her young partner might not be up to this, Riley had seen enough corpses not to be daunted by the prospect.

Without further hesitation, Wightman gently lifted away the cover.

The sight of the corpse actually took Riley aback.

The body was in a considerable state of decay from having been buried for a long time. But the truly weird thing was that the victim was wearing a skeleton costume, a black outfit with white bones printed on it.

A skeleton dressed up as a skeleton, she thought.

Before Riley could ask any questions, she heard Ann Marie let out a sharp cry—but it wasn't a cry of distress.

"Oh, this is so *interesting!*"

Ann Marie's face expressed pleased fascination as she crouched down beside the corpse. She leaned forward for a closer look at the remnants of flesh and hair clinging to the bare human skull.

This was hardly the reaction Riley had expected from this youngster. She wondered what other surprises her new partner might have in store for her.

Chapter Five

Riley watched with surprise as Ann Marie peered closely and curiously at the corpse's face. The victim's head was little more than a skull with dried skin stretched over it. It eerily mirrored the costume skull mask that had been removed and was lying next to the face.

The young woman seemed to be perfectly used to this kind of thing. In fact, she took out her cell phone and began to snap pictures of the corpse.

Riley was startled.

Doesn't she know the guys here have surely taken pictures already? she wondered.

Riley almost told her to stop, but she didn't want to criticize Ann Marie right here at the crime scene with others watching.

Ann Marie glanced up at the medical examiner and said, "I've not seen many bodies in this condition before. Most of the ones I've looked at have been . . . well, fresher, you might say. This one's a 'she,' isn't it?"

Tyler just nodded in response.

Ann Marie asked, "How long do you figure she's been buried here?"

Tyler shrugged slightly. "It's hard to say," he told her. "Quite a few months, I guess. I'll have a better idea when I've done an autopsy."

Sheriff Wightman added, "We're quite sure that the victim's name was Allison Hillis. She disappeared a little more than a year ago. M.E. Tyler will do some tests to make sure this is the same person. But Allison was wearing exactly this sort of costume when she went missing."

Ann Marie shook her head and clicked her tongue.

"How sad that she wound up like this," she said. "But I guess a year's a long time to be missing. Hard to expect somebody to turn up alive after all that time."

Then peering again at the face she said, "But there's something unusual about her. She wasn't just buried a year ago, right after she'd been killed, was she?"

Tyler tilted his head with interest.

"Why do you say that?" he said.

Snapping a tight close-up of the corpse's hand, Ann Marie said, "Well, I haven't seen many exhumed corpses, and the ones I *have* seen came out of coffins, not straight out of the ground. And even the ones that were buried recently looked a lot more decayed than this one—pretty much falling apart, really. The skin's more intact on this one—almost like she was mummified or something."

"Yeah, I noticed that too," Tyler said with interest.

"I've got a little theory, if you don't mind hearing it," Ann Marie said.

The middle-aged M.E. stroked his mustache and smiled—just a bit flirtatiously, Riley thought.

"I'd love to hear it," Tyler said.

Ann Marie said, "Well, I think she might have been frozen for a while before she was buried here. That might help explain the unusual preservation."

Pointing to a spot on the neck, she added, "See these cracks? Those look like freezing damage to me, not regular decay."

Tyler's eyes widened with surprise.

"Well, I'll be damned," he said. "I was thinking pretty much the same thing."

A bit flirtatiously herself, Ann Marie winked at him and said, "Well, you know what they say about great minds."

Tyler's squinted with curiosity. He said to her, "Hey, did you say that your last name was Esmer?"

Ann Marie nodded.

Tyler asked, "You wouldn't happen to be related to Sebastian Esmer over in Georgetown?"

Ann Marie's eyes twinkled.

"He's my dad," she said with a note of pride.

Tyler's smile broadened.

"I should have figured," he said with a shake of the head. "The apple doesn't fall too far from the tree."

"I don't guess it does," Ann Marie said.

Riley felt thoroughly dumbfounded now.

Who is this kid? she wondered.

And why the hell does she know so much about corpses?

But now was no time to sort all that out. She still knew next to nothing about what they were doing here.

She asked the sheriff and the M.E., "Has the cause of death been determined?"

"Maybe so," Sheriff Wightman said.

"We're not sure, though," Tyler added. "I'll show you what I mean."

Riley crouched down beside the corpse with Ann Marie and Tyler.

Tyler pointed to a place where the costume had been cut open to reveal a wound in the center of the chest.

"She was stabbed through the sternum, straight into the heart," Tyler said. "But not with a knife."

He fingered the peculiar wound and added, "As you can see, the opening is almost perfectly round. It looks as if she were stabbed by something extremely sharp and cylindrical."

A stake through the heart? Riley wondered as Ann Marie snapped a picture of the wound.

Surely not.

But the details about this murder were striking her as weirder and weirder by the moment.

Riley asked, "Do you have any theories about what kind of weapon might have been used?"

Before Tyler could reply, Ann Marie gasped.

"Oh, look at these!" she said.

Now she was taking pictures of indented marks on the costume.

Tyler said, "Yeah, those are really strange. Take a look right here."

He showed Riley and Ann Marie another place where he had cut the costume for a better look at the flesh underneath, revealing that the marks in the costume were matched by indentations in the body. It looked like the body had been beaten by something heavy and hammer-like.

What really struck Riley was the odd shape of the marks. They were sort of pear-shaped, but they were divided down the middle. Before Riley could bring to mind exactly what they looked like, Ann Marie spoke up.

"They look like hoof prints."

"I think so too," Tyler said.

Riley felt a prickle of confusion.

She asked, "Are you saying the woman was trampled to death by some hoofed animal?"

Tyler shook his head. "I'm not saying anything just yet. I'm still not sure whether these marks were made before or after the wound to the chest. But my hunch is that they came afterwards, after the victim had already been stabbed."

Ann Marie gasped again.

She said, "And the object that stabbed her was shaped like a hoofed animal's horn! Like she was gored to death!"

"It does look that way," Tyler said.

Riley could hardly believe what she was hearing.

She said, "Are you saying this woman was gored in the chest by some large animal, which then trampled her body?"

Tyler shrugged, "Like I said, I'm not saying anything yet."

Ann Marie asked, "But what kind of animal might we be talking about?"

Sheriff Wightman spoke up with a surprising note of certainty.

"A goat."

Riley looked at the sheriff. She could tell from his expression that he meant exactly what he said.

"I don't understand," Riley said.

"Neither do I," Wightman said. "But I am pretty sure more people are going to wind up dead if we don't put a stop to this. I'll show you why when we get back to the station. I'm hoping you BAU folks can help make sense of it. Do you think it's OK for Tyler and his team to take the body to the morgue now?"

"That would be fine," Riley said.

As Tyler began giving orders to his team, Wightman said to Riley and Ann Marie, "Let's go on over to the station. You can follow me in your car. When we get there, I can brief you completely on what we know so far."

Riley's mind boggled as she and Ann Marie headed back toward their vehicle. This murder was much stranger than she'd imagined—too strange, she suspected, for the local police to deal with on their own.

Was this going to turn out to be a true FBI case after all?

As she and her new partner got into the car and started driving behind the sheriff's vehicle, something else nagged at Riley—Ann Marie's behavior at the crime scene. It seemed as though the chief M.E. knew more about Ann Marie than Riley did. That situation had to change.

Riley tried to think of a tactful way to broach the subject. But her impatience got the best of her, and she blurted aloud to Ann Marie, "Who *are* you, anyway?"

Chapter Six

As those four blurted words seemed to echo through the car, Riley immediately regretted the bluntness of her question.

"Who are *you, anyway?"*

Ann Marie was staring back at her with surprise. The rookie seemed to be trying to understand what Riley was asking.

Riley stammered, "What I mean is . . . you know so much about dead bodies . . . and the M.E. seems to know who you are . . . and . . ."

Ann Marie broke into a smile.

"Oh, that," she said. "Yeah, I guess I must have seemed kind of, you know, ghoulish back there. Well, I grew up around corpses."

"Huh?" Riley said.

"My dad runs a mortuary in Georgetown—Esmer's Funeral Home."

Then she laughed and added, "It's a thriving business, believe me. Rich people die as much as everybody else. Who'd have thought it, huh? Anyway, Dad's got a really good professional reputation throughout this area, so even a lot of forensics guys know who he is. That's why the M.E. recognized my name."

Riley tried to keep her eye on the road and the car she was following. But she couldn't help glancing at Ann Marie, trying to imagine her as a child—maybe even a toddler—hanging around a funeral home. What kinds of things had this fresh-faced kid witnessed in her life so far? Had she maybe even watched as her father carried out embalmings? If so, how young had she been the first time?

As if in reply to Riley's unspoken questions, Ann Marie said, "I guess I know the business pretty much backwards and forwards. Which is why Dad's still not happy that I decided to go into law enforcement. 'There's no money in it,' he keeps telling me. What he really means is, he always wanted me to take over the family business someday."

Ann Marie shrugged and said, "Which I used to think would be fine with me—until I solved that murder case and got recruited into the FBI Honors Internship Program. Now I'm really hooked on *this* business."

Business? Riley thought.

She had never in all these years thought of what she did as a "business."

Now Riley's curiosity was growing. There seemed to be a whole lot about this kid she didn't know.

She asked, "Tell me about that case you solved."

Ann Marie let out a self-effacing laugh.

"Oh, it was nothing," she said. "It would bore you, I'm sure."

I doubt that, Riley thought.

But now was not the time to hear the story. The sheriff was pulling into the police station parking lot, so Riley followed and parked near where he did. She and Ann Marie got out of their car and walked with the sheriff to the station.

The station was a large, handsome colonial building. As they walked inside, Riley saw that the place was fully remodeled and modern-looking. Riley felt sure it was well equipped with the latest law enforcement technology. The people inside seemed focused on their work. It certainly appeared that Sheriff Wightman was running a competent force, not the primitive kind of local outfit Riley and Bill often had to deal with.

She found herself wondering if any FBI agents were needed here after all.

For one thing, she still had no idea why the sheriff thought they might be dealing with a serial killer, not just a one-time murderer.

As they walked by employees' desks, everybody seemed to look up and smile at Ann Marie, and she met their eyes and smiled back at them and waved slightly.

She's likeable, I guess, Riley thought.

To everybody but me, apparently.

What bugged Riley was that the girl seemed to *know* she was likeable—and pretty. She was clearly basking in all the attention she was getting from the people around her. It didn't strike Riley as an especially professional attitude for an aspiring BAU agent.

Riley and Ann Marie followed Sheriff Wightman into a large conference room, where a case folder lay on the table. They all sat down, and the sheriff opened the folder and browsed through its contents.

"I guess I'd better start at the beginning," he said. "Last year on Halloween night, a girl went missing—seventeen-year-old Allison Hillis."

Wightman pushed a picture of the smiling teenager across the table for Riley and Ann Marie to see. Although she made no comment, Riley couldn't help comparing it to the skull on the body that had been removed from the grave. Could that have been what became of this healthy-looking youngster?

She knew that it very well could be. Certain kinds of monsters liked to prey on the young and attractive.

Wightman continued, "She was last seen walking on her way to a party, dressed in a skeleton costume. Her family started calling around for her that night, and called us the next morning. A few more days went by with no sign of her, and of course her family panicked, and so did everybody else who knew her. Nobody thought of Allison as the kind of kid who might just run off. Of course, my people and I did everything we could to find her, to no avail."

Fingering a piece of paper, the sheriff added, "A week later, this note was dropped off at the station."

He laid the paper in front of Riley and Ann Marie. It was a message made out of cut-out print letters pasted onto a sheet of blank paper. It read:

LOOKING FOR THE GIRL DRESSED LIKE DEATH?
GOOD LUCK.
NOW THE GOATMAN WILL TAKE HIS TURN
SINGING THE GOAT SONG.

"You can imagine that really got our attention," Wightman said.

Riley nodded and said, "'Dressed like death'—that sure sounds like Allison's Halloween costume."

"Right," Wightman said. "Frankly, it also scared the hell of us. Because there was something else enclosed with the message."

He laid out another sheet of paper—a photocopy of a map with a small red rectangle drawn on it.

Wightman explained, "This is a map of Ironwood Park. And the marked spot shows the exact place where we were just a few minutes ago."

Wightman shuddered a bit at the memory.

"I took several of my guys out there, and we found a mound of dirt that looked just like a fresh grave. We expected the worst, naturally. We thought for sure we'd find Allison's body at the bottom of that grave. But we dug out all the dirt that had been shoveled into the hole—and nothing was there."

Wightman shrugged slightly.

He said, "Naturally, we thought it was a prank—a sick joke at police expense, and also the expense of poor Allison's family. With the girl still missing, some bastard must have thought it was cute to send us out digging up an empty hole."

Wightman let out a weary sigh.

"Well, almost a whole year has gone by," he said. "Every single day since then, we've been trying to find out where Allison disappeared to. Try as we might, we haven't come up with any answers. Then last night we got another note."

He pushed another piece of paper across the table—another message with cut-out, pasted letters:

STILL LOOKING FOR THE GIRL DRESSED LIKE DEATH?
EXPECT BETTER LUCK THIS TIME.
THE GOATMAN IS STILL HUNGRY.
HE WILL FEAST AND SING AGAIN
ON THE HALLOWED EVE

The sheriff showed them yet another piece of paper—a map just like the other one, with a red rectangle in the same spot.

"This came with the note," the sheriff said, tapping the map with his forefinger. "Well, naturally, we took this to be another cruel prank. I had half a mind to ignore it altogether. But I couldn't do that—not if there was even the slightest chance of finding Allison."

The sheriff leaned toward Riley and Ann Marie.

He said, "So a couple of my guys and I went out again late last night with flashlights and shovels. When we got to the spot, it wasn't freshly dug like before. It looked like maybe nobody had touched it for a long while, maybe since we'd filled the hole back up a year ago. But I had my guys dig there anyway."

"And that's when you found her," Riley said.

Wightman nodded. "Somebody must have buried her there sometime during the course of the year without anybody else noticing. I wish we'd thought to keep watch over the spot. But how could we have expected anything like that?"

"You had no reason to think it was anything but a prank," Riley agreed.

"But the whole thing was weird beyond my imagining," Wightman replied. "I knew I had missed some possibilities and I might miss more. So this morning I told my guys to hold the crime scene in place and called the BAU to ask for help. We haven't even worked out a timetable on just when was Allison actually killed, and how soon afterwards she was buried."

Ann Marie spoke up.

"Well, the M.E. agrees with me that the body was frozen for some period of time before it was buried."

Wightman commented, "So if the body was frozen, that really affects what he can tell us about when this victim died."

Ann Marie nodded and added, "Maybe he can get a better timetable when he conducts an autopsy. But I doubt that he'll ever be able to figure out exactly when she was killed. Maybe she died shortly after she disappeared. Or maybe it was quite a while after that. Maybe she was held captive for a while."

Riley felt weird hearing the girl talk like a forensics expert.

What other surprises does she have in store? she wondered.

Wightman sighed and said, "All I know is, I'm worried sick about whatever's going to happen next. The new note says the Goatman will 'feast and sing again on the hallowed eve.' Obviously, that means Halloween. Which is the day after tomorrow."

Riley's head was buzzing with questions. She said to the sheriff, "Do you have any idea what 'Goatman' refers to?"

The sheriff's lips twisted into a grimace.

"As a matter of fact, I do," he said. "The Goatman is a Maryland urban legend. According to the most common version, a mad scientist who was experimenting on goats accidentally turned himself into a hybrid creature—half man, half goat. He's said to roam the countryside, hungry for human blood."

The sheriff drummed his fingers on the table and added, "The Goatman legend actually isn't even indigenous to this part of Maryland. He's said to prowl near Beltsville along Fletchertown Road. But stories like this get around. I've heard of Goatman 'sightings' elsewhere in the state."

The whole thing was starting to make some weird, sick kind of sense to Riley. She thought back to the corpse at the crime scene.

She said, "The body was marked with hooved footprints, like those of a goat."

Ann Marie added, "And the fatal wound did look like it came from animal's horn. But goats are vegetarian, aren't they? And they're actually kind of cute."

"It's just a legend," Wightman grunted, "I don't assume any of us believe Allison was gored by a goat which then trampled her—much less that she was killed by some kind of half-man, half-goat. But whoever *did* kill her wanted things to look that way."

Riley nodded and said, "And he would love it if the public started to believe the Goatman was real—and 'hungry,' as the note says. Are these notes public knowledge?"

Wightman shook his head.

"The only people who know about them are me and the guys who did the digging. Even after we got the first one, I swore the guys to secrecy. Back then, I didn't want to give the bastard who sent the note the public attention he obviously wanted."

"That was a good call," Riley said. "Try to keep things that way. I assume that word has already gotten out that Allison Hillis was murdered. But we've got to keep the details secret for as long as we can. This whole 'Goatman' element could make the case a lot harder to solve if it takes hold with the public. Things could turn into a real circus."

Riley thought quietly for a moment, staring at both of the notes.

She felt sure of only one thing—that Wightman had been right to call in the BAU. They might or might not be dealing with a serial killer. But they were definitely dealing with a unique kind of psychopath.

Then Riley asked Wightman, "Does the phrase 'Goat Song' mean anything to you?"

Wightman shrugged. "Just part of the story, I guess. I've never heard about it, myself. But you know how it is with these urban legends. There are all kinds of variants and differences. Maybe the Goatman is supposed to sing in some versions."

Riley knew that he might be right. Even so, she felt a prickle of suspicion that the phrase had some kind of significance they'd better not overlook.

Wightman said, "What scares me right now is the reference to 'the hallowed eve.' Do you think the killer might try to abduct somebody else the night after tomorrow?"

"I don't know," Riley said. "And I don't want to start a panic by putting out some kind of warning just yet. If we hunker down and do our jobs, we might catch the killer before then."

"What do we do next?" Wightman asked.

Riley paused and thought for another moment. Then she asked, "Does Allison Hillis's family live here in Winneway?"

Sheriff Wightman nodded.

Riley said, "I'd like to pay them a visit and ask them some questions."

Wightman sighed and said, "Agent Paige, I don't know if that's a good idea right now."

"Why not?" Riley asked.

"As you can imagine, this has been an ordeal for Allison's parents ever since she first disappeared. They never stopped hoping their daughter would turn up alive and safe. I sent a couple of my people over to their house this morning to tell them about the body we'd found."

"How did they take it?" Riley asked.

"Allison's father, Brady, wasn't at home. He's in London on business. But my guys talked to her mother, Lauren. They told me she's in a deep state of denial. She keeps saying the body isn't her daughter, it must be somebody else dressed in the costume she was wearing that night."

Wightman shrugged again. "There's not a doubt in my mind that the body is Allison's. But I can't prove that yet. We could take Lauren to the morgue and see if she can identify the body—although I'm not sure she can, given the condition of the remains. I'd rather wait until Tyler can confirm the girl's identity with a DNA test. Then maybe Lauren will accept the truth. Meanwhile, I'd rather not bother her."

Riley squinted with thought.

She said, "Sheriff Wightman, I appreciate your concern. But I want to get moving as soon as possible, and as far as I'm concerned, my first order of business is to talk to the mother. I'd like to go over to their house right now."

Wightman nodded reluctantly.

"I'll call Lauren and tell her we're coming over," he said.

The moment he took out his cell phone, Riley's own phone rang. She saw that the call was from Bill. She almost answered right then and there, but she quickly decided she'd better find some place where she could talk to Bill more privately. She stepped out of the conference room into the empty hallway.

Bill's voice sounded agitated when she took the call.

"Riley, talk to me. I'm going crazy here. Meredith is keeping me at the BAU, and I'm supposed to be doing research, but I don't know where to start. Tell me what's going on."

Riley briefly filled Bill in. She went into a fair amount of detail as she retold Sheriff Wightman's account of all that had happened since Allison Hillis's disappearance, including the contents of the two messages. She also told him about the condition of the body.

"Frozen, huh?" Bill said. "It sounds like maybe I should track down large freezer units—the kind that get used in restaurants and grocery stores and such. Maybe someone in that area has bought something like that recently. I can check out local sales and purchases."

Riley agreed. It sounded like a long shot, but at least it was a place for Bill to get started.

"Anything else?" Bill said.

Riley thought for a moment. Something about those messages had been nagging at her.

She said, "Try to find out if there's any significance to the words 'goat song.' Maybe it's just part of the Goatman's urban legend. But I've got a feeling there's more to it than that."

"I'll get on it," Bill said.

Then a silence fell between them.

This is where we're supposed to end the call, she thought. But it seemed as though neither of them was quite ready to do that.

Finally Bill said what both of them were thinking.

"This is weird."

Riley smiled.

"Yeah, it really is," she said.

Bill said, "I really don't like being benched like this when you're out on a new case."

"I know, Bill," Riley said. "And I don't like working without you. But we may have to get used to quite a few changes now that..."

Her voice faded as she wondered, *Now that what?*

Things would surely be very different right now if Meredith hadn't called to interrupt her lunch date with Bill. Right now their whole relationship seemed to be made up of unanswered questions.

"We've got a lot to talk about," Riley said. "But now's not the time."

"I understand," Bill said. "Maybe later this evening."

"That would be good," Riley said.

Another silence fell.

This is getting to be ridiculous, Riley thought.

Finally she said, "We'll talk soon."

"Right," Bill said.

Then they ended the call. Riley stood staring at the phone for a moment, wishing Bill was here right now.

When she walked back into the conference room, she found Ann Marie chattering away while Sheriff Wightman listened. Riley quickly realized that Ann Marie was regaling the sheriff with stories about mortuary work. Sheriff Wightman seemed to be utterly fascinated.

Riley guessed that he was less intrigued by the stories themselves than by the pretty young woman who was telling them.

"We need to get going," Riley said to the pair.

The conversation ended, and Riley and her two colleagues headed out of the building.

Riley kept glancing at Ann Marie as the three of them walked toward their vehicles.

Everybody likes her, she thought again.

And she likes being likeable.

Riley had never thought of likeability as being a particularly useful trait in law enforcement.

She didn't think this partnership was going to work out very well.

Chapter Seven

The rookie agent's reaction to their surroundings told Riley something new about her young partner.

"Oh, what a nice neighborhood!" Ann Marie cooed. "It looks a lot like where I grew up!"

Riley was driving their car behind Sheriff Wightman's, following him into the area called Aurora Groves. Everything here looked expensive, like the rest of Winneway. It wasn't a gated community, but it was well-planned with curving streets designed to keep traffic low. There were ponds and meadows and gardens amidst the enormous lawns.

If Ann Marie was from a neighborhood like this, it indicated something specific to Riley.

Her family's kind of rich.

Of course, Riley wasn't really surprised. Ann Marie had struck her as well-off pretty much from the start.

As Riley continued to follow the sheriff, Ann Marie took out her cell phone and searched for information about the neighborhood, eagerly sharing her findings.

"Aurora Groves is a lot newer than the rest of Winneway. Look, you can see that some of the houses are still for sale. You can buy some of these places for just a little over five hundred thousand, even though others are closer to a million."

Ann Marie nodded with approval.

"This isn't the richest area around here. But I like houses like these a lot better than real mansions. Mansions always make me feel lonely. I'm glad I grew up in a more modest area like this."

More modest? Riley thought.

The area certainly didn't look "modest" to her. The houses were far too big for her taste, and she didn't even find them very attractive.

Many of the houses they'd seen in the rest of Winneway had been authentic and historical, even if they were cluttered by anachronistic features like swimming pools. These houses were pseudo-traditional, and Riley didn't like them. But apparently Ann Marie felt right at home in these surroundings.

At least she knows how to do online research, Riley told herself.

Not that what Ann Marie was finding out seemed particularly relevant to Riley right now.

When Sheriff Wightman pulled over and stopped in front of one home. Riley parked behind him. Like other houses on the street, this one had a broad porch, narrow shutters beside the wide windows, and lots of gables. Riley and Ann Marie followed the sheriff to the front door. When they rang the doorbell, they were met by a well-dressed, conventionally good-looking man about Riley's age.

Sheriff Wightman introduced him as Allison's uncle, Walker Danson.

The sheriff quickly added, "*State Senator* Walker Danson."

Wightman added the title as if he were speaking of royalty.

Danson shook hands with Riley and Ann Marie.

"I'm Lauren's brother," he said. "Her husband, Brady, is in London, so I've been here all morning, keeping her company. She's very shaken by this new development. I hope you're not going to upset her further."

He said it as if it were a command and not a request. Riley, of course, didn't reply. She doubted very much that this meeting was going to make Lauren Hillis feel better about things.

As Danson started to lead them into the house, he paused and said something to Riley and Ann Marie.

"I understand that you're with the BAU."

Riley nodded.

Danson tilted his head and asked, "Do you happen to know Carl Walder?"

Riley tried not to wince at the sound of the name.

"Yes," she said. "He's . . . Special Agent in Charge at the BAU."

"Yes, I know," Danson said.

Danson stood looking at them for a moment with an inscrutable expression.

Riley asked him, "Do you know him?"

"Indeed I do," Danson said.

Riley felt a chill at how he said that.

Without further comment, Danson led Riley and her two colleagues on into the house. Riley felt distinctly uncomfortable now. Did this Maryland politician have some kind of personal relationship with her nemesis at the BAU? Riley could only hope it wouldn't lead to trouble.

Walder liked to boast of friends in high places, and some of those friends had been a nuisance to Riley in the past. The last thing she needed right now was some high-ranking disgruntled family member complaining directly to Walder about her work.

The front entryway led into an open, thoroughly modern interior, a continuous open space leading from one area into another.

They soon arrived in a large living room with a high ceiling. The walls were sparkling white, and the pale hardwood floors were very nearly white as well. Bursts of color from cushions on the furniture matched the hues in abstract paintings on the walls.

Seated on the couch directly in the center of their view of the room was a woman dressed in plain, subdued colors that contrasted with the rest of the room. Danson introduced her as his sister Lauren Hillis, Allison's mother.

Her eyes brightened.

She said to Riley and Ann Marie, "Oh, you're the FBI people who Walker said were on their way over. I'm so relieved to see you. Today has been terrible."

She turned toward Sheriff Wightman with an angry expression.

"Emory, I can't believe how awful your police were when they came with the news this morning. They tried to convince me you've found Allison's body. That's ridiculous and you know it."

Wightman looked stricken.

He began, "Lauren, I'm sorry, but—"

Lauren interrupted, "Now don't you go trying to convince me of it too. I know, the body you found was dressed in a skeleton costume. But that doesn't mean anything at all. Allison bought that outfit at a costume shop, all kinds of people go there. Anybody could have bought a costume like that."

Her frown grew more severe as she added, "And the police who came this morning told me the body had been buried for a long time. It hadn't been positively identified. How could it be? It must be in a terrible state of decay. Emory, you saw the body. Can you honestly say it looked anything like Allison at all?"

Not giving the sheriff a chance to reply, she spoke again to Riley and Ann Marie.

"You two are FBI people. I've been trying to get Emory to call in the feds this whole time. You understand what I'm talking about. You're experts at this sort of thing. You know better than to jump to mistaken conclusions."

She nodded sharply at Riley and her new partner.

"Now I want the two of you to get right to work and do what Emory and his—his *amateurs* haven't been able to get done for a year now. Find my daughter. She's alive, I feel it in my bones, and a mother knows such things. My own guess is that she's got amnesia, can't remember who she is. She must feel terribly lost. But I'm sure you can find her in no time flat. I'm counting on it."

An awkward silence fell. Sheriff Wightman shuffled his feet and looked at the floor.

Coming here was a mistake, Riley thought.

She remembered how Wightman had told her at the station that Lauren Hillis was in "a deep state of denial."

I should have listened, she thought.

But this was much worse than she could have expected. The poor woman had spent a whole year hoping and grieving, trying to resign herself to the worst and yet yearning for good news, all at the same time. Confusion and trauma had clearly taken a terrible toll on her. Riley sensed that she was barely in her right mind anymore.

In a quiet voice, her brother said, "Perhaps the three of you would like to sit down."

Riley wanted to say no, that she and her colleagues needed to leave and get on with their work. She couldn't imagine that Lauren could give lucid, coherent answers to any questions at all. Even trying to ask them would surely be both an intrusion and a waste of time. But leaving abruptly didn't seem like an option either.

It would be too cruel, she thought.

Riley and the sheriff sat down in a couple of straight-back chairs in front of the couch. Riley was startled that Ann Marie sat down on the couch right next to Lauren.

She was even more startled when Ann Marie took hold of the woman's hand.

No! she thought.

This was completely inappropriate. Didn't the girl have the sense not to make such intimate contact while conducting an interview? Riley feared an impending emotional catastrophe.

Then Ann Marie purred in a soft, gentle voice.

"Ms. Hillis, we're terribly sorry for how hard this has been for you."

Ann Marie's tone seemed to have an immediate calming effect on the woman.

"You have no idea," Lauren Hillis said.

"No, of course I don't," Ann Marie, still holding Lauren's hand. "Nobody else can possibly understand what you're going through."

Then she and the woman sat looking at each other for a moment. Riley quickly realized what her rookie partner was doing.

She's acting just like a mortician.

She'd undoubtedly watched her father comfort loved ones through all sorts of states of despair. But this realization didn't make Riley feel better about what was going on.

We're FBI agents, not morticians.

This is completely crazy.

She wanted to yank Ann Marie away and drag her out of the house and give her a sharp lecture on professional behavior. But she couldn't do that—not right now, not without making things even worse. She just had to hope that the situation wasn't going to get as bad as she thought it might get.

Still in that soft, cozy voice, Ann Marie said, "Ms. Hillis, I need for you to do something for me. Is that all right?"

Lauren nodded.

Ann Marie let go of the woman's hand and got out her cell phone and began to tap on it with her finger.

What's she doing now? Riley wondered.

Then Ann Marie said, "I took this picture at the crime scene this morning. Did your daughter have a mole on her right cheek. One like this?"

Ann Marie showed her the picture on her cell phone. Lauren's eyes widened and she grew a little paler. Then she let out a long, strange sigh of surprise that somehow sounded both anguished and relieved.

She looked straight into Ann Marie's eyes.

"It's her," she whispered. "It's really her."

Ann Marie nodded and said, "We were afraid so. I'm sorry."

To Riley's surprise, the woman didn't burst into tears. Instead, she looked at the sheriff, then at Riley, and then at Ann Marie again. She spoke in a voice that hinted of deep anger.

"You've got to find whoever did this to her."

Ann Marie nodded. "That's what my partner and I are here to do. We'd really appreciate your help."

"Of course," Lauren said.

Riley felt a tingle of unexpected optimism. Lauren was suddenly much more lucid than she had been.

Maybe it won't last, Riley thought.

Maybe the truth hasn't fully sunk in yet.

But in the meantime, maybe Lauren could answer some of their questions.

Riley said, "Could you tell us about the last time you saw your daughter?"

Lauren nodded.

"It was about eight thirty in the evening on Halloween night. She'd just put on her skeleton costume and she came into the living room—right here—to show it off to her father and me. We were all quite amused by it. She said she was going to leave for the party right then."

"The party?" Riley asked.

"Over at Patsy Haley's house, in her family's rec room," Lauren said. "Patsy was a friend of Allison's, and we've known her family for years. They had a Halloween party every year, and Allison always had fun there. Brady and I were sure everything would be fine."

"How did she get to the party?" Riley asked.

"She walked," Lauren said. "The house is just a few blocks away, and our streets are normally so safe."

Lauren stared into space for a moment, then repeated, "We were sure everything would be fine."

The woman fell silent, but Riley knew better than to coax her with questions.

She'll talk on her own.

Sure enough, Lauren soon continued, "Then at about nine thirty, Patsy called our house. She asked to talk to Allison. She wanted to know why she wasn't at the party yet. She laughed and said, 'I called to tell her to get her butt over here.' I told Patsy . . . Allison wasn't here and . . ."

Lauren's voice faded, then she said, "That was when Brady and I started to worry."

Her face darkened as she glared at Sheriff Wightman.

She said, "That was when I called *you*, Emory. I told you that Brady and I didn't know where Allison was, even though she was supposed to be at a party, and I asked you to try to find her."

Lauren's lips twisted angrily.

She said to Wightman with a slight growl, "You told me not to worry. You said it was Halloween and Allison could be lots of places. Teenagers were having parties all over Winneway, you said. Allison might be at any one of them, you said."

The sheriff looked stricken now.

"Lauren . . ." he said.

The woman continued, "I told you something was wrong. I told you it just wasn't like Allison to go someplace without telling anybody. And that was when you got testy. 'It's Halloween night,' you said. 'Do you want me to send out some kind of a search party? All of my people are busy dealing with kids playing pranks.'"

Lauren looked away from the sheriff and added, "You promised everything would be all right. It was only after she was gone all night that you started looking for her. And by then it was too late."

A grim silence followed. Riley felt sorry for the sheriff. It was obvious from what Lauren was saying that he hadn't done anything wrong. In fact, Riley knew that most sheriffs wouldn't have bothered even starting to search the next day. Days might have passed before they started to take the situation seriously.

Finally Lauren let out a choking sound and started to cry.

"She's gone," she gasped. "She's really gone."

Ann Marie handed Lauren a handkerchief. Then she took Lauren's hand again and patted it gently.

Riley knew the interview was over. But it hadn't turned into the catastrophe that she'd expected. Even though the information Lauren had given them must have long ago been told to the police, it did confirm a starting point for Riley's investigation.

Riley rose from her chair and said, "Ms. Hillis, thank you for your time and help. We'll do everything we can to find whoever did this terrible thing to your daughter."

Lauren nodded, sobbing.

Her brother said, "I'll see the three of you out."

Senator Danson escorted Riley, Ann Marie, and Sheriff Wightman to the front door. Riley saw that his expression was stern as he stepped out onto the porch with them.

Danson spoke to Riley and her partner.

"How soon do you expect to catch this killer?" he asked.

Riley was startled by the question. It didn't sound like a question at all. He sounded as if he expected them to precisely schedule the murderer's apprehension and arrest.

"I don't know," Riley said. "But we will find him."

Danson crossed his arms, looking anything but satisfied, but he said nothing more.

As she and her two colleagues stepped down off the porch, Riley looked around at the neighborhood. It was getting dark now, and lawn lights were starting to come on to illuminate the houses. She could see the bright orange of a Halloween decoration in front of a house on the other side of the street.

Halloween was nearly here. Was this killer going to strike again soon? If he did, would it be here, in this same upscale community?

She asked Sheriff Wightman, "I assume you canvassed the neighborhood after you found out that Allison was missing."

Wightman nodded and said, "Like you wouldn't believe. We interviewed at least half of Aurora Groves. Nobody had any idea what had happened to her."

Riley stood thinking for a moment. She felt sure that Wightman and his team had done a thorough job.

Then Riley said, "I'd like you show me the way Allison would have walked to her friend's party."

Wightman let out a weary sigh.

"Easier said than done," he said, pointing. "The Haleys live over that way, less than a half mile from here. But the way these streets curve and interconnect here in Aurora Groves, she might have gotten there in several different ways. Nobody has any idea exactly which route she chose. Of course all of them are just like this, an apparently safe route through the neighborhood."

He hung his head, looking exhausted and discouraged. "It's been a hell of a long day," he said to Riley and Ann Marie. "If it's all the same to you, I'm heading home for the night."

Riley nodded sympathetically. After the way Allison's mother had spoken to him just now, Riley was sure he was emotionally at the end of his tether.

She said to him, "My partner will keep looking around for a while. Just tell me the address of the Haleys' home. Also, maybe you could recommend a motel where we can stay while we're here."

Wightman told them the information Riley wanted, then headed for his police car. As she and Ann Marie walked away from the house, Riley glanced back and saw that Walker Danson was still standing on the porch. He was staring at them with his arms crossed.

Riley didn't like the looks of him.

Worse, she didn't like that he had some kind of relationship with Carl Walder.

Was Danson going to report her progress or lack of it back to the BAU chief, a man who was constantly looking for ways to discredit or even get rid of Riley?

Nothing bodes well, she thought.

Chapter Eight

As the two agents walked along a curving street that led away from the Hillis home, Riley wasn't feeling good about anything they'd accomplished today. They had just left a mother grieving over her daughter's death and a politician who seemed likely to make trouble for their investigation. They were making no progress on the case

Looking around at the comfortable, untroubled-looking neighborhood, Riley turned her thoughts to the disappearance of Allison Hillis.

It happened on a night like this.

On that Halloween, nearly a year ago, the houses would have looked much as they did now, with macabre Halloween decorations in many of the windows, front porches, and yards.

As they walked along, they passed a pale ghostly apparition floating from a nearby tree. At another walkway, a standing figure suddenly came to life, greeting them with an evil cackle and brightly lit eyes.

"O-o-oh," Ann Marie squealed. Then she laughed. "I love the ones that are activated by motion detectors. These people really go all out with decorations."

Riley knew that her townhouse neighborhood would have some jack-o'-lanterns set out, mostly to indicate where kids might stop for treats. That seemed incredibly tame compared to this.

As they passed another house, a lighted life-sized plastic skeleton grinned at them from the yard. The white bones and bare skull echoed a more grisly sight they had encountered just hours ago. Apparently that decoration even made Ann Marie uncomfortable

"Well" the rookie said, "I guess this family would have no way of knowing about…" Her voice trailed off for a moment. Then she became more cheerful. "Of course, on Halloween night, there would have been a lot of people out and about—all kinds of costumed kids roaming these streets knocking on doors. It's a perfectly charming neighborhood."

Riley wasn't feeling charmed. It was be getting darker out by the moment, and she found something odd about the way lawn lights illuminated these immaculate houses.

The houses look like toys, Riley realized.

Had the killer thought the same thing?

Had these houses seemed unreal to him—and perhaps the people inside as well?

Had that feeling of unreality made it easier for him to abduct and kill a young woman from this neighborhood? Riley wished she had a stronger sense of who the killer was and what had driven him.

Was he really threatening to kill again—and if so, where?

So many unanswered questions.

Meanwhile, she found that she didn't know what to say to her young partner. Should she congratulate Ann Marie and perhaps even thank her for how she'd handled Lauren Hillis a few moments ago?

She couldn't make up her mind. She winced a little as she remembered that moment when Ann Marie had taken the woman's hand.

It was wholly inappropriate, she thought.

And yet the results had proven to be productive. Lauren had opened up and answered questions much more readily than Riley had dared hope.

More than that, Ann Marie had helped the woman come to terms with the simple fact of her daughter's death.

Still, the whole episode had left Riley feeling uneasy. For one thing, she felt troubled about Ann Marie's sheer skill at handling such an emotionally fraught moment. Remembering how Ann Marie had spoken softly, patting the woman's hand, something now occurred to Riley.

She hadn't sensed any true empathy from her partner.

No real feeling.

Like a true mortician, Ann Marie had seemed to go through the motions of comforting a bereaved parent with consummate skill, and yet without feeling anything herself. She couldn't help but think of Ann Marie as emotionally shallow and insincere. She didn't strike Riley as possessing the maturity needed to really succeed as a BAU agent. And yet…

Everybody seems to like her.

Everybody except me.

Riley doubted very much that she was going to warm up to this rookie before this case was solved. And she found herself hoping that she'd never have to work with her again.

Before Riley knew it, they'd arrived at the house where the Haley family had held their Halloween party last year.

Ann Marie broke the silence again. "The sheriff is right. We could have taken any of several routes to get here."

Riley stifled a sigh as she looked at the house. She realized she'd been distracted by her complicated feelings about her new partner. It wasn't like her to let her thoughts drift like that.

"What do we do now?" Ann Marie asked.

Riley shrugged. "Walk back to the car, I guess. Take a different route along the way. If we don't see anything, we should probably call it a night. We can get a fresh start tomorrow morning."

As Riley and Ann Marie wended their way back toward their car, Riley noticed a small, well-lit park that extended along a side street. She felt a tingle of interest.

Pointing, she said, "Let's head over there."

"Why?" Ann Marie said. "There's no way the girl would have walked in that direction. That park is not on the way to her friend's house at all. In fact, it's pretty much the opposite direction."

"I want to go there anyway."

"But it doesn't make any sense," Ann Marie said.

Riley felt a flash of impatience. Ann Marie clearly didn't understand that Riley sometimes acted on pure instinct, without any rational reasons. Her hunches didn't always prove to be right, but they often steered her in the right direction.

Riley said, "Look, it's OK with me if you don't want to come along. Go back to the car if you like."

Riley was surprised by the sharpness in her own voice. She could see that her words had hurt Ann Marie's feelings.

Ann Marie shrugged slightly and said, "OK, fine."

She turned away and walked away.

Riley almost called out to apologize and tell the rookie to come back, but she quickly thought better of it. Having Ann Marie around was already having a detrimental effect on her ability to focus. Maybe just a few minutes without her was exactly what she needed right now.

She walked into the park and looked around. As Ann Marie had said, most of the park extended away from the direction they'd been checking. But this narrow end of it was close to this sidewalk that the missing girl might have been using.

Riley walked onto a path that wound across the well-groomed grass and tried to imagine what this area had looked like on Halloween night. Had there been lots of kids roaming these paths?

No, she thought. *They'd have been busy going house to house.*

Besides, their parents would probably have warned them away from here. The paths were well-lighted, but there were also bushes and small wooded areas where someone might lie in wait. This was not a good place for kids to play at night.

But Ann Marie was right about one thing. There was no apparent reason for Allison Hillis to have taken a detour in this direction.

Unless . . .

Had someone perhaps enticed her into the park?

If so, how?

She couldn't quite make sense of it. Even so, a familiar feeling started to come over her—a sense of the killer's presence, of what he might have been thinking and feeling as he'd lurked in any of a dozen places she saw around her.

Riley breathed long and slowly.

Yes, it had been a good thing to get Ann Marie out of the way. These instinctual moments were Riley's greatest asset as a BAU agent. There was nothing psychic or supernatural about her feelings of connection with a killer, and sometimes her gut feelings turned out to be flat-out wrong. But often enough, they led to productive insights.

She kept breathing slowly as she walked along and let her mind drift where it might. She wished she could guess which of these wooded or bushy spots the killer might have chosen for a hiding place.

She stopped at the first patch of shrubbery she came to and stepped behind it and crouched there. Sure enough, she could see that he'd had a clear view of the lighted street if he'd chosen this particular spot. He could have watched kids wander up and down the street without his presence being suspected.

It was easy for Riley to imagine how he might have felt as he crouched in wait.

Mysterious.

Powerful.

Dangerous.

Riley also guessed that he didn't experience those feelings in his everyday life. Far from it, he might well feel weak, inadequate, and ineffective.

But here he felt like . . . what?

The Goatman, Riley thought.

She remembered what Sheriff Wightman had said about the Goatman legend. It was the story of a hybrid creature, half man and half goat, hungry for human blood.

Did the killer actually imagine himself to *be* the Goatman?

Riley didn't know. Perhaps he fancied himself more as the Goatman's minion, his loyal helper. In any case, his sense of connection to the Goatman legend elevated him above the blandness of ordinary everyday life.

Still looking toward the street, Riley wondered . . .

What might he have been waiting for?

And who?

Did he know his victim already—well enough to know what route she'd take while walking to a party on Halloween night? Riley somehow doubted it. She was sure he'd come here fully prepared to kill, but she got the feeling that his choice of victims was impulsive, almost random.

Or maybe not quite random.

Looking through the branches, Riley imagined how the killer's heart would have quickened to see the specter of death walking alone along the street. Of course he would have known that it wasn't really a walking skeleton but a young person wearing a costume.

But even so, the girl in that costume would have seemed the perfect prey, as if fate had dropped her into his waiting hands.

And she had been alone.

But how had he approached her?

Maybe he didn't approach her at all.

Riley reminded herself of her feeling that he had somehow *enticed* his victim.

But how could he have done that?

How could he have lured the girl away from the safety of a well-lighted street into the murkier park?

She remembered something from one of the notes the killer had sent.

NOW THE GOATMAN WILL TAKE HIS TURN
SINGING THE GOAT SONG.

Did he sing to her? Riley wondered.

Or maybe whistle?

The sheer absurdity of the idea struck her in an instant.

Singing or whistling behind a bush was hardly any way to *entice* a young girl off the street and into the park.

In fact, it was surely the perfect way to scare her away.

Riley's sense of connection of the killer suddenly evaporated with the ridiculousness of the notion.

She sighed aloud. She knew from experience that she wasn't going to be able to slip back into that state of mind—not here, not right now.

It's over, she thought. *I might as well head back to the car.*

When she got back to her feet, her cell phone rang.

Her spirits rose to see that Bill was the caller.

She sighed with relief.

Just who I need to hear from, she thought.

Chapter Nine

Bill's heart warmed at the sound of Riley's voice answering the phone.

He'd never enjoyed working at his desk, but he'd been hunkered down in his office doing research at his computer for hours now. He really wanted to get out of here soon, but even though he didn't have anything really urgent to report to Riley, he did want to talk with her rather than just email her the results of his investigations.

Working separately from her was feeling downright intolerable right now, and her voice sounded incredibly sweet.

Remember, this is business, he reminded himself.

"Did I catch you at an OK time?" he asked.

He heard Riley let out a sigh.

"I don't think *you* could catch me at a bad time," she said. "I'm not in the middle of anything, anyway. What have you got for me?"

"Maybe something, I'm not sure," Bill said. "I've been poring over purchases of large freezing units in the Winneway area. Most of them look legitimate enough—restaurants and supermarkets and the like. And most of the sales were years ago. But I found one that looked rather odd."

"Tell me about it."

Bill peered at the information he'd brought up on his computer.

He said, "Last year late in October a guy named Gabriel Ballard bought a freezer chest—definitely a commercial unit, but it was delivered to his private residence, not some food-related business."

"The timing sounds right," Riley said. "He could have bought the chest in preparation for the murder."

"That's what I figured," Bill said. "I did a quick check on his name. He's done short time for assault and battery but that was some years back."

"Do you have an address for him?" Riley asked.

"Yeah. It's there in the Winneway area—345 Magnolia Road."

Riley said, "Sounds like my new partner and I ought to pay him a visit."

"How are things going with the kid?" Bill said.

"Don't ask," Riley grumbled.

"That bad, huh?"

"Well, let's just say she's a work in progress. She's left me alone for a few minutes, which is a relief."

Bill was pleased to hear that. It would be nice to talk to Riley privately, even if it was only about work.

Riley asked, "What about that other thing I asked you to look into? Some possible significance for the words 'goat song'?"

"I think maybe I've found something on that too," Bill said.

He brought up a new page on the screen. "The Greek word 'tragedy' literally means 'goat song.'"

"No kidding?" Riley said, sounding quite interested.

"Nope, no kidding," Bill said. "Nobody seems to know exactly how the word 'tragedy' originated. But this article says that the ancient roots of drama were in religious ritual, and also in choral song and dancing. Scholars think it's possible that a goat was sacrificed as part of those rituals."

"Hence the name 'goat song,'" Riley said.

"Yeah. Do you think maybe our killer is aware of that connection?"

"What do you think?" Riley asked.

Bill thought for a moment, then said, "What was the wording in his notes? Regarding the goat song, I mean."

"Well, let's see. In the first note, he wrote, 'Now the Goatman will take his turn singing the goat song.'"

Bill scratched his chin. "Maybe he's saying that the goat is tired of being the sacrificial animal. It's time for *humans* to become the sacrifice. It's a case of 'the worm turning,' so to speak. The goat will have his revenge."

"That's an interesting idea," Riley said. "In his second note, he says, 'He will feast and sing again.' It's still a sacrifice, still a ritual with song and dance. But the rules have changed."

Bill nodded and said, "Of course, it's just a theory at this point."

"Yeah, but a pretty good one. It sure sounds like he could be playing with that kind of idea."

Bill asked, "So are you thinking that this killer actually believes himself to be the legendary Goatman?"

"I've been wondering that myself," Riley said. "I'm not sure. For one thing, he keeps referring to the Goatman in the third person—as 'he.' Maybe he's more of a worshipper or a disciple or something."

She chuckled a little and added, "That is, if we're not just letting our imaginations run away with us. For all we know, we're concocting this whole ritual idea out of thin air. Maybe he's just some sick, crazy bastard who likes goats. Or who's just messing with our heads. Have you got anything else?"

Scrolling on the screen, Bill said, "Well, the Maryland 'Goatman' story didn't appear out of thin air. There's a whole body of myths and legends from all over the world about creatures who were half-man and half-goat going back thousands of years—satyrs, for example. I couldn't even scratch the surface of all that kind of lore."

"Well, you've found out a lot," Riley said. "I appreciate it. Maybe you should call it a night, go home and get some sleep."

"What about you?" Bill said.

"I'm not sure," Riley said. "It's kind of late, but I'm thinking that maybe my rookie partner and I might pay Gabriel Ballard a friendly visit, maybe ask what he's doing with that big freezer of his."

"You be careful," Bill said.

"I will," Riley said. "I always am."

She fell silent for a moment.

No, Bill thought. *You're not always careful. That's why I should be there.*

Then she said, "But I wish we were doing this together."

Bill felt his throat catch a little.

"Yeah, me too," he said. "Do you think this is a temporary assignment or that Meredith wants to split us up for good?"

"I don't know why he would." Riley groaned, then asked, "What do you think?"

"We're a great team," Bill replied. "Our record is outstanding. But it could be that he's going to want both of us to help to break in new agents from now on."

"I guess somebody's got to do it," Riley muttered. "But it never occurred to me that being good at our jobs might get us split up after all these years. It's a change I don't even like to think about."

"I know," Bill said. "And that's not all that's changing."

"Of course not," she replied.

"You've always been my best friend, Riley. You've always meant the world to me. But now..."

He paused, knowing that now he was no longer thinking about business. But these were words he wanted to say, so he went on.

"But now you mean more than that to me. More than my job. More than the world."

"I know. I feel the same way."

A silence fell between them.

Bill thought, *This is where one of us should say "I love you."*

Or maybe both of us.

It seemed odd, in a way, that neither of them had said those words aloud.

But isn't it true?

As if wondering the same thing, Riley said, "We've still got a lot to talk about, don't we?"

Bill nodded. "We certainly do."

"But face to face," Riley said. "Not over the phone."

"I agree," Bill said. "So hurry up and finish this case so we can get together. I miss you more than I can say."

"I miss you too," Riley said.

They ended the call, and Bill sat staring at the phone in his hand.

He wondered how many other BAU partners had fallen in love like this—and how they'd dealt with it when they had.

His thoughts were interrupted by a familiar voice.

"Working late, Agent Jeffreys?"

Bill turned to see the babyish freckled face of Carl Walder. The Special Agent in Charge was standing in Bill's office doorway.

Bill's heart jumped.

I should have shut the door, he thought.

But at this hour, he hadn't expected anybody to drop in like this—least of all Walder, who was well known to avoid personally staying late even though his teams sometimes worked on into the night.

In answer to Walder's question, he replied nervously, "Just doing some research."

Walder's lips shaped themselves into a smirk.

"Research, eh?" he said.

He crossed his arms and leaned against the door frame.

He said, "I hear Agent Paige is working on a case over in Maryland. I'm surprised you're not there with her."

"Yeah, well... things came up," Bill said.

"Things sometimes do," Walder said.

With a knowing smile, Walder nodded and headed on down the hall.

Bill breathed a sigh of relief that he was gone. Even under the best of circumstances, Walder was hardly the sort of guy Bill wanted to have a chat with. And these weren't the best of circumstances. And now Bill couldn't help feeling paranoid.

How long was he standing there?

How much did he hear?

Did he know I was talking to Riley?

Of course Bill and Riley both knew that they couldn't keep whatever was happening between them a secret forever at the BAU. But Bill hated the possibility that Carl Walder might be the first to find out.

He could make real trouble for us, Bill thought. *And he's always happy to do that.*

Chapter Ten

The materials on the table before him appeared to be everything the man needed for what he was about to do—a blank sheet of paper, a bottle of glue, a pair of scissors, and a small pile of magazines to cut words and letters from. But he just sat there in his basement, staring at them by the glow of a single bare light bulb.

He knew that the most important thing was still lacking . . .

Inspiration.

But he waited patiently. He had no doubt that inspiration was coming. In fact, he felt hints of it tingling in his bloodstream already.

"Come to me, Pan," he murmured aloud. "I'm waiting. I'm ready."

He spoke a little louder, "Sing me the message."

He knew that Pan would sing to him soon.

As he waited, he thought back to how he'd been chosen for this. When he was just a kid, others had tried to frighten him with tales of a monstrous Goatman. Then they had him left him all alone there in the dark woods.

He laughed aloud now, remembering how he had embraced the very thing they expected him to fear. He had felt the touch of real power before he emerged from those woods. Over the years he had recognized just how mighty the thing that visited him was. The shabby local Goatman legend was just a shadow of the demon deity known as Pan.

And over the years that power had visited him again and again, telling him what to do and giving him the strength and stealth to carry it out. Pan had guided his every step, just a few days ago singing the message that he had sent to the police—a message that had led to the discovery of the young woman's body.

Exactly as Pan had intended.

The foolish police would never figure it out.

They've got no imagination, he thought.

People were such herd-like animals, after all. Which was why Pan, the eternal keeper of flocks, found such ready ways to trick them. Pan was now wreaking his revenge for all the hoofed animals that people had so wantonly sacrificed in their futile rites and rituals—the sheer *tragedy* of it all. It was humans' turn to be sacrificed to the god. And someday Pan would unleash the full force of his terrible power and set all of humankind into a vast stampede of universal panic.

For as the man also knew, the very word "panic" came from the god's name.

"When will it come—your sacred panic?" he asked the god in a whisper.

No reply came. Of course the man knew that Pan wouldn't answer such a question, not even when he arrived tonight, even when he sang his song. The man was a mere mortal, after all, and he wasn't meant to know such divine secrets.

But what an honor it was to be Pan's instrument!

How privileged he felt to feel his power flowing through him!

And not just his power, but his genius.

For the man knew from experience that the god Pan was possessed of uncanny intelligence, especially when it came to human nature. He remembered last year on All Hallows' Eve when he was full of the god, how he'd crouched behind a bush in that park in Aurora Groves, watching the lighted street for the arrival of Pan's prey. Children in costumes were coming and going. But Pan didn't seem interested in any of them.

After a while Pan had spoken in a clear, flute-like voice that no one but the man could hear.

"There she is!"

And there she'd been indeed—a young woman dressed as a skeleton.

How appropriate, the man had thought.

But how, he'd wondered, did the god want him to seize his prey this time?

As if in reply, he'd heard his own voice cry out.

"Mew."

That was all—just a high-pitched "mew."

The man hadn't even understood why Pan wanted him to make that sound.

But then the young woman stopped walking and looked toward the park.

"Mew," the man had said again.

And the young woman had called back in a gentle voice, *"Kitty?"*

Then the man had understood Pan's clever trick.

The woman thought a lost kitten was in that park nearby.

She turned off the street and came walking toward him on the park path, murmuring words of comfort and reassurance as she searched for the source of that sound. He'd kept uttering "mew" with increasing pathos and desperation.

Until finally . . .

She'd crouched down beside the bush looking for the poor, lost animal that was calling for help. He hadn't had to move from his spot to reach out and seize her once and for all.

It had been brilliant—absolutely brilliant.

And it had been the god's scheming and doing, not his.

Of course, there had been other sacrifices—people in graves the police had no idea about.

Did Pan intend to reveal all those graves sometime soon?

Would he use that revelation to unleash his apocalyptic panic?

It's up to the god.

It's Pan's will.

His ears perked up as a sound started coming from the concrete walls around him—a musical incantation.

Pan's song—at last!

He picked up his scissors and got ready to cut out the message of that song, feeling possessed by the primal powers of the universe.

For he knew the true meaning of Pan's name...

All.

Chapter Eleven

Riley slowed the car down as the headlights fell on a battered-looking rural mailbox with the number 345 on it.

"This must be the place," Riley said. "345 Magnolia Road."

Ann Marie muttered from the passenger seat, "I don't like the looks of this."

I don't either, Riley thought, although she didn't say so aloud.

Their surroundings had changed a lot during the last half mile or so. As they'd followed their GPS directions to the address that Bill had given Riley over the phone, they'd passed large country homes, small farms, and occasional clusters of houses.

Everything had struck Riley as fairly prosperous, not like the rough rural areas she'd known during her childhood. But they hadn't passed any houses for a while now. And even though they'd come to a mailbox, there was no house in sight.

Instead there was a wire fence with barbed wire on top and a gate with a sign that read NO TRESPASSING. The sign was crudely hand-painted, as was the number on the mailbox. The gate was secured with a chain and padlock

Riley drove slowly past the gate and the mailbox.

"Where are we going?" Ann Marie asked.

Riley thought the rookie was sounding a bit worried.

Maybe we should both be, Riley thought.

Riley didn't reply, just drove on for about an eighth of a mile until she came to a broad shoulder in the road. She pulled over and parked their vehicle, then turned off the engine and the headlights.

"What are we doing?" Ann Marie said.

"We're going to walk back," Riley said. "I don't want to announce our approach."

"But it doesn't look like anybody lives anywhere near here."

Riley felt a flash of impatience.

"There was a mailbox back there," she said. "Where there's a mailbox, there's a house. And a big freezer got delivered to that house about a year ago. I want to find out why and who it was delivered to. I want to check out that house. There are a couple of flashlights in the glove compartment. Hand me one, and keep the other for yourself."

Ann Marie handed a flashlight to Riley, and they both got out of the car. The night was chilly and dark. No other vehicles came into sight as they walked back along Magnolia Road toward the gate and the mailbox.

"What are we looking for, anyway?" Ann Marie asked.

She sounded like her teeth were chattering—and not from the cold. Riley couldn't help but be amused.

"We'll know it when we find it," Riley said. "*If* we find it. You sound kind of scared for a kid who grew up around dead people."

Ann Marie sighed and said, "Yeah, well, in case you never noticed, mortuaries aren't exactly spooky places. They're designed to look peaceful and pleasant, nice lighting and pretty pastel colors and all. I'm not used to wandering around outside at night—at least not in a wilderness like this."

Riley smiled at the irony.

My partner is a mortician's daughter who's afraid of the dark, she thought.

She wondered what else she was going to learn about Ann Marie before the night was over. The rookie still hadn't told Riley the story of that case she'd solved—the case that had gotten her recruited into the FBI Honors Internship Program. Riley figured now was still not the time to ask her about that. It might turn out to be a long and involved story.

But Riley had another question on her mind, and she thought it was an important one. Now seemed like as good a time as any to ask it, but Riley wasn't sure how to say it.

"You've seen a lot of corpses," Riley said cautiously. "But have you ever . . . ?"

Riley's voice trailed off.

Ann Marie said, "Seen anybody get killed? No. I haven't even seen anyone die from natural causes. I was just never around when any of the older people in my family died. Kind of weird, huh? I guess that's likely to change now that I'm an FBI agent."

It sure is, Riley thought.

She hoped they could finish this case without Ann Marie going through that particular rite of passage. Riley wasn't at all sure the girl would handle it well, and she didn't much want to be the one to help her through it.

When they arrived at the gate, they could see that the dirt road beyond it led into a wooded area. Riley shined the flashlight along the road, but they could see nothing beyond those impenetrable trees and underbrush.

Ann Marie said, "I don't see an intercom button to push to tell anybody we're here."

Riley almost laughed at what seemed to her like a rather silly idea.

Ann Marie added, "Um... the sign says 'no trespassing.'"

"So it does," Riley said. "And this is where you learn that signs aren't always there to be obeyed."

In spite of the padlocked gate and barbed wire on the fence, she saw how they could get inside. There was a fair amount of space between the gate and the fence.

Riley squeezed through the space to the other side of the gate.

"Come on through," she told Ann Marie.

The girl just stood there, eyes wide and mouth hanging open.

"Did you hear me?" Riley asked.

Ann Marie nodded nervously and squeezed through herself.

They started to walk along a dirt road that suddenly seemed oddly familiar to Riley. Then she realized it reminded her of the drive that had led to her father's cabin up in the Appalachian Mountains. Although she had sold the place after he died, she had walked that road many times in earlier years. This one wasn't uphill like her father's drive, but the dirt and stones crunched underfoot in much the same way.

She also remembered that her father was sometimes prone to welcome unwanted visitors with a shotgun, especially at night.

"Be ready for anything," Riley said, fingering her sidearm.

"OK," Ann Marie replied nervously.

As Riley and her partner followed the road through the woods, they kept their flashlights tilted downward, still trying not to advertise their presence.

Riley could see that the drive was riddled with potholes, but fresh tire tracks showed that it was recently and frequently used by some large vehicle.

Finally a bungalow came into view, situated in a small clearing that was overgrown with weeds. The house was completely dark. Riley avoided shining her flashlight directly onto the house, but in the moonlight she could see that it was in bad need of repair and a new coat of paint.

"It doesn't look like anybody lives here," Ann Marie said.

"Let's find out," Riley said.

They made their way through the weed-infested yard to the house and climbed up a handful of rickety steps onto the porch. With one hand on her weapon, Riley knocked on the door.

She called out, "Is Gabriel Ballard here? This is the FBI. We'd just like a word with you."

There was no reply.

Ann Marie said wishfully, "There's nobody home. I guess we'd better leave, come back tomorrow or something."

"Let's look around first," Riley said.

Ann Marie let out a sigh of wordless disapproval. They stepped down off the porch, and Ann Marie followed as Riley waded through the weeds around the side of the house. Riley soon detected a faint but horrible smell.

"Oh my God," Ann Marie muttered.

"You smell it too, huh?" Riley said.

"Uh-huh," Ann Marie said.

"And you know what it is?"

"Uh-huh."

Riley wasn't entirely surprised. As a mortician's daughter, the rookie must have had some familiarity with the vile smell of death with its hint of disgusting sweetness. Not all the corpses her father had dealt with would have been in pristine condition.

Riley turned and retraced their steps back to the front of the house.

"What are we doing?" Ann Marie asked.

Riley didn't reply as they climbed the front steps again. When they got to the door, she reached into her purse for her lock-picking kit.

She asked her partner, "How are your lock-picking skills? I assume they still teach that at the Academy, don't they?"

Ann Marie's eyes widened with alarm.

"We're not going in there, are we?" she asked.

"Why wouldn't we?" Riley said.

"Well, it would be . . . breaking and entering, wouldn't it?"

Riley said, "I think we both agree that there's something dead in this house. And we're investigating a murder. I'm pretty sure that gives us cause."

"But not *completely* sure?" Ann Marie asked.

Riley stifled a growl of impatience. She knew perfectly well that her rookie partner wasn't nearly as worried about the legality of entering the house as she was about whatever they might face in there.

She said, "Go ahead, get on your cell phone and call a lawyer. Or better yet, get us a search warrant. Let me know how that works out for you. Meanwhile, I've got a lock to pick. Give me some light to work by, OK?"

Ann Marie nodded and pointed the beam at the door lock. Riley used a pick and a tension wrench to twist the lock, then turned the door handle and pushed. The door squeaked as it swung open. Riley and Ann Marie stepped inside.

Riley's partner felt around the wall for a light switch.

"Don't do that," Riley said. "If somebody's anywhere in the area, I'd rather they not notice that we're here."

Riley and Ann Marie shined their flashlights around the small living room. There was a decrepit-looking stuffed armchair near the fireplace, but the other furniture was covered with dingy white sheets.

Ann Marie said, "It really doesn't look to me like anybody lives here."

For a moment, Riley almost agreed. But her eye was caught by a telltale glint from the fireplace. She walked over and looked inside. Sure enough, she could see the glow of warm embers.

"There's been a fire here recently," Riley said. "Somebody uses this place for something, even if he doesn't live here."

She sniffed and added, "That smell is stronger in here than it was outside. Can you tell where it's coming from?"

"No," Ann Marie said.

"We'd better find out," Riley said.

They moved on through the house, checking it out room by room without finding anything unusual. When they got to the kitchen, they saw that the sink was piled high with dirty dishes.

A different kind of stench emerged when Riley opened the refrigerator door and its bulb came on to reveal a grubby interior with moldy food and containers. She quickly shut the door and looked around. She still hadn't seen any sign of that large freezer chest.

Then Riley heard Ann Marie say, "Agent Paige, I think the smell is coming from over here."

Riley turned and saw her partner standing outside a door. Riley checked it out and saw that it was locked with a hasp and a padlock. Again using her pick and tension wrench, she quickly snapped the lock open.

She opened the door. As she'd expected, the doorway led down into a basement. And the smell was much stronger and more unpleasant than before.

A feeling of dread was starting to creep over Riley. She felt sure she wasn't going to like what she found down there. And given Ann Marie's current state of mind, she doubted that her partner would be able to deal with it.

She said to Ann Marie, "Go back to the living room and keep watch out front. If you see anybody coming, let me know."

Ann Marie nodded and went back through the house. Riley shined her flashlight down the basement stairs. There was a light switch on the wall, but she still didn't want to turn it on in case the basement had windows.

Slowly, she moved down the creaking wooden stairs. Once she heard something scurrying, but she couldn't catch it in her flashlight beam.

Rats, she realized. That made her hesitate, but then she turned her light back on the steps continued on down.

At the bottom, she used her flashlight to see that she was in an unfinished basement with bare cinderblock walls and a concrete floor. There was quite a bit of clutter on the floor, including buckets and ice chests.

A shotgun and several rifles were in racks on one wall. She saw other weapons on another wall—bows and arrows, including a couple of crossbows. Those were certainly powerful enough to kill a person as well as an animal.

Riley remembered the roundness of the murder victim's chest wound. Might it have been made by the shaft of an arrow?

She thought the wound was too large to have been made by the arrows she saw here.

Unless the arrow was specially designed, she considered.

Then her flashlight fell on something that made her gasp.

It was a wooden table was covered with blood. Some of the blood was dried and black, but some of it looked fresh, sticky, and red. Riley no longer had any doubt that this had been the scene of some violent act.

Beyond the table against the far wall, Riley saw what she'd come here looking for and now that she paused to listen, she could hear it faintly humming. It was a large white chest-type freezer, more than big enough to hold a human body.

She hurried over to it.

Her fingers trembled as she reached for the latch and lifted the lid.

Chapter Twelve

Ann Marie was positively shivering. Ever since Agent Paige had disappeared down into the basement, she had felt her own fear of the dark rising. She knew it was irrational, and she had no idea where it came from.

She wasn't scared of most other things that frightened other people. Nothing about Dad's mortuary ever upset her. But when she was little she'd been terrified of her own dark closet and imaginary things under her bed. Now, standing here alone in this strange dark cabin, she felt a powerful impulse to turn on the lights.

Nevertheless, she resisted the urge and made her way back into the living room with her flashlight shining in front of her. She held the light tilted low to keep its beam from spilling too much.

Some fearless BAU agent I am, she thought.

And of course, Agent Paige had noticed.

"You sound kind of scared for a kid who grew up around dead people," Agent Paige had said.

She knew that this would be just one more thing for Agent Paige to find fault with. So far, Ann Marie's senior partner hadn't said a single encouraging word to her—not even about how she'd coaxed Lauren Hillis into answering Riley's questions. Ann Marie thought she'd handled the grieving mother pretty well. If Agent Paige didn't think so too, why didn't she just say so?

She just doesn't like me, I guess.

Ann Marie wasn't used to people not liking her. It was a strange and uncomfortable feeling.

As Ann Marie made her way back into the living room, her flashlight fell again on the sheets covering most of the furniture, making them look ghostly and even vaguely threatening. And of course there was still that awful smell. It reminded her of one time when an unusually putrid corpse had been brought to the mortuary. An elderly woman had been found in her house after she'd been dead for a month.

Nope, there's no mistaking that smell.

Ann Marie had no doubt that Agent Paige was going to find a dead body down in that basement. That was no big deal as far as Ann Marie was concerned. She only wished her partner would find the damned corpse and come back upstairs so she wouldn't be alone in this darkness.

Meanwhile, she remembered what she was supposed to do.

"Go back to the living room and keep watch out front," Agent Paige had said.

Ann Marie went to the front door and pulled it open. Then she realized that anyone outside might see the glow of her flashlight, and snapped it off. She thought she could see the road reasonably well by moonlight.

Nothing seemed to be stirring out there except a rising wind.

Then a weird whistling sound came from somewhere behind her . . . somewhere inside the house.

Ann Marie gasped. She whirled around and snapped her flashlight back on.

On the other side of the living room, a curtain was moving slightly over one of the windows.

Was somebody trying to get in there?

Gathering her courage, she hurried across the room. Reaching out a shaking hand, she pulled the curtain aside. Then she let out a nervous giggle.

A pane of glass had been broken in one corner. The wind was moving the curtain and making that whistling sound.

She felt foolish for reacting so sharply.

Calm down, she told herself.

Then she heard yet another sound—or was it her own heart pounding?

She listened and heard it again. It was coming from the front porch.

It was a squeaking sound, like someone taking a step on rickety floorboards.

And she hadn't closed the front door. It was still standing open.

She rushed back to the door and shined her flashlight through the opening, but all she could see were the rickety porch floorboards.

Then she heard the sound again.

And again.

Her heart was pounding now, and her breath was coming in gasps.

Someone must be on that porch. Someone or something.

She wanted to call out and demand to know, *"Who's there?"*

But when she opened her mouth, no words came out.

Suddenly, being scared out of her wits didn't seem so irrational anymore.

In fact, it made pretty good sense.

After all, if there was a dead body in the basement, then surely whoever was walking on the front porch must be . . .

A murderer.

As she stepped toward the doorway, it felt like she sometimes did in a dream when she tried to run but could barely move.

What was she supposed to do in a situation like this?

It vaguely came back to her . . .

Identify myself as an FBI agent.

Draw my weapon.

But before she could do either of those things, a large man leapt into the doorway in front of her flashlight beam. He lunged toward her.

Ann Marie's flashlight fell from her hand and rattled across the living room floor. The next thing she knew, somebody was holding onto her with a vise-like grip.

"Just who the hell are you?" her attacker snarled.

At the sound of a scream upstairs, Riley slammed the freezer door shut. With her gun in one hand and her flashlight in the other, she bounded back up the basement stairs. When she got to the living room, she saw that Ann Marie's flashlight was lying on the floor, still spinning around from having been suddenly dropped.

Riley's own flashlight beam fell upon a big man wearing a hunting outfit. He was holding Ann Marie tightly against him with one arm. With the other he was holding a large knife to her throat.

Riley's mind clicked away as she assessed the situation.

From what she had discovered in the ice chest downstairs, she was sure that this man was no murderer.

And she doubted very much that he was really going to hurt Ann Marie.

Looking at her, the man growled, "What the hell are you two up to?"

Pointing both her weapon and her flashlight beam at his face, Riley said, "We're Agents Paige and Esmer with the FBI."

Still holding the knife to Ann Marie's throat, the man said, "FBI, huh? Care to show me some ID?"

Riley had a gun in one hand and a flashlight in the other, and at the moment, she didn't want to put either of them down to fetch her badge.

She said, "Let go of my partner and she can show you."

His expression wavered for a moment. But Riley could see in his eyes that he had no intention of turning this into some kind of hostage situation. After all, he had no reason for it. Sure enough, he released Ann Marie from his grip. She took out her badge and showed it to him.

Returning his knife to a sheath on his belt, the man growled, "Just what business has the FBI got trespassing around my place?"

Holstering her own weapon, Riley said, "It depends. Are you Gabriel Ballard?"

"Folks normally call me Gabe—but yeah, I'm him."

He flicked on the overhead light switch. It took Riley's eyes a moment to adjust, but she quickly saw that the house was even dirtier and more decrepit than she had originally thought. Gabe had a dull, unintelligent face, and at the moment he looked seriously rattled.

Riley said, "And would you describe yourself as a law-abiding citizen, Gabe Ballard?"

Ballard shrugged uneasily. "Well, I ain't done nothing illegal enough for the FBI to come after my ass."

"No, just hunting out of season," Riley said.

"Hey, it ain't out of season for bow hunting. I'm an archer, at least during this time of year."

Riley said, "Judging from the amount of deer meat you've got in that freezer downstairs, I'd say you've killed over your limit—*way* over your limit. And you sure do keep a disgusting place here."

"What are you talking about?"

"I'm talking about that smell," Riley said.

"What smell?"

Riley scoffed and said, "I guess I shouldn't be surprised that you're used to it. You've got pieces of butchered deer all over the place down there, and whole buckets full of entrails. It's an out and out health hazard."

Ballard shrugged again and said, "I just never get around to cleaning things up, I guess. What business is it of yours, anyway?"

That's a good question, Riley had to admit to herself.

"Look, just explain a few things to me, OK?" Riley said. "Why did you just threaten my partner with a knife?"

Ballard snorted. "Hell, I didn't know who the two of you were—a couple of strange people coming around here at night. Couldn't tell anything about you. You were trespassing and I didn't know why. Thought you must be after something."

"Do you live here?" Riley asked.

"Naw, I live over in town. I keep this place for hunting, storing weapons and deer meat and such. I was just driving over here to check on things when I saw your car way up ahead, slowing down and checking out my gate. I turned off my headlights and watched you driving slowly on. I thought something might be up, so I pulled over and stopped and waited. Sure enough, I saw the two of you came walking back, then slip through the gate."

"Why didn't you say anything to us then?" Riley asked.

"For all I knew, you might be armed. I didn't have a gun on me. So I followed way behind on foot, watching your flashlights as you walked down the drive. I was still down the road a piece when I saw that you got through my front door somehow. Picked the lock, I guess. I could have called the cops on you right then, but I didn't want them poking around either. It took a little while before I got up the nerve to come on into the house to find out just why you'd broke in here."

He's got some reasonably good stalking skills, Riley thought. She could appreciate that after having a father for a hunter.

Then Ballard pointed at Ann Marie and said, "Then I came inside, and I got blinded by the beam of this girl's flashlight. I figured she was liable to shoot me, so I grabbed hold of her fast as I could. I asked who she was, and she didn't say a word."

Riley turned and glared at Ann Marie. She stopped herself from asking aloud, *You didn't introduce yourself as an FBI agent?*

Ann Marie lowered her eyes ashamedly. She obviously knew what Riley was thinking.

Ballard then said, "Now maybe the two of you would like to tell me what the hell you're doing, breaking into my place like this?"

Riley stifled a discouraged groan. She owed the man an explanation. But just how much should she tell him?

"We're investigating a murder," Riley said.

Ballard's eyes widened.

"Murder? Are you talking about the missing girl who turned up dead today? I sure didn't have anything to do with that."

Ann Marie demanded, "Really? Because we've got a few questions we need answers to. For example, where were you last night?"

Ballard snapped back, "Last night I was over at Tim's Bar, having a few drinks with buddies."

Ann Marie persisted angrily, "What about Halloween a year ago?"

He looked puzzled for a moment, then replied. "Back then I was out in the next county, at a hunting lodge with a bunch of bow hunters. It's absolutely legal, you know."

Riley remembered the crossbows in the basement. Although she hadn't seen the exact dates for this year, she knew that bow hunting season usually opened before the regular season. Her father had looked down on that kind of hunting. He'd said it was done just to show off skill, for bragging rights rather than for food needs. Bow hunting too often resulted in wounded animals rather than clean kills. But even so, it was certainly legal in season.

Ballard broke into a grin. "See, ladies? I've got lots of friends who'll tell you everywhere I've been."

Ann Marie looked like she was about to continue trying to drill him, but Riley silenced her with a gesture across her throat.

Then she said to Ballard, "We came here by mistake. We're sorry."

Ballard grunted loudly. "You're *sorry*?" he said. "Sorry don't cut it. I went to school, I know my rights. The law can't come busting into somebody's house without a warrant. It's illegal."

Riley shrugged slightly.

"Yeah, and so is hunting over your limit," she said. "I guess that makes us just about even. I'm sure neither of us wants to make a big deal out of things. Let's just call it a night, OK?"

Without another word, she walked out of the house with Ann Marie following her.

As they headed back down the road by the beams of their flashlight, Ann Marie chattered disapprovingly.

"Where are we going? We've got to ask him more questions!"

"Like what?"

"Like where he was when Allison Hillis disappeared or—"

Riley interrupted, "That man didn't kill anybody."

"How do you know?"

Riley groaned aloud and said, "His alibis are going to check out. Besides, didn't you hear what I said back there? His freezer is stuffed full of deer meat. That freezer was the only reason we suspected him in the first place. He's not a killer, just some jerk who keeps a smelly hunting lodge."

"Oh," Ann Marie mumbled sheepishly.

Riley felt her frustration rising as they walked in silence for a few moments.

Finally she said in a voice tight with anger, "Ann Marie, we've got some things we need to discuss."

Chapter Thirteen

The tension between Riley and Ann Marie was palpable. They walked a little farther along the dark dirt road without talking.

Finally Riley spoke up, "Just what the hell happened back there?"

"I'm sorry," Ann Marie said. "I screwed up."

"I'll say you screwed up," Riley said. "But I need to hear your version of it."

Ann Marie sighed deeply.

Then she said, "It was dark. I heard a noise out on the porch. I thought someone was out there. I wasn't sure."

Riley said, "And you didn't call out to whoever it was?"

"No."

"You didn't announce that you were FBI?"

"I was too scared."

Riley struggled to imagine the incident from Ann Marie's point of view. She found it hard to do.

"So you thought you might be in danger?" Riley asked.

"Yeah."

"But you didn't draw your weapon?"

"No."

"Why not?"

Ann Marie's voice sounded choked with emotion.

"I don't know. I just froze, I guess."

"Froze?" Riley said. "Ann Marie, you were trained—no, you were *drilled* on what to do in these situations. Are you telling me you just forgot everything you'd learned at the academy?"

"I remembered," Ann Marie said. "I just . . . well, froze. I was just so scared. I'm sorry. It won't happen again. I promise."

Riley found it hard to control the anger in her voice.

"How can I know it won't happen again? Suppose we'd been right, and the killer really lived there, and it was *him* you heard on that porch. What do you think would have happened?"

"I don't know."

Riley scoffed. "Well, I'm pretty sure I *do* know. You'd have gotten killed. And I might well have gotten killed as well. We both could have ended up missing and buried somewhere, like that girl we saw earlier today."

They'd arrived back to the gate at the end of the drive. They squeezed between the gate and the fence again and continued walking toward the car.

Riley shook her head. "Ann Marie, I can't train you from scratch. I've got to be able to count on you when the going gets tough. You need to be ready to do this job. Do you think you *are* ready?"

"I think so," Ann Marie said.

She doesn't sound very sure of herself, Riley thought.

They got into the car, and Riley started driving them back to Winneway. They didn't say another word to each other during the whole drive. They found the motel that Sheriff Wightman had recommended and checked in.

As they walked toward their rooms, Ann Marie said, "Agent Paige, please let me finish this case. You have no idea what becoming a BAU agent means to me. I'll do better. I promise."

"We'll see," Riley replied sternly.

Ann Marie ducked her head and hurried off to her room.

Riley went inside her own room and stood there for a moment trying to decide what to do next. She knew that her first order of business was to report in to Brent Meredith. After all, when she and Ann Marie had met with him this morning, he hadn't believed this was going to turn out to be a real BAU case. She remembered what he'd said.

"You'll probably go there and turn right around and come back again."

Riley didn't think things were turning out that way after all. It was true that they had only one murder to investigate. But the killer's odd messages combined with the sense of him that she'd experienced in the park had her intuitions tingling. She felt a rising suspicion that this "Goatman" was a true serial killer, the kind of monster she had dedicated her career to hunting. She couldn't give up on this case until she found him and stopped him from killing again.

It was too late to phone Meredith, so she opened her laptop and wrote him an email reporting much of what had happened today.

Then she threw herself on the bed. It was very late, and it had been a long, discouraging day. She felt tired, and unsure what to do next. She had half a mind to call Meredith first thing in the morning and tell him that Ann Marie just wasn't cut out to be a BAU agent.

But the rookie's plea echoed through Riley's mind.

"Please let me finish this case. You have no idea what becoming a BAU agent means to me."

Riley scoffed aloud to herself.

I've got no idea, huh?

Did the girl really think no other rookie agent had ever felt the same way—the same depth of commitment, the same feeling of being called to a noble task?

But Riley found it hard not to sympathize with her. She remembered something else Ann Marie had said earlier today about the choice she'd made to go into law enforcement, and how her father had disapproved.

"He always wanted me to take over the family business someday."

She knew it was no small thing to defy a father's expectations.

Ann Marie might seem like a shallow twit, but Riley figured there must be grit and commitment somewhere inside her.

Maybe she deserves another chance.

Besides, now that Riley had some time to think, she realized she was at least as angry with herself as she was with Ann Marie. She hadn't been at her best today. In fact, the whole debacle back at that hunting lodge was more her own fault than Ann Marie's.

She knew that she had jumped too eagerly on Bill's discovery that a commercial-sized freezer had been delivered to that house a year ago. It ought to have occurred to her that the area was hunting country, and a hunter might use such an enormous freezer to store deer meat.

Or at least a hunter who's been shooting over his limit.

Sure, she should have followed up on Bill's tip. But rushing out there with Ann Marie at night and breaking into the place was a bad call on her part. If one or both of them had gotten killed, it would have been on Riley's head.

I'm definitely off my game.

But what was wrong, exactly?

Was it having to work with a green, awkward rookie instead of with Bill? Or did it have something to do with how her relationship with Bill was changing? Maybe she was letting their budding romance distract her from her work. If so, did she have any business scolding Ann Marie for making rookie mistakes?

Another lingering worry floated into her mind.

Was there any chance at all that this new thing with Bill was going to turn out well—for either of them?

Were they going to ruin the best relationship either one of them had had in their whole lives?

She wondered if maybe she should call him right now and talk all this through.

Or maybe she should call the kids at home.

She smiled as she remembered how satisfied she'd felt just to get her quarreling kids off to school this morning, and what she'd said when April had complained that her solution to their argument "didn't make sense."

"It doesn't have to make sense. I make the rules here."

Now that she thought about it, that was one of the beautiful things about being a mother. Things didn't always have to make sense. She could exercise a little arbitrary authority from time to time.

Being a BAU agent was different. Making sense of things was the whole point of her work. There had to be an answer to everything. But sometimes that seemed to be impossible. How could anyone make sense of a twisted, homicidal mind? How was she going to make sense of a killer who wrote messages about a "Goatman"?

How could she make sense of sheer madness?

Maybe it would be nice to get out of law enforcement and settle down to the daily challenges of raising a family.

Maybe that was something that she and Bill could do together.

Still lying on the bed, she looked at her watch and saw that it was much too late to call home. She got up and took a shower and got ready for bed.

Riley found herself outside in the dark, walking along a curving street in an upscale neighborhood. She knew she'd been here before. And once again, she thought the houses all around her looked like toys.

But what am I doing here? *she wondered.*

She turned to ask her partner and realized that no one was with her—neither Ann Marie nor Bill. Whatever task was at hand, she was going to have to figure it out for herself.

Something to do with Halloween, *she thought.*

There was plenty of evidence of that along this street. The whole neighborhood was decorated for Halloween, with ghosts floating in the trees and life-sized plastic skeletons hovering in the yards.

Then the street began to fill with trick-or-treaters—kids and teenagers dressed up as vampires and zombies and mummies and such.

Riley was discouraged to see the young people out and about.

All these make-believe monsters, *she thought.*

They're perfect camouflage for a real one.

For all she knew, that dancing skeleton with a bag of candy might really be a killer.

To add to the confusion, the mechanical apparitions were coming down from the trees and yards and porches and mingling among the trick-or-treaters on the street. She was finding it harder and harder to tell the costumed kids from the costumed toys.

And now a whole chorus of recorded spooky noises—howling and growling and screaming—was so loud that she could barely hear herself think.

Or were they recordings? That screaming sounded very real.

Was somebody being brutally murdered nearby?

Don't let your imagination run away with you, *she told herself.*

Then she saw a new costumed character on the street ahead. Draped in a sheet like a Halloween ghost, the figure was walking directly toward her. As it grew closer, she could see that it was also wearing an oversized mask with enormous eyes and an anguished, open, downturned mouth.

She recognized that image.

The theatrical mask of tragedy.

Then she heard a voice speaking through the mask.

No, not speaking, *she realized.*

Chanting. Singing.

She struggled to remember something she was supposed to know. It was something Bill had said to her over the phone . . .

"The Greek word 'tragedy' literally means 'goat song.'"

Riley stifled a gasp of alarm.

Is this him?

Is this the killer I'm looking for?

Then the apparition halted in its tracks. Riley took a couple of hesitating steps in its direction. Suddenly the figure was changing, morphing, taking on a completely different form, until it became . . .

A goat.

Or rather, a hybrid creature—half man and half goat.

The creature stood on two legs glaring at her with an insolent, grinning expression.

And blood was dripping from its horns and teeth.

Singing louder than before, the goat turned and begin to walk away.

I've got to stop him, *Riley thought.*

I've got to stop him before he spills more blood.

But she realized to her horror that she couldn't move from where she was standing.

Riley was awakened by the sound of her phone buzzing. Struggling to shake off the nightmare, she picked up the phone.

She was alarmed to see that the call was from Sheriff Wightman.

She took the call and asked, "Has something happened?"

"Something, yeah," the sheriff said. "I'm not sure what it is yet. It might—just might—be another body. I'm going to check it out, and I want you and your partner to join me."

Wightman gave Riley a street location. She jumped out of bed and got dressed as fast as she could.

Had she been too slow? Had the Goatman killer struck again even while she was trying to figure things out?

Chapter Fourteen

Riley had just gotten dressed and was pulling on her jacket when she heard a knock on her motel room door. She hurried to answer and was surprised to see Ann Marie standing there carrying a little cardboard tray. The smell of coffee reminded Riley that she had been about to rush out without any kind of breakfast.

"I was already dressed when you messaged me," Ann Marie said. "So I went by the motel breakfast buffet. Got coffee and doughnuts." Looking a little nervous, she added, "Unless you'd like something different..."

"Great idea," Riley told her. "We can eat in the car on the way."

"What's going on?" Ann Marie asked.

She showed Ann Marie the piece of paper where she had jotted down the information Sheriff Wightman had given her over the phone.

Riley said, "I don't know yet, but the sheriff wants us to meet him at this location. Come on, let's get going."

Ann Marie's face erupted into a smile. Riley could see that she was thrilled to be getting another chance. But she could also tell from the redness around Ann Marie's eyes that she'd been crying a lot.

Riley felt a pang of sympathy.

The poor kid didn't get a lot of sleep last night, she thought.

It was small wonder that she was up and ready to go already. She'd probably given up on trying to sleep. Riley only hoped that the rookie would handle herself better today than she had yesterday.

For both of our sakes.

With Ann Marie still carrying the food tray, they headed toward their car. As they crossed the parking lot, Riley's phone buzzed and she pulled it out of her pocket. She sighed to see that the call was from home. At this early hour on a school morning, it was bound to be about some kind of problem.

When she answered, she heard April's voice.

"Mom, Jilly's being impossible."

"What's the problem?" Riley asked.

"She insists that I also wear a costume when I take her trick-or-treating tomorrow night."

"What's wrong with that?" Riley said.

"Mom, I'm sixteen years old. Yesterday you said that *Jilly* was too old to go trick-or-treating. I can't go walking around the neighborhood in a costume like a kid."

When they reached the car, Riley tossed the car keys onto the little food tray, indicating that Ann Marie should drive. Riley climbed into the passenger seat and continued the phone conversation.

"I don't see why not," Riley said. "You wanted to go to a Halloween party. I'm sure you wanted to wear a costume there."

"Yeah, but that would be different. I'd be around other kids my age."

Riley felt her teeth clench.

One more word of this and I'll get a splitting headache, she thought. Gratefully, she reached for the coffee that Ann Marie had just settled into the cup holder. She took a sip before she replied.

"Mom," April's voice protested, "are you still there?"

"Of course," Riley snapped. "April, you and your sister have to work this out between yourselves. I just got called in to work, which might mean that a dead body is about to be dug up. That'll be the second one since yesterday."

A brief silence fell.

"Oh," April said sheepishly.

"Now you two girls get ready for school. Gabriela's surely got breakfast ready for you by now."

"OK," April said.

Setting up their destination in the vehicle GPS, Ann Marie glanced over at Riley as the call ended.

"Did I hear you say there might be another body?" Ann Marie asked.

"I don't know," Riley said. "That's what we're on our way to find out."

The younger agent pulled the car out of the motel parking lot and followed the GPS directions through Winneway. On the way they both downed coffee and doughnuts. By the time they arrived at the location Sheriff Wightman had spoken of—a parking lot behind Pater High School—Riley felt primed to deal with whatever they might find there.

The back of the parking lot was already crowded with police vehicles. Several of those vehicles and three cops blocked off part of the parking lot, making sure that nobody came into that area. The guards recognized Riley and Ann Marie and allowed them to pass on through.

More cops were clustered just off of the paved area, near a row of small trees. From their bright red leaves, Riley realized that they were maples. But since they were only about four feet or so tall, they couldn't be very old.

Two cops were energetically digging into the ground around one of the little maples. Several other men stood a few feet away, watching them work. One of those was Sheriff Wightman, who stepped toward Riley and Ann Marie when he saw them arrive.

"We got this message this morning," Wightman said, holding out a sheet of paper.

Like the one they'd seen yesterday, this message was made out of cut-out print letters pasted onto a sheet of paper. It read:

BLOOD RED FROM THE ROOTS
THE SAPLING GROWS NICELY NOW.
ON THE HALLOWED EVE
GOATMAN WILL SING A NEW SONG.

"I don't know what it means," Wightman added. "But I sure don't like it."

Riley felt her heart sink. The threat to someone's life on Halloween, tomorrow night, confirmed what she had been expecting. But a sapling with blood red roots was a new image and it didn't bode well for what they might find here.

Like the other two messages, this one was attached to a map. Riley saw at a glance that the map showed the school and its environs. The row of trees was clearly visible on the map, and a rectangle was drawn directly over the tree where the digging was now taking place.

One of the cops looked up from his digging and complained to Wightman, "I don't see how anybody could have buried anything under here. Are we sure this isn't like the first time? It'll be a shame to kill a tree for no good reason."

"Just keep digging," Wightman replied. Then he glanced at Riley and Ann Marie and shook his head.

"I sure as hell don't know what to expect," he grumbled.

Riley understood just what the sheriff meant. Given the prankish nature of the killer, the cops might well be digging up an empty hole, just like they had a year ago. On the other hand, the words in the message suggested that something sinister could be beneath this small red-leafed tree…

BLOOD RED FROM THE ROOTS

Another cop started an electric chain saw and began to gnaw away at some of the exposed roots.

Riley saw that one of the men who had been standing with the onlookers had turned and begun to pace back and forth in the parking lot.

"Who is that?" she asked.

"The school principal," Wightman replied. "You should meet him."

Wightman led Riley and Ann Marie over to the restless man and introduced him as Principal John Cody.

Wringing his hands, Cody said to Riley and Ann Marie, "Sheriff Wightman told me that you found a dead body yesterday. What do you expect to find here?"

Rather than try to answer his question, Riley asked, "What can you tell us about this row of maple trees?"

Cody said, "One of our graduating classes planted them—just a couple of years ago, I believe. Yes, that was the year when…"

Cody's voice faded away for a moment, and his eyes widened with alarm.

"Oh, God," he said.

Sheriff Wightman said, "Take it easy, John. We don't know anything yet."

"How long is this going to take?" Cody demanded. "Rumors are already flying around the school. The media is bound to get out here soon. Parents will be asking questions."

"We'll find out soon enough," Wightman told him. "Just help us keep everybody away from this area."

Cody nodded, but he looked more miserable than ever.

Wightman patted the principal the shoulder, then led Riley and Ann Marie back toward the excavation.

Speaking quietly, he told them, "Two years ago, the vice principal of this school disappeared without any notice. Yvonne Swenson was her name. Naturally Cody is worried...and to tell the truth, I'm worried too. It never made any sense for that lady to just go off like that, but we never found any trace of her."

They heard one of the cops who was digging call out.

"Hey, Sheriff. You'd better have a look at this."

When they got back to the excavation, the little tree had been cut free of its roots and laid to one side. The two cops were staring with horror into the hole they'd been digging.

Riley saw that they'd exposed what looked like a shoulder bone.

"Aw, damn," Sheriff Wightman said.

Everyone watching fell silent as the two cops continued digging carefully with smaller tools, then just pulled dirt away by the handfuls. Soon a ribcage draped in tattered clothing came into view.

Even Riley found it an unsettling sight.

Tree roots had wound between the ribs and continued on into the ground. The body was both penetrated and webbed with a mesh of tendrils. Thus the little tree had truly been blood red from the roots.

The cops kept scraping dirt away from the macabre remains, and they soon revealed a skeletal hand clutching the battered remnants of a purse. With gloved hands, one cop opened the purse. He reached inside, carefully removed something, and laid it on the ground next to the excavation.

It was a wallet. When he nudged it open, a driver's license with a photo and a name was clearly visible.

Sheriff Wightman leaned down to look at it, then let out a groan of despair.

"It's her, all right," he said. "It's Yvonne Swenson."

"I don't understand," a voice behind Riley groaned.

She saw that Principal Cody had joined them. Now he tottered dizzily, then crouched down to keep from fainting.

"This doesn't make any sense." he murmured, obviously struggling not to burst into tears. "I was here when the students planted this tree. I watched them do it."

He squinted at Riley and her colleagues and added, "In fact, Yvonne was here too, helping them plant it. How is this even possible?"

That's a good question, Riley realized.

Then she heard Ann Marie speak up rather shyly.

"I've got kind of a theory about that, if anybody would like to hear it."

Riley's young partner was now crouched beside the body, taking pictures of it like she had with the one yesterday. While even Riley herself felt somewhat startled by the grotesque state of these remains, she saw that Ann Marie's attitude seemed cool and utterly clinical.

Ann Marie said to the principal, "I take it the trees were planted *before* Halloween a couple of years ago?"

Principal Cody nodded and said, "Yes, two or three days before Halloween, if I remember right."

Ann Marie stood up and murmured to Riley and the sheriff, "I don't think the principal should hear what I've got to say."

Sheriff Wightman took his cue and asked one of his cops to escort Principal Cody back to his office. He also ordered another cop to call the M.E. and tell him to bring his team to the scene. Then he looked expectantly at Ann Marie.

The young agent spoke clearly and confidently. "We know the trees were planted just two or three days before Yvonne Swenson disappeared. We also know that the killer doesn't always bury his victims as soon as he's murdered them."

Riley agreed. "He seems to have frozen Allison Hillis's body for a while before he actually buried her."

Ann Marie nodded and continued, "My guess is that the killer snatched Yvonne on Halloween, maybe killed her right away, but put her in deep freeze—just for a couple of weeks, maybe."

Riley was starting to understand what Ann Marie was getting at.

She said, "The tree would still have still been freshly planted after that amount of time."

Ann Marie added, "Yes, digging would still have been easy in the newly turned soil, and the trees would have been just foot-high saplings at that point.

The killer might have brought the frozen body back late at night. He could have easily removed the tree, buried the body right here, then replanted the tree above the body."

Riley observed, "If he did it skillfully enough, nobody would have noticed that anything here had changed."

"Right," Ann Marie said. "And that would explain how these roots grew down through her remains."

Riley nodded slowly and said, "That's a pretty good theory, Ann Marie."

The rookie smiled and went back to snapping pictures.

Suppressing a bitter sigh, Riley said, "Now we know for sure that we're dealing with a serial killer. He's murdered two victims, and unless we stop him, he'll kill more."

Sheriff Wightman said, "I'm afraid things might be even worse than that."

Riley saw that Wightman's face had gone pale from some awful realization.

He stared at her for a moment, then said, "Come on, let's head over to the station. I'll explain it there."

Chapter Fifteen

Riley's apprehension grew as she and Ann Marie followed Sheriff Wightman's car to the police station. Now that they'd found a second body, this case was obviously much worse than she had first expected. But Wightman's perspective seemed to be even more dire.

"I'm afraid things might be even worse than that," he'd said.

Riley's mind boggled at what he might possibly mean. What was so important that he insisted they return to the police station to discuss it?

When they arrived, she parked their car next to Wightman's vehicle. As she and Ann Marie got out and followed him toward the building, Riley's heart sank at what she saw.

A group of reporters was gathered at the front door.

It's started, she thought.

She'd known all along that it was only a matter of time before the media started hounding them for information. Not only did this case involve the murders of two local women, it had some bizarre aspects that the press would love to run with.

But just how much of all that had they found out?

Riley and her colleagues just kept walking and pushed among the reporters without answering any of their questions. As harassed as Riley felt by all their shoving and prodding, she was relieved not to hear any questions about the "Goatman," or about cryptic messages threatening of another abduction on Halloween night. The reporters knew that a second body had been found this morning, and they also knew the victims' identities, but not much else.

This could be worse, Riley thought.

But she wondered how long they could keep some of the more sensational details from leaking out.

As they entered the building, the receptionist at the front desk stood up and spoke to Wightman.

"Senator Danson called again just now. He really wants to talk to you."

"Damn it," Wightman grumbled to the receptionist. "If—or *when*—he calls again, tell him we're doing the best we can. Tell him I'll get back to him . . . well, when I can."

"Right," the receptionist said.

"Walker Danson's been calling every several hours," Wightman said as he led Riley and Ann Marie into his office. "He even called me at home last night. I'm sure he's heard by now that we've got a new body. I wish he could get it through his head that we're liable to do better work if he's not pestering us."

Riley got a sinking feeling as she and Ann Marie sat down in front of Wightman's desk. She remembered the state senator's inscrutable expression when he'd asked her whether she knew Carl Walder.

It was bad enough that Danson was constantly calling to check on their progress. She was even more worried that Danson seemed to have some kind of personal connection to Walder. If they didn't solve the case soon, would Danson complain directly to the BAU's special agent in charge? Politicians had done that before, and it had always raised problems for the investigation.

If that happened now, how long would it be before Walder started breathing down Riley's neck, holding her job over her head as he often did? Tangling with Carl Walder was the last thing she needed while she was trying to solve a murder case.

At least he doesn't know about Bill and me yet, she thought.

But of course, it was only a matter of time before he did. Whenever that happened, she was sure Walder was going to make things uncomfortable for her—and for Bill as well.

Wightman took several folders out of his filing cabinet then sat down behind his desk.

He opened up one of the folders filled with reports.

"Here's what we've got on Yvonne Swenson, the vice principal at Pater High School. As you already know, she disappeared two years ago—on Halloween night. The last time she was seen, she was walking home from a Halloween party that had been held in the school gym."

Wightman shook his head wearily.

"I can't describe what a toll her disappearance took on the community—and frankly, on myself, personally and professionally. Not everybody got along with her, but just about everybody respected and even admired her. She was a widow, dedicated to her work. Nobody could seriously believe she would just run off without telling anybody. We worked like demons trying to find out what had happened to her. Of course we failed."

Riley thought hard about what she was hearing.

She said, "I take it you thought the date was just a coincidence when Allison Hillis disappeared on Halloween last year."

"Well, of course it made us wonder whether their disappearances might be connected," Wightman said. "So we looked for some common thread between Allison and Yvonne, but we couldn't find a thing. They lived in different neighborhoods, didn't know each other personally, and didn't have any acquaintances in common—or any enemies, for that matter. There didn't seem to be any actual connection between their disappearances—until just now."

Riley found herself holding her breath. She doubted that she was going to like whatever he was about to say next.

He said, "You know, in a town like this, folks disappear from time to time. Sometimes we can figure out why they disappeared, and even where they went. Sometimes we can't. But that doesn't necessarily indicate foul play. People can run off for lots of reasons. It just happens."

Wightman opened up the other two folders and showed Riley and Ann Marie their contents.

He said, "For example, a woman named Deena McHugh vanished four years ago. Her husband was unfaithful and as mean as hell, so even he figured she just wanted to get away from him and didn't want him to ever be able to find her. Four years before that, a thirteen-year-old kid named Henry Studdard disappeared. He lived with an abusive father, so everybody figured he just ran off as well."

Wightman took a long, slow breath.

He said, "The thing is—both Deena McHugh and Henry Studdard disappeared on Halloween."

Ann Marie's eyes widened. She said, "But you never had any reason to think anything of it until now."

Wightman scowled. "No bodies had ever turned up. We had no reason to think they'd been murdered. All that's changed now that we've got Yvonne Swenson's corpse. What scares me now is..."

His voice trailed away.

Finishing his thought, Riley said, "If their disappearance on Halloween *is* significant, that means there might have been two more murders—and two other buried dead bodies that nobody's ever found."

Wightman nodded silently.

Riley's mind clicked away as she tried to process what she was hearing.

Of course, it might merely have been coincidence that two other people had disappeared on Halloween over a period of several years. Riley had long since learned that coincidences were an inevitable part of investigative work. And as the sheriff had said, people sometimes simply disappeared in a town like this.

But if they're not coincidences...

She suppressed a shudder as she considered the possibilities. Just as Wightman was obviously thinking, perhaps this "Goatman" killer had claimed at least four victims so far, not just two. That would mean there were two undiscovered graves out there somewhere.

And of course, there was still the killer's lingering threat:

THE GOATMAN IS STILL HUNGRY.
HE WILL FEAST AND SING AGAIN
ON THE HALLOWED EVE.

And Halloween was tomorrow night.

This killer's schedule sped up, Riley realized. There would be no more gaps of a couple of years between murders. He was on an annual schedule.

And the clock is ticking.

Before Riley could ask any questions, the sheriff's office phone rang. When he answered, Riley could tell that he was talking to his receptionist—and judging by his tone of voice, he wasn't at all happy.

"Oh, God," he groaned on the phone. "Not *her* again! How the hell did she find out...?"

He shook his head and said to the receptionist, "Well, I guess it's public knowledge now, damn it. What a pain in the ass. Just tell Madge I'll get back to her as soon as I can."

The sheriff rolled his eyes as he listened.

"Well, *keep* telling her that every time she calls!" he said.

The sheriff let out a deep sigh and said, "OK, put her through."

He covered the receiver and said to Riley and Ann Marie, "I'm sorry, I've got to take this call. I'll be right back with you."

Soon Riley could make out another voice babbling irritably on the sheriff's phone.

In reply, Wightman said, "Yeah, Madge, we found another body just this morning. And it looks like... well, we're sure, really... that it's Yvonne."

Riley could hear more shrill chatter.

Then Wightman said, "Damn it, Madge. I just came from the crime scene myself. I didn't have a chance to call you and let you know. And frankly, I've got other priorities. For one thing, I had to call the M.E."

The chatter got louder and shriller.

Wightman said, "Madge, you're not helping. I've got work to do. If you want me to find out who killed Yvonne, you've got to let me do my job. I'm hanging up now. Goodbye."

He hung up the phone and stared at it in exasperation.

Then he looked at Riley and Ann Marie and said, "I'm sorry for the interruption. That was Madge Torrance, Yvonne Swenson's next-door neighbor. She means well, I guess, but she's a busybody, and she's got a head full of theories and doesn't know what she's talking about. I'm afraid she's going to start making a thorough nuisance of herself. We'll just have to try to ignore her."

Riley's ears perked up at the sheriff's words. *"She's got a head full of theories."*

Another thing she'd learned over the years was that even crackpots sometimes have important ideas.

"I want to talk to her," Riley said to Sheriff Wightman.

"Huh?" Wightman said with surprise.

"Is she at home?" Riley asked.

Wightman shrugged and said, "Well, yeah, but—"

"Good," Riley said. "Let's drive right over and pay her a visit."

Without waiting for a reply, she grabbed Yvonne Swenson's case folder off the desk, then headed out the door with Ann Marie and Sheriff Wightman hurrying after her.

Chapter Sixteen

As soon as Riley had pulled in and parked behind the sheriff's car, Ann Marie reached over from the passenger's seat and tapped her arm. Then the young agent pointed to a window in Madge Torrance's little house.

"Agent Paige, look," Ann Marie said with a slight giggle. "Sheriff Wightman said she was a busybody."

Following her partner's direction, Riley saw what she meant.

A pair of suspicious spectacled eyes was peeking out at the cars from behind a curtain.

I guess Wightman is right, she thought.

She figured that not much happened in this neighborhood that the woman didn't find about. She just hoped that some of that neighborhood gossip might turn out to be helpful.

When the two agents and the sheriff got out of their vehicles and walked toward the house, the curtain fluttered and the eyes disappeared.

The house was a modest duplex with two front doors and a single roofed porch across the front. One of those doors swung open as soon as they stepped up on the porch.

A tiny, elderly woman wearing a bathrobe and smoking a cigarette popped out of the door and confronted Wightman.

"I didn't expect you to show up," she snapped. "Not after the way you talked to me on the phone just now."

Wightman grunted irritably.

He said, "Yeah, well, coming here wasn't exactly my idea, Madge."

He introduced the woman to Riley and her partner.

"FBI, huh?" Madge said with a note of stern approval. "Well, it's about damn time someone called in the big guns."

Shaking a finger toward the sheriff, she turned to Riley and Ann Marie. "Maybe the two of you can teach this yokel a thing or two about how to do his job. Come on inside, the three of you."

Riley and her colleagues followed Madge into her apartment. Riley almost coughed in the thick haze of cigarette smoke and noticed that an ashtray on the coffee table was overflowing with cigarette butts.

Madge herded Riley, Ann Marie, and Sheriff Wightman into a crowded threesome on her small couch. Then she sat down in a rocking chair and puffed away at her cigarette.

"I guess Wightman here told you I was the one who first reported Yvonne missing. I knew something was wrong by midnight that night. She was *always* home by then, no matter what else might be going on. And I called the police right away, but they blew it off. Nobody got worried until she didn't show up to school the next morning."

Madge added with a grunt, "I guess Wightman has also told you what a pain in the ass I am. Well, the feeling's more than mutual. I'm telling you FBI gals, this guy's a public menace."

"Now look here—" Wightman began to protest.

But Madge paid no attention to him and continued to address Riley and Ann Marie.

"My neighbor's dead because he didn't do his goddamn job. If he'd only listened to me two years ago, Yvonne would still be living next door instead of the noisy, smelly bums who inhabit that place now. It's a damned shame."

Riley leaned forward and said to her, "Sheriff Wightman said that you had some theories."

Madge scoffed. "Theories, hell. I call 'em *facts*."

"For example?" Ann Marie asked.

"For example, I know exactly who nabbed and killed poor Yvonne—and that other girl too."

Before Riley could ask her who she meant, Madge was laying into the sheriff again.

"And from what you said on the phone, you *still* haven't arrested him! What are you waiting for? And now he's sending you crazy notes about being the Goatman. What's all that about, Sheriff?"

Wightman's eyes widened with alarm.

"Now how did you find out about—?"

"Well, it's true, isn't it? And what do you make of it? Do you think he's gone off his rocker, or is he just trying to scare folks? All I know is, you'd better go scoop him up right away, now that he's threatening to do it again tomorrow night. The note says something about the Goatman being 'hungry,' the way I hear it."

Riley could see that Sheriff Wightman was having trouble keeping his temper.

He snapped at the woman, "Now look here, Madge, we've talked about this, haven't we? I don't want you talking to my men behind my back, getting them to tell you things nobody's supposed to know."

Madge shrugged and said, "What if your boys *like* talking to me? Can I help it if I'm sociable? Running a tight ship and stopping up leaks is your responsibility. I'm just an engaged and interested private citizen. I consider it my civic duty to know all the goings-on here in Winneway. There's too much apathy in this town."

Struggling to get a word in, Riley spoke up.

"Who do you think killed Yvonne and the girl?"

Madge nodded brusquely. "Why, Brad Cribbins, of course."

Wightman tried to interrupt, "Now, Madge, we went through all this—"

Madge kept right on talking.

"Brad was a senior at Pater High School when Yvonne disappeared—or at least he was until she expelled him. She told me all about him. We used to sit right out there on the porch just about every evening, having a drink and talking together. She was a tough disciplinarian as a vice principal—tough but fair. She expelled Brad early in first semester of his senior year, then she disappeared about a month later."

It was obvious to Riley that this particular busybody had access to far more than neighborhood gossip. Her interest piqued, she turned to the sheriff and asked, "What can you tell me about him?"

Wightman shrugged and said, "Brad Cribbins was a bad kid—or he used to be. He began vandalizing churches and graveyards when he was nine years old. Started stealing bicycles soon after that, then graduated to stealing cars. He got into lots of fights, landed a couple of guys in the hospital. He still gets into trouble from time to time."

"Why did he get expelled?" Riley asked.

Madge started explaining before Wightman could say another word.

"Yvonne told me all about it. Some scared students told her that Brad had brought a knife to school—and not some nice little Boy Scout job, but a real fighting knife. Yvonne ordered a search of his locker, and sure enough, they found enough knives in there to start his own street gang." She paused for a moment to be sure she had their full attention. Then she added, "He also had a list of people he had it in for."

"A list?" Riley asked.

"Yes," Sheriff Wightman said tiredly, as though he'd been through all of this before. "Yvonne's name was on that list. She expelled him right away, and she also reported the incident to me. Naturally, when she disappeared, Brad was at the top of our suspect list. But by then he'd settled into a janitorial job at a local mall. His coworkers confirmed that he'd been working there on the night when Yvonne disappeared."

Riley's interest was mounting by the second.

"What else can you tell me about the list?" she asked Wightman.

Wightman said, "You'll find it in the case file you brought along with you."

Riley opened the folder that she'd picked up off Wightman's desk before they'd left the station. She'd tucked it beside her seat in the car and then carried it in with her, but hadn't had a chance to open it. Now she flipped through some pages until she came across the list. Across the top of the sheet was written in large, crude block letters…

FOR TERMINATION

Underneath those two words was scrawled a skull and crossbones. Then came the list itself, with Vice Principal Swenson's full name at the top, followed by a roster of first names and nicknames:

Buzz, Smitty, Carla, Jerry, Earl, Ally…

Riley's eyes stopped short on that last name.

"Ally!" she murmured aloud.

Was it a nickname for Allison Hillis?

Riley looked up at Madge and asked, "Did Yvonne ever mention Allison Hillis to you?"

"You mean the poor kid that got dug up yesterday?" Madge asked. "I can't say she did."

"Are you sure?" Riley asked.

"I've got a pretty good memory," Madge snapped.

Sheriff Wightman said to Riley, "I don't think the 'Ally' on that list is the same person as Allison Hillis. She didn't even go to Pater High School. And remember, we searched hard for any other connections between her and Yvonne Swenson. We didn't find a thing."

Riley thought hard and fast. Sheriff Wightman was making good sense, and she had no doubt that he'd done thorough and competent investigations of both disappearances.

But still . . .

She asked Wightman, "Do you know where Brad Cribbins lives now?"

Wightman shrugged. "Yeah, he lives with his dad over on the far side of town, but—"

"I want to pay him a visit," Riley said.

Wightman scratched his head.

"Well, like I said, he had an alibi when Yvonne Swenson disappeared, so I don't understand why—"

To Riley's surprise, Ann Marie interrupted the sheriff.

"If Agent Paige says she wants to see him, you can be sure she's got a good reason. In case you don't know, she's kind of a law enforcement legend. She really knows what she's doing."

Riley saw that Madge had a big smile on her face as she stared hard at the sheriff.

Finally, Wightman sighed and got up from the couch.

"OK, then," he said. "Let's get going."

As Riley and her partner got up to leave, Ann Marie winked at her.

She's trying to get on my good side, Riley realized.

And at least for the moment, Ann Marie was succeeding pretty well.

Riley paused to thank Madge, who was using the lighted end of the cigarette she was smoking to light yet another one.

"Glad to help out," Madge said. "I'm glad to see you two girls on the job. Wightman's badge is bigger than his you-know-what. Now go and kick some ass, you hear?"

As they continued out the door, Wightman told Riley and Ann Marie that he'd drive ahead and lead them to where Brad Cribbins lived. Riley and her partner got into their vehicle and started to follow the sheriff.

Riley said, "Thanks for speaking up for me back there."

"Glad to help out," Ann Marie said. "But I'm not sure I understand what we're doing or why. Sheriff Wightman said the guy had an alibi. Don't you believe him?"

"Well, I believe Wightman believes what he told us," Riley said. "But in my experience, killers can be awfully clever about cooking up alibis. For one thing, they often have loyal pals who will stand up for them. The sheriff might have been wrong. I've seen it happen more than a few times."

She took a long breath and added, "And I've really got a hunch about this guy we're going to see."

"Well! This should be interesting!" Ann Marie said enthusiastically.

It had better be more than interesting, Riley thought.

With Halloween coming up tomorrow, they didn't have any time to lose. She remembered what Ann Marie had said about her just now.

"She really knows what she's doing."

Riley sure didn't want to prove the kid wrong.

Chapter Seventeen

As Riley drove behind Sheriff Wightman's vehicle, she noticed that her partner in the passenger seat was busily jotting down notes. Ann Marie seemed completely focused on whatever she was writing.

"What are you working on?" Riley asked.

"Just doing a bit of math," Ann Marie said.

Math? Riley wondered. They were following Wightman toward the neighborhood where Brad Cribbins lived. What could math have to do with that?

Riley almost asked why, but decided to let it go. Ann Marie just kept scribbling.

After a moment, Ann Marie tapped her eraser on her notepad and stared ahead thoughtfully.

She said, "If Brad Cribbins got expelled from high school two years ago, that would make him—what?—nineteen or twenty now?"

"I imagine so," Riley said, starting to sense what Ann Marie might be getting at. "Unless he got held back a grade or two. Then he might be older."

Ann Marie said, "According to Sheriff Wightman, Deena McHugh disappeared four years ago. Brad might have been fifteen or sixteen then. And Henry Studdard disappeared eight years ago. Henry was thirteen then, and Brad would have been . . ."

Riley nodded and finished her thought.

"Just a kid himself. I know. But we know that Brad Cribbins has a criminal record all the way back to when he was nine years old, and he's always been a fighter. He might have been capable of a lot more than vandalism and stealing bikes and cars. Even though it's rare, children have been known to commit murder."

As Riley continued driving, it occurred to her that Ann Marie's query was really quite sensible. Brad Cribbins's age might well turn out to be a factor in determining just how viable he was as a suspect. Her scribbling wasn't irrelevant after all.

She's smarter than she seems, Riley thought. *Maybe just not the kind of smarts that lends itself to BAU field work.*

Riley couldn't forget how the rookie had frozen during her confrontation with the hunter yesterday. If the man had actually been dangerous, Riley and her partner might both have been hurt or even killed. Ann Marie was going to have to start doing a lot better than that if she hoped to stay on this job.

Again Riley wondered about the murder case Ann Marie had helped solve—the one that had gotten her recruited into FBI training. Riley figured she ought to ask Ann Marie to tell her that story.

As they approached the edge of town, Riley observed a marked change in their surroundings. The houses here were small bungalows, not unlike the duplex where Madge Torrance lived. But unlike those in more upscale areas, these buildings were set close together, with tiny front yards and only a dozen feet or so in between the houses. And these little homes were all in serious need of paint and repairs.

Ann Marie commented, "This looks like a whole different town."

It does indeed, Riley thought.

Not that she was surprised that even an upscale town like Winneway had its seamier side. She'd found similar neighborhoods just about everywhere she had visited.

Even though it had never been affluent, this had probably once been a comfortable little suburb. Even in their rundown state, the houses retained a bit of character. But poverty had overtaken this community, just as had so many others that hadn't benefited from upticks in the national economy. The cars and clutter in the streets and yards indicated that many of the houses probably had a lot more people living in them than they had been designed for.

Sheriff Wightman's vehicle pulled up to the curb, and Riley parked right behind him. The little house they had come to wasn't the most rundown on the block, but it definitely needed repair and paint.

Riley and her colleagues got out of their cars and climbed up a steep row of concrete steps onto a small front stoop. Sheriff Wightman knocked on the door.

A moment later, an enormous man with a hairy belly protruding from under his T-shirt opened the door. Riley could smell the beer on his breath more than a yard away.

Sneering, he said, "Well, well, well. Sheriff Wightman. To what do I owe this honor?"

Wightman introduced Fred Cribbins to Riley and Ann Marie, who showed him their badges.

"We're here to see your son," Wightman said.

"He ain't here," Cribbins said.

"When do you expect him back?" Wightman asked.

"Who said he's coming back?" Cribbins said. "Who said he even lives here?"

Wightman grunted and said, "Fred, don't play games with me. You and that boy of yours have had your share of run-ins with the law. I don't need to tell you what 'obstructing an investigation' means. I also don't need to tell you it's against the law."

Cribbins smiled and chuckled sarcastically.

"Hey, there's no need to get snippy about it. Come on inside, let's discuss this like civilized folks."

He opened the screen door. Ann Marie stepped inside first, followed by Riley and Sheriff Wightman. Then Cribbins turned his head and spoke in a louder voice that was obviously directed toward somebody else in the house.

"After all, it's not every day I get the pleasure of a visit from the FBI."

Riley felt a surge of adrenaline as she realized what was happening.

Sure enough, she heard a clatter of footsteps from somewhere farther inside the house, and then the sound of a door opening.

Before anybody else had time to react, Ann Marie was in motion, dashing past Cribbins and back through the house, after the unseen occupant who was apparently leaving. Riley started after her, but Cribbins blocked her way.

The towering, obese man presented a vast and formidable obstacle, and at the moment the sheriff didn't seem inclined to take him on. But the sounds from behind him told her that Ann Marie had just followed someone out a back door.

Cribbins said to her, "Hey, little lady, don't be rude when I'm trying to show some hospitality. Where are you and that girl rushing off to? Why don't you and my pal the sheriff sit down and make yourself comfortable and let me fetch y'all some cold brewskis?"

Riley knew she had no time to play this game. A physical confrontation would just slow her down. She lurched sharply to one side and then pushed past the slower, hulking man and hurried on through the house.

Cribbins and Wightman can just deal with each other, she thought.

As she passed through an archway into a dirty kitchen, she could hear the two men arguing back in the living room. And now she could see the back door standing open.

She rushed to the door and looked outside. A chilly breeze was blowing a few pieces of litter about an overgrown backyard, but nothing else in sight was moving. Beyond the uncut grass was a narrow alley.

From where she stood, Riley could see no sign at all of Ann Marie or the man she was pursuing.

Where did they go?

Chapter Eighteen

As Riley stood listening in the doorway, she heard Ann Marie's voice call out. The sound was coming from somewhere beyond the yard—off to the left, she thought.

Ann Marie yelled again, "Halt! FBI!"

It was obvious that the guy they had come to interview was on the run. And Riley's young partner was in pursuit.

Riley dashed out of the house and across the little back yard. When she reached the alley, she could see Ann Marie running hard away from her. It was easy to guess that Brad Cribbins must be somewhere ahead of the rookie, but Riley couldn't see him. She thought for a moment of calling out to her partner, but she didn't want to stop the chase. They'd surely lose their suspect if he got out of Ann Marie's sight.

Riley broke into a run herself. As she charged frantically down the alley, she didn't know whether to hope Ann Marie could catch up with the young man, or to hope that she couldn't. After yesterday's debacle with the hunter, Riley didn't know how Ann Marie might fare in a one-on-one confrontation with a possibly violent criminal.

The way this guy had slipped out of the house when he heard the FBI was there meant that he was likely to be the killer they were looking for.

Riley sped up her pace. She wanted to catch up with that young man before Ann Marie did. But she wasn't actually gaining on the rookie, and there didn't seem to be much chance of getting ahead of her.

Suddenly Ann Marie veered sharply to the left and dashed between two small sheds, apparently still on the young man's tail. Riley followed after her and found herself in another cluttered back yard. Now she was closer to Ann

Marie, who seemed to have tripped over a toy truck in the next yard over. Although the rookie was stumbling, she didn't fall.

A couple of back yards beyond them, Brad Cribbins had paused to look back. It was the first glimpse Riley had gotten of him, and what she saw wasn't encouraging. He was a big man like his father, but very lean and muscular. Riley didn't look forward to tangling with him. And she doubted that Ann Marie was up to the task at all.

When he spotted Riley, he gave a laugh, then turned and ran again. Ann Marie was already charging after him, and Riley followed. Soon they were wending wildly through neighboring back yards, trailing Brad among beat-up shacks, garages, old cars, garbage cans, and random junk.

He knows this neighborhood well, Riley realized.

He was also extremely agile, leaping and dodging to evade various obstructions. But Riley could see that Ann Marie was showing remarkable agility herself and actually closing some of the distance between them.

If only I can keep up, she thought.

At forty-one she knew she must be marginally slower than the two young people up ahead of her. But she also knew she had exceptional endurance, and figured she could outlast either of them if the chase continued for very long. The demands of her work and the required obstacle-course scores at Quantico had kept her in remarkably good shape.

Even so, Riley's spirits sank as she saw Brad Cribbins hurdle a five-foot-high wooden fence. He obviously kept up some kind of fitness routine himself.

We're going to lose him, she thought.

But Ann Marie put a hand on the top board and leaped over the fence right after him, almost as deftly as he had. On the other side she landed well and pounded away after the suspect.

Without slowing down, Riley followed. She grabbed the top boards with both hands and vaulted, clearing the fence but landing in a painful squat on a concrete surface on the far side. She could feel her muscles strain as she rose to her feet.

Now Ann Marie had turned out of a back yard and was running between two houses toward the front yards. Riley regained her stride and followed in time to see the rookie darting toward the street.

Again, Brad was nowhere in sight. He must have already crossed the street and disappeared. There seemed to be two likely places where he might have gone between houses on the other side.

Heedless of an approaching car, Ann Marie dashed into the street. The car screeched to a stop just short of hitting her, and the driver honked his horn indignantly. Ann Marie froze in front of the vehicle for a startled moment, then continued on after the suspect.

Her knees still aching a bit from the hard landing, Riley also dashed toward the street. She saw Ann Marie waver for just a second or two, trying to decide which route Brad had taken. Then the rookie made a blind choice and continued on between two of the houses.

Riley got across the street during a break in traffic. She was catching up with Ann Marie, but she was afraid that they both had fallen hopelessly behind the man they were pursuing. She decided to split from the rookie's direction and follow the runner's other possible route between two of the houses. Moving fast again now, she crossed an open back yard and entered another alley.

For a moment, she stood face to face with Brad Cribbins. He was about ten feet away from her, catching his breath and watching to see if he was still under pursuit. The young man's eyes widened with alarm, and he whirled and dashed away from her.

"Halt!" Riley yelled.

She wasn't surprised that he disobeyed and kept right on running. She broke into a run after him but quickly realized that her knees were aching now, slowing her down. She couldn't pick up the speed she needed.

Just when Riley despaired of catching him, Ann Marie appeared from the far side of a garage, heading him off. Even though Brad was much bigger and obviously stronger than Ann Marie, the young rookie threw herself forward and tackled him.

Both of them sprawled writhing on the concrete, but then Brad rolled sharply away from Ann Marie. As he leapt to his feet, he drew a large hunting knife from an ankle sheaf.

Ann Marie also struggled up off the ground, but he kicked her backward. By the time the rookie regained her balance, he was holding the knife in front of her face.

Riley came to a halt and reached for her Glock, but before she could even get it out of its holster, she saw Ann Marie execute a shrewd and swift maneuver. She tore off her jacket and whipped it in front of her, using it to knock Brad's knife out of his hand.

With a roar of frustration, Brad turned to lunge for his fallen knife, but found himself facing the barrel of Riley's gun.

"Put your hands above your head," Riley growled. "You're under arrest."

Looking shocked, he did as she demanded.

Riley tossed her handcuffs to Ann Marie, who cuffed the surly suspect as Riley read him his rights.

When she heard someone approaching behind her, she glanced back and saw that Sheriff Wightman had just arrived.

He said sheepishly, "Uh . . . I'm sorry I'm late." Then he bent over gasping with his hands on his knees, looking completely exhausted.

Riley realized that he must have been trying to follow them through the obstacle course that Brad Cribbins had run. But the sheriff was definitely not up to this sort of chase.

Chuckling hoarsely, Wightman said, "I've got to say, you two gals can be pretty hard to keep up with."

"Thanks for coming to look for us," Riley said with a tired laugh.

"Glad to oblige," the sheriff said. "Not that you needed my help. I can see the two of you've got things pretty well under control."

We sure do, Riley thought.

Moments later, Sheriff Wightman was escorting the handcuffed and subdued Brad Cribbins toward his parked vehicle. Riley and Ann Marie agreed to meet them at the police station.

As she walked alongside Ann Marie back toward their own car, Riley realized that she was limping slightly, but the rookie seemed as spry as ever.

Riley told her, "You handled yourself pretty well back there."

Ann Marie's eyes glowed and face was flushed with excitement.

"Yeah, I guess I did, didn't I?" she said.

"Where did you learn a move like that?" Riley asked.

Ann Marie let out a chuckle.

"Hey, I went to the academy too, you know. Besides that, I took a few Krav Maga classes back when I was in high school."

Riley smiled. "Krav Maga. I should have known."

She had first encountered that Israeli fighting system before she was even an agent, when her father had decided she needed to know it to defend herself. His lessons had been rough, but she'd had more practice after she joined the FBI. By the time her father had died, they hadn't been on speaking terms, but the wild combination of boxing, wrestling, karate, and ruthless street fighting techniques was built into her automatic defenses.

Her rookie partner had just used the classic Krav Maga tactic of using a makeshift weapon—her jacket—to thwart her opponent. And she had used it well.

They climbed into their car and headed for the police station.

In a breathless, ecstatic voice, Ann Marie said, "Wow, that was . . . a *rush!* Does it always feel like that? Taking down a bad guy, I mean?"

Riley smiled. At the moment, she felt little else except aches and pains. She didn't feel the least bit elated.

"Not always," she said.

"Too bad," Ann Marie said. "I could get to like it."

As Riley continued to drive, she found herself unexpectedly curious about her new partner. Meredith had said that Ann Marie skipped some of the requirements for entering the FBI Academy, just as Riley had. Like Riley, she had impressed a senior agent by solving a difficult case on her own, and had been admitted based on recommendations.

Riley had been pushed into thinking about a serial killer because he had murdered her own college roommate and another friend. She had nearly been killed herself.

What, she wondered, had pushed Ann Marie? What kind of case had she solved?

Riley said, "Maybe it's time you told me a little more about yourself, Ann Marie Esmer."

Chapter Nineteen

Driving close behind Sheriff Wightman's car, Riley waited for Ann Marie to answer. But the young agent just turned and looked at Riley as if she had no idea what she meant.

Of course she doesn't, Riley realized.

She explained, "You got recruited because of a murder case you solved. I'd like you to tell me about it."

Ann Marie laughed a little.

"Oh, that," she said. "That was just a silly thing."

A "silly thing"? Riley wondered. She found it weird to think of a murder case as a "silly thing."

Ann Marie continued, "Anyway, it had to do with these twins in Georgetown..."

Riley couldn't help but interrupt.

"Twins? Do you mean the Bristow twins case?"

"Yeah, that one," Ann Marie said. "So you've heard of it?"

"Yeah," Riley said, trying not to sound too startled—or too impressed.

There had been quite a bit of talk around Quantico last year about the Bristow case. Riley hadn't been involved with it, but from what she'd heard, it was a peculiar one, even by her standards. She didn't know many details about it, just that it had some kind of twist to it that investigators had almost missed.

Riley was glad that she was apparently going to hear all about it now from someone who had actually been involved. She'd never have guessed that her young partner would know anything about that semi-notorious case.

"Please fill me in," she added.

Ann Marie shrugged. "Well, one day at Dad's mortuary, this guy named Glenn Bristow brought his identical twin brother's body in for cremation.

They'd been rock climbing, and his brother, Ethan, had fallen to his death. Dad asked me to conduct the bereavement interview while he was preparing the body for cremation."

She sighed happily. "I really like that part—talking to people about their grief, I mean. I'm good at it, I really know what I'm doing. I guess it's because I'm such a people person."

Riley wasn't surprised to hear her say that. She remembered vividly the rookie's skillful professionalism when she'd interviewed Allison Hillis's mother. She also remembered finding Allison's performance to be shallow and insincere. But Lauren Hillis hadn't seemed to feel that way at all. Ann Marie had managed to put that bereaved woman fully at ease in a way that Riley couldn't have pulled off.

She really is good at it, Riley had to admit to herself. *A real people person.*

But Riley still wasn't sure if she herself was one of those "people" that Ann Marie did so well with.

The rookie went on, "Glenn had come to the mortuary with his wife, Barbara. They were really leaning on each other for support. In fact, Glenn seemed to be taking his brother's death hard. They'd been pretty much inseparable their whole lives, he said."

Riley said, "And they really were *identical,* right?"

"Well, to look at, yes," Ann Marie said. "But in some ways they apparently weren't so similar. Glenn said the whole thing was horribly ironic. Although they sometimes climbed together, it wasn't one of Glenn's main interests in life like it was his brother's. Ethan was the better climber and was actually in much better shape. That day he was leading the way like he always did. But he fell. Glenn said he just barely managed to keep from falling too."

Riley said, "That can happen. Even the best of climbers sometimes make mistakes. It can be because of overconfidence."

Ann Marie agreed and added, "This time it was an equipment failure, but that could be put down to carelessness because of overconfidence. Glenn said he felt awfully guilty about it, even though the accident obviously hadn't been his fault. No one ever blamed him at all. To me it looked like a classic case of survivor's guilt."

"I suppose morticians see that sort of guilt all the time," Riley said.

"Oh, they sure do," Ann Marie said. "But there was also something about the whole situation didn't feel right to me. In fact, when I thought about it, I got to tingling all over. It was a really weird feeling, like nothing I'd ever experienced before."

Riley was startled. A tingling sensation usually signaled her that she was getting an important hit on a killer's way of thinking.

When Riley didn't reply, Ann Marie added, "But I guess you know that feeling well."

Riley nodded and said, "It's the way you feel when a hunch is coming on. Paying attention to it can be important."

"Right, well, I didn't understand that at the time," Ann Marie said. "But I definitely noticed how Barbara didn't seem to share Glenn's grief over his brother's death. Even though she was going through the appropriate motions, she just seemed kind of—I don't know, cold about it."

With a tilt of her head, Ann Marie added, "Pretty soon Glenn got really overcome and he couldn't talk anymore. He said he had to get out of the room for a few minutes to collect himself, and I found myself alone with Barbara."

"What happened then?" Riley asked.

"Well, Barbara confided to me in a whisper that she didn't feel sorry for what happened to Ethan at all. He might have been Glenn's identical brother, but except for their physical resemblance, she said they couldn't have been more unlike each other. Glenn was a responsible man and a wonderful husband. Ethan was a bum and a ne'er-do-well, she said, and he sponged off of Glenn a lot."

"What else did she say?" Riley asked.

"She said she'd also been worried about them going rock climbing together. Glenn just wasn't as good at it as his brother. She was annoyed with her husband for even going up again. Ethan had never had a bad fall, never even broken a bone. But just a couple of years ago, Glenn had suffered a short fall when they were out together. He'd broken an ankle and had promised her he wouldn't climb again. But his brother really wanted them to go up together, and Glenn could never say no to him."

"And the better climber fell," Riley commented.

Ann Marie shrugged. "Anyway, the wife agreed with Glenn about one thing. It *was* ironic that Ethan wound up getting killed. But it was clear that as far as Barbara was concerned, it was no great loss."

"That *does* sound cold," Riley said.

"Oh, she was positively icy, at least about Ethan," Ann Marie said. "But she really did seem to love Glenn and be truly concerned about him. Anyway, I was around when Dad put the body in the cremation chamber. As usual, it took a couple of hours to cremate the body. During that time, Dad and I heard some small popping sounds. Dad wasn't bothered by it. Sometimes that sort of thing happens during a cremation. But I just had this feeling…"

Ann Marie shuddered a little.

"After the cremation process," she said, "Dad and I took the remains out of the oven, and they cooled off for a while. I insisted on helping Dad with the next step, which was picking out any metals that might still be mixed up in the remains—stray jewelry, pins and screws from surgery, that kind of thing. Sure enough, I found something odd."

Riley waited for her to continue.

"I found three bone screws in the remains," Ann Marie said.

Riley was starting to understand the role Ann Marie had played in the case.

"So the question was…" Riley began.

Finishing her thought, Ann Marie said, "What the heck was a man who'd 'never had a broken bone' doing with those screws in his body? They were the kind of thing that might be used to repair a broken ankle. It didn't make sense—but of course it really did."

"Did you go straight to the police?" Riley asked.

"Oh, you bet we did, Dad and I both, although Dad was pretty confused about the whole thing. I showed the cops the screws and told them what I thought was going on."

Riley nodded and said, "That it was Glenn's corpse you'd cremated, not Ethan's."

"Right. I figured Barbara and Ethan must have been having an affair, and they both decided to get poor Glenn out of the way so Ethan could take his place as Barbara's husband. So Ethan was still alive and now he had a wife and property and a good income. The two guys looked so much alike, they didn't think anyone would notice the switch."

"What did the cops say?" Riley asked.

"They acted like I was crazy," Ann Marie scoffed. "They said they'd already investigated the accident and found no evidence of foul play. They even said that it would be no surprise if a longtime climber had some kind of break repaired. They really just didn't want to open a case against the man they thought was Glenn Bristow, a well-respected citizen. But I insisted that they check again, and this time I helped them. And sure enough, I found very slight plier marks on the harness that had failed in Glenn's climbing equipment. The cops just hadn't looked carefully enough, because they'd had no reason to suspect foul play. But I proved it was sabotage, pure and simple."

Riley said, "I guess the rest of the case must have been pretty cut and dry."

"Oh, yeah," Ann Marie said. "There were no medical records of Ethan ever having had any kind of surgery, but his brother had definitely had an ankle repaired a couple of years back. After that, they could get warrants to check fingerprints and even DNA, and it turned out my theory was right. The cops were impressed with me, and the FBI got word of what I'd done, and... well, you know the rest."

Riley did know the rest, indeed. Ethan Bristow and Glenn's widow were both found guilty of murder and sent to prison. They might have gotten away with it if it weren't for Ann Marie.

Ann Marie added with a shy laugh, "Anyway, like I told you—just a silly thing. Nothing at all like the cases you're used to solving. Nothing like the one we're working on now."

Riley figured it was small wonder that her partner had been recruited into the summer intern program, then into the academy. The kid obviously had potential.

But potential for what?

The case Ann Marie had solved was hardly a typical field case, and there was a sort of Nancy Drew quality to how she had solved it. It was all quite cerebral and free from physical risk. Riley wondered—might the kid be more suited to a career in forensics of some sort, for example forensic medicine?

But then Riley reminded herself of how well Ann Marie had handled herself just now, starting at the very moment when Brad Cribbins took off through the back door of his house. She'd been fast, shrewd, and even athletic. If it hadn't been for Ann Marie, Cribbins might still be on the loose.

She did good work back there, Riley had to admit.

And maybe, with some luck, they had caught the killer they were looking for. If so, maybe they'd find out when they questioned him at the police station. Riley certainly hoped so.

Again she remembered what the killer had said about the Goatman in his message . . .

HE WILL FEAST AND SING AGAIN
ON THE HALLOWED EVE

Riley shuddered deeply as she parked behind the sheriff's car in front of the police station.

Halloween's tomorrow, she thought.

We don't have time for mistakes.

Chapter Twenty

Riley kept getting flashes of déjà vu. The room on the other side of the two-way mirror looked like a thousand interrogation rooms she'd seen before—the same soundproof panels on the walls, the same battleship-gray table, the same stark lighting.

As she watched and listened to Sheriff Wightman badger Brad Cribbins with questions, the grilling seemed all too familiar as well. Even so, she was aware that the rookie standing beside her was following the proceedings with considerable interest.

Every interrogation is different, Riley reminded herself. She needed to watch closely to spot the differences in this one.

Ann Marie nudged her and asked, "I don't get it. Why aren't *we* in there asking the questions?"

"We'll get our chance," Riley said.

"But—"

Riley interrupted a bit impatiently.

"Just listen," she said. "You might learn something."

In fact, that was what she was hoping for herself. As far as she was concerned, Sheriff Wightman was laying the groundwork for her own questions. And she was already getting a strong sense of just who Brad Cribbins was.

As she'd observed when they'd chased him down, he was a big, muscular man—at least on the outside. But she sensed a weakness lurking just beneath that physical strength, a kind of vulnerability that was rooted in profound insecurity.

Many of the killers she'd hunted down had shared the same characteristic.

She could also tell that Wightman and Brad had acted out this scene together many times before. She remembered Wightman telling her that Brad

Cribbins had always been a "bad kid," with run-ins with the law dating back to when he was nine years old.

These two know each other well, she thought.

Right now, Wightman was trying to get the younger man to come up with an alibi.

"We've been through all that," Brad said. "I was working over at the mall."

Wightman snapped impatiently, "I'm not talking about when Vice Principal Swenson disappeared. I'm talking about when Allison Hillis went missing."

Riley could see Brad wince at the sound of Allison's name. She wondered why.

Brad said, "I've got no idea where I was."

"Are you sure?" Wightman said. "It was Halloween night, a year ago tomorrow."

Brad shrugged and smirked.

"So maybe I was trick-or-treating."

It was obviously a wise-ass answer, but Wightman didn't let himself be goaded by it.

"You weren't at work?" he asked.

"I think maybe I was between jobs around then," Brad said.

"You have trouble holding down a job, don't you?"

"Can I help it if nobody wants me?" he replied despondently.

Riley was startled by his change in tone. He wasn't being wise-assed now. He seemed to sincerely feel unwanted. And Riley didn't doubt that that was true.

"Aw, don't make me cry," Wightman said in a mock whine. "At least your dad puts up with you. But then, I guess that situation isn't all that great, maybe for either one of you. Tell me, are you going to live with that drunken old bastard forever?"

Brad grimaced bitterly and didn't reply. But Riley sensed a whole world of meaning in his reaction. She remembered the hulking, drunken man who had met them at the door. She'd known right then that Fred Cribbins must have been a violent, abusive father. Brad had almost certainly grown up in a state of what she'd heard psychologists call "learned helplessness."

Sadly for Brad, Riley guessed that he'd grown up without even realizing that he had become physically much stronger than his father, who was now pretty much a wreck from years of drinking. Fred Cribbins probably still beat his son whenever he felt like it. Brad didn't know how to fight back—and he didn't know how to move out and live on his own.

Riley's interest mounted as the interview continued. The sheriff wasn't getting a lot of information out of him, but Riley was still gaining useful impressions. Brad kept slipping into that wise-ass attitude of his—an attitude Riley was sure he'd shown Yvonne Swenson during the many times he'd been called into the vice principal's office.

This told Riley a lot about how Brad dealt with people. He didn't dare stand up to his father, so he took his aggression out on other authority figures, usually in the form of snide insolence.

He felt like he had little to fear from people like the sheriff and Yvonne Swenson. After all, it wasn't like they were going to beat him. Getting arrested now and again didn't seem like such a big deal.

The guy's a sad case, she thought.

But was he a murderer?

Riley couldn't yet tell.

Finally Sheriff Wightman seemed to tire of Brad's smirking evasions. He came out of the interrogation room into the booth with Riley and Ann Marie.

"I'm done," he growled. "He's all yours."

As she and Ann Marie went into the interrogation room, Riley had four case folders tucked under her arm—not only the ones for Yvonne and Allison, but for the earlier disappearances of Henry Studdard and Deena McHugh. Riley had already instructed Ann Marie to always let her take the lead during the questioning.

Not that Riley didn't want the rookie to speak up at all. Riley knew that her "people skills" would probably come in handy as the interview went on.

Meanwhile, Riley knew that she and Ann Marie both needed to play the "good cops" after the surly performance Sheriff Wightman had just given. They needed to put the suspect at ease, at least for the moment.

Riley smiled warmly at Brad as she and Ann Marie sat down across the table from him.

As she set the folders on the table, she said in a kindly voice, "I'd ask how you're doing, Brad. But I don't guess you're having a very good day right now."

Brad slumped and sighed. "No, I can't say that I am," he said.

"Well, Agent Esmer and I will try to keep this short. Maybe this is all a misunderstanding."

"Does that mean I can get out of here soon?" Brad asked.

Riley tilted her head sympathetically.

"Not right away, I'm afraid," she said. "You resisted arrest back there. A bit roughly, I might add. You know that's against the law, and you might get charged for it. But if you just answer my questions, maybe we can make things a whole lot easier. Maybe we can kind of play down the knife, for example."

"That sounds good," Brad replied, looking interested for the first time.

Riley opened the folder for the Deena McHugh case and showed him a picture of the middle-aged woman.

She said, "Tell me, Brad—do you recognize this woman?"

Brad shook his head.

"Are you sure?" Riley said. "It's really important for you to be sure."

Brad scoffed. "Hey, I'm not sure of much of anything right now. But she doesn't look familiar to me."

Riley exchanged a glance with her partner, inviting her to pitch in.

In her kindly, mortician-like manner, Ann Marie said, "Her name was Deena McHugh. Does that name sound familiar?"

"No," Brad said. "Did something happen to her?"

Riley gave Ann Marie a nudge, signaling her not to answer the question. If Brad really was the serial killer they were looking for, it was best not to complicate things by telling him things he already knew. Their goal was to get him to tell them everything himself.

Riley opened the folder for the Henry Studdard case and showed him the picture of the long-missing boy.

"What about this boy?" she asked. "His name was Henry Studdard."

Brad shook his head again.

"Are you sure?" Riley asked again. "The picture's pretty old."

"I guess I'm sure," Brad said. "Should I know him?"

Again, Riley didn't volunteer an answer.

Instead, she studied his face closely. She remembered the "math" Ann Marie had done in the car. Henry had been thirteen when he'd disappeared, and Brad was probably twelve or thirteen. Riley tried to imagine Brad as he might have been in the beginning of adolescence—slighter, more awkward, but full of raging emotions.

Would such a boy have been capable of murdering a younger boy?

She wasn't yet sure, but she thought maybe he might be.

She opened the folder for the Yvonne Swenson case and showed him a picture of the slain vice principal.

"I'm sure you know who this is," she said, not disagreeably.

"Yeah, but what's the point of getting into that?" he said in a defensive tone. "The sheriff and his cops really put me through hell when she went missing. It was a waste of time. I had an alibi."

Scanning the report, Riley said, "Yeah, you were working at the mall, and your workmates vouched for you. Sorry to dredge up ancient history, but we've got to be thorough. I hope you understand."

Brad let out a grunt of dismay.

"Anyway, you definitely knew Ms. Swenson, right?" Riley said.

"Oh, yeah," Brad growled. "And if you want to know if I'm sorry about what happened to her, I'm not."

"You didn't get along?" Riley said.

"Nope."

"Why not?" Ann Marie put in.

Brad snorted. "You'd have to ask her—if you could. She just took some kind of dislike to me, that's all. I can't explain it. I wasn't the only one she was hard on, though. Lots of kids thought she was a bitch."

Riley was pleased with what she was hearing. The "good cop" tactic was paying off, and Brad was starting to let out some genuine feelings.

It's time to start leaning in a little more, she thought.

She thumbed through the file until she came to the notorious list with "FOR TERMINATION" written across the top. She pointed to where the vice principal's name was written under the scrawled skull and crossbones.

"Why did you put her name on this list?" Riley asked.

Brad rolled his eyes.

"Come on," he said. "You're not going lay this on me again, are you? I was still a kid. I got pissed off with some people. I wrote this list to let off steam. I didn't mean anything by it. And I sure as hell didn't expect anyone else to go reading it."

Riley ran her finger down the page until she got to the name "Ally."

She said, "'Ally' is a girl's name, right?"

Brad said nothing, but his face looked pained and sad.

Riley added, "And you were pissed off with her too, right? That's why you put her name on the list, right?"

Brad actually started trembling a little.

Riley felt a sharp tingle of expectation.

"Just who is 'Ally,' Brad?" she said.

He opened his mouth to say something, then stopped.

I've hit a nerve, she thought.

She spoke again in a gentle voice. "I think you'd better tell us about Ally."

Chapter Twenty One

It was obvious to Riley that Brad was struggling to keep his emotions under control. She just waited to see how that worked out, but her expectations were rising by the second.

If he breaks down now, everything might come out, she thought.

In a choked voice, Brad said, "I never meant Ally any harm."

Ann Marie leaned toward him and asked, "Just who *was* Ally?"

Brad didn't reply. He was fighting back his tears.

"Ally is—was—Allison Hillis," Riley said. "Am I right?"

Brad nodded.

Riley said, "If you didn't mean her any harm, why did you put her on this list?"

"I'm sorry about what happened to her," Brad said. "It was terrible what happened to her."

Riley studied his face closely. She wondered—what was he feeling at the moment?

Guilt?

Grief?

Both?

She was pretty sure that she and her partner were about to find out. She thought the boy was reaching a point where he *wanted* to tell them about Allison. He probably needed to let out some long-pent-up feelings.

Ann Marie asked, "You and Allison went to different schools, right?"

Brad nodded again.

"So how did you know each other?" Ann Marie asked.

"We met at a basketball game," Brad said. "Our schools were playing against each other. We caught each other's eyes in the stands across the court from each other. Through the whole game, she kept smiling at me, and I kept smiling at her. It was like we . . . already knew each other."

He sighed at the memory.

"It was like . . . well, I can't tell you what it was like. The girls at my school weren't interested in me at all. I never knew why. And here was this pretty, sweet girl across the basketball court smiling at me like we'd always been lifelong friends. It was magical."

Ann Marie asked, "Then what happened?"

"After the game, she got away from her friends and we managed to find each other. We walked and talked for an hour or so. We had so much to say to each other. I had a car, so I drove her home—she lived over in Aurora Groves. And when I walked her to the door, we kissed. It was . . ."

He shook his head as if unable to find the words for how he'd felt.

"Well, I couldn't sleep at all that night. I kept worrying that I'd wake up and it would turn out to be a dream. But in the morning I texted her, and she texted me back, and she seemed as happy as I was to get in touch. She told me she'd had trouble sleeping too."

He seemed to slip away into memory for a moment. When Ann Marie opened her mouth to ask a question, Riley gave her glance that signaled not to. They'd reached a point in this interrogation that was familiar to Riley. Right now it was important to let the suspect speak on his own.

He continued, "We communicated a lot during the next few days—text messages, emails, video chats, phone calls. But it wasn't enough—for me, at least. I kept suggesting we get together for a real date. She sort of kept avoiding the idea. Finally I just got her on the phone and asked her what the problem was."

His jaw clenched tightly.

"She said she was sorry, but her parents would never let her date a guy like me. She hoped I'd understand."

He drummed his fingers on the table.

"Oh, I understood, all right," he said. "I felt like an idiot for ever thinking I could get anywhere with a rich girl from Aurora Groves—not a guy like me, living in a dump of a house, working at odd jobs to help my drunk of a dad pay the rent, with a police record going all the way back to when I was just a kid. No, I just wasn't in her league."

Brad's face twitched.

"I got mad. I told her she should have told me where things stood between us from the start. I accused her of leading me on, getting her kicks from slumming with a poor kid from the wrong side of Winneway. She got upset and hung up. I can't say I blamed her."

He shook his head and added, "I guess I got a little crazy after that. I kept sending her texts and emails and leaving voicemails, begging her to give me another chance. She didn't reply to any of them. Well, finally I got the message. I know when I'm not wanted, I'm used to it, believe me. But..."

His voice choked again with emotion.

"I sent her one last text, with just one word. 'Bitch.'"

He raised his manacled hands to his face and wiped away a tear.

"I never heard from her after that, and she never heard from me. And now..."

He couldn't force the words out, but Riley knew what he was starting to say.

"And now she's dead."

He was weeping softly now.

"I was mad at her when I put her name on that list," he said. "I guess I was kind of mad at the world. I still get that way from time to time. But I never meant her any harm. I liked her a lot. She was a wonderful girl. Too wonderful for a guy like me. I should have just accepted that. That last text I sent... I shouldn't have been mean like that... I should have just said, 'I understand.'"

He kept crying quietly.

Riley felt startled. Whatever she was expecting to hear from him, this wasn't it.

Was he the murderer they were looking for?

Maybe, Riley told herself. *Don't count him out yet.*

This show of grief could all be an act. A true sociopath could fake all the emotions Brad was showing right now. On the other hand, his emotions could be authentic. Even if he really was the killer, he could genuinely feel guilty about killing this particular girl.

But Riley was far from sure of what to think.

She reached into her mind for a different approach, and something started to occur to her. In the research Bill had done yesterday, he had found a connection between the killer's messages and the origin of the word "tragedy."

He'd told her about it on the phone.

"The Greek word 'tragedy' literally means 'goat song.'"

Maybe that's the key, Riley thought.

She leaned across the table and spoke in a sympathetic voice.

"I'm sorry. It was a real... *tragedy,* wasn't it? Not just for Allison, but for you too."

He glanced up at her when she emphasized the word tragedy. Riley studied his face, trying to gauge his reaction. Did the word evoke anything in him? Did it seem to have any significance for him?

Then Brad shrugged and said, "I guess so, if you want to put it that way. I just... hate feeling this way about it. I feel so bad."

Try as she might, Riley simply couldn't read his expression. But she didn't sense that the word had any significance to him. As he slumped down in his chair, she tried to think of yet another approach. She hastily considered details of the case that weren't yet public knowledge, even though Madge Torrance knew more about them than she ought to.

She said cautiously, "Brad, what do you know about the Goatman?"

Brad looked up at Riley in apparent surprise.

"What?" he asked.

Ann Marie put in, "Have you heard of him? The Goatman?"

Brad wrinkled his brow.

"You mean that monster people talk about over around Beltsville? What's that got to do with anything?"

Brad wasn't crying anymore. He just looked confused, but Riley sensed that it wasn't because she had touched a nerve. Instead, she got the strong feeling that he really had no idea why she'd mentioned the Goatman. The question had just seemed weird and out of the blue to him.

She also sensed that he'd told them everything he was going to tell them.

Before Ann Marie could ask any more questions, Riley spoke to him.

"Thanks for your time, Brad."

"Wait a minute," Brad said. "Aren't I getting out of here?"

"That will be up to Sheriff Wightman," Riley said. "Like I said before, resisting arrest is a crime."

Without another word, Riley got up from the table. Ann Marie followed her out into the adjoining room, where they found Sheriff Wightman pacing impatiently.

"Why did you quit questioning him?" Wightman asked. "He was about to crack. He was about to confess."

"No, he wasn't," Riley said.

"Why not?" Wightman asked.

"I don't think he had anything to confess," she replied. "Because in spite of all his shortcomings, he's not our killer."

Riley felt a chill to hear herself say that. She hadn't been sure of it herself until now that the words were out of her mouth.

Wightman's eyes widened.

"What do you mean, he's not our killer? Hell, you got him to admit that he knew Allison Hillis—not only knew her, but was angry with her. And they didn't even go to the same schools. Do you call that a coincidence?"

"Yes, I do."

"That's crazy."

Riley stifled a groan of frustration.

Apparently she was going to have to educate this seasoned lawman about a basic fact of investigative work.

"Coincidences happen, Sheriff Wightman," she said. "In fact, they're inevitable in our line of work, and they can be really misleading. You ought to know that."

Wightman's face reddened. He obviously didn't like being contradicted.

"I'm sure as hell not going to let him go," Wightman said.

"Then don't," Riley said. "Like I told him just now, it's your decision. He's guilty of resisting arrest, but he has been cooperative during questioning." She took a breath then added, "We're not finished with this case yet. If I'm right, there's still a killer out there, and—"

Wightman interrupted, "And I'm sure you're wrong. We've got our man, and we can prove it. That's what we should focus on. I'm going in there and I'm going to keep questioning him."

"Go ahead," Riley said.

Wightman continued, "And I'm going to wrap this up once and for all. If we keep chasing after somebody who doesn't exist, we'll just be spinning our wheels and wasting resources and taxpayer money. I won't have it."

"What are you saying?" Ann Marie asked.

Wightman scowled.

"I'm saying I won't be needing BAU help anymore. You're here at my request, and you stay at my pleasure. I'm telling you to go back to Quantico. The sooner the better."

Riley was angry as well. But she knew better than to lose her temper.

Things are bad enough as it is.

She said in a tight, controlled voice, "Whoever the killer is, he said he's going to strike again tomorrow—or try to. At least impose a curfew for tomorrow night."

Wightman scoffed. "And call off Halloween?"

Riley nodded.

Wightman shook his head incredulously.

"The whole town will be furious," he said.

"So what if they are?" Riley said. "It isn't your job to make everybody happy all the time. Are you sure you want to risk the public's safety? Do you want another murder on your head?"

Wightman's eyes narrowed, and he fell silent for a moment.

"I'll order the curfew," he said. "But I won't be needing the two of you anymore."

Riley nodded brusquely. As she and Ann Marie headed out of the booth, Sheriff Wightman was already on his way into the interrogation room to continue questioning Brad Cribbins.

As they left the building and walked toward the car, Riley saw that it was getting dark outside, and the reporters who had besieged them earlier had given up and left for the day.

When they climbed into the car, Ann Marie said, "Well. That was kind of a bummer."

That's an understatement, Riley said.

Ann Marie added, "Maybe we should get something to eat before we drive back to Quantico. Have we got enough gas for the trip?"

Riley didn't reply. She thought hard as she sat at the wheel without turning on the ignition. Sheriff Wightman had made himself more than clear just now.

"I won't be needing the two of you anymore."

She knew that it was also true that she and Ann Marie were here at his pleasure, and he could order them to go whenever he wished.

But still...

She turned to Ann Marie and asked her, "Do *you* think Brad Cribbins is our killer?"

Ann Marie crinkled her brow, as if surprised at the question.

"No," she said. "No way."

Riley felt relieved that she and her new partner were in agreement.

"Good," she said. "It looks like we'll be spending another night in Winneway. Let's go get something to eat."

Chapter Twenty Two

The man was enjoying the dancing clatter of Pan's cloven feet as they capered to the faint flutelike sound. Soon the tune would grow louder and these feet would leave their mark on a new sacrifice to the ancient god of chaos.

For a moment, he stopped the feet from dancing and admired his handiwork. He'd carved these two actual-sized wooden goat's feet out of hickory himself. He'd done the job according to Pan's instructions and design without knowing what they were for. The wooden feet had been ready when Pan had told him to sacrifice that young boy some eight years ago.

After he'd strangled the boy, Pan told him exactly what to do. He held the carved feet against the boy's dead flesh, then struck them repeatedly with a hammer until they left hoof-shaped indentations. The pounding took a good deal of effort and strength, especially around the victim's chest, where ribs had to be broken. But when he finished, he could see the effect was remarkable.

The body looked as if a goat—or rather the two-legged "Goatman" of Maryland legend—had danced all over it.

Absolutely brilliant, the man thought.

He only hoped that the public would start reacting to the Goatman connection at long last. The police had shrewdly kept the contents of his messages secret. So far, only the cops had known that he was attributing the killings to the Goatman.

But lately he'd started telling everyone he met about a "rumor" that the Goatman was at large and killing people—and he came into contact with a lot of people daily. With some luck, the idea would catch on and add to the public hysteria.

Meanwhile, it seemed rather sad that the boy's body still lay buried, and that the exquisite touch remained unappreciated. The man wondered—if the body were found someday soon, as he had reason to hope it would be, would the hoof prints still be visible? Or would they be erased by physical decay?

He also wondered about the woman he had killed four years ago, and whose body had never been found. It would be a shame if impressions were no longer visible.

But Pan truly had an extraordinary imagination. He had also instructed the man to compose clever messages, at first teasing the dull-witted police with an empty grave, and now a year later revealing the locations of the most recent victims.

The man smiled at the thought of the girl he'd killed last Halloween.

The footprints must definitely have been visible on her.

The body wouldn't have been as decomposed as the others, and the prints had made an especially sharp impression in the skeleton costume she'd been wearing.

As for the woman from the high school, Pan had been especially inspired on that occasion. What a stroke of sheer brilliance it had been to "plant" the corpse underneath a maple sapling! The roots of that tree must have been charmingly intertwined with the woman's bones. He only wished he could have seen how the body had looked when it had been disinterred this morning.

In his dictated message, Pan had described the spectacle in words of sheer poetry.

BLOOD RED FROM THE ROOTS
THE SAPLING GROWS NICELY NOW.

The glory would go to Pan someday—perhaps very, very soon. Perhaps the time was near when Pan would finally release his stampede of universal panic upon the whole human race.

Pan's shrill melody was already growing louder now. Giggling, he set the feet in motion again, tapping them against the top of his coffee table, making them dance ecstatically. A familiar exhilaration was rising inside of him. Pan was filling him with a wild, jubilant power created by thousands of years of legend.

And tomorrow night, on the Hallowed Eve, he would do Pan's will again.

Chapter Twenty Three

The next morning, the silence at breakfast was making Riley feel tense and uncomfortable. She and Ann Marie were sitting at a table at one side of the motel breakfast area, having an actual sit-down meal and coffee in real mugs for a change. All around them families and other groups of people were chatting away, but at their own table there was only the occasional faint clink of a fork against a plate.

Riley was sure that her young partner was waiting for her to say something—to come up with some brilliant plan. After all, it had been Riley's idea yesterday to stay here in Winneway and not drive back to Quantico. Riley had hoped that she'd have some idea what to do today after a good night's sleep.

But morning was here, and she still had no ideas. In fact, her sleep hadn't even been all that great. She had awakened from hazy dreams she couldn't quite remember... something about ghosts and goblins, she thought. They hadn't been friendly kids in cute costumes, but something definitely more dangerous.

And now it was Halloween. The kids in cute costumes would be out tonight, at least until the curfew. She was sure that at least one real monster would be out there too. She was sure that the killer who called himself the Goatman would strike again tonight. She didn't yet know how to stop him.

She remembered how indignant the sheriff had been yesterday when Riley had told him she thought Brad Cribbins was not their murderer.

"We've got our man, and we can prove it," he'd snapped.

Riley hated to imagine how he'd react if they showed up again at the police station this morning, having blatantly ignored his order to leave. But she felt much too certain about this not being over to pull out of town and leave the residents to face whatever happened. She wondered if there was there anything she and Ann Marie could do quietly on their own, so Wightman might not even know they were still in Winneway—at least not until they'd made a break in the case.

Probably, she thought. *There are always possibilities.*

But right now, she just couldn't think of what those things might be.

She felt completely stymied.

Every time she looked up from her coffee and her egg biscuit, she found herself wishing she'd see Bill looking across the table at her instead of Ann Marie. She and Bill always clicked especially well in moments like these, when tough decisions had to be made. If he were here right now, they'd be brainstorming away about tactics and strategy without worrying about whether or not every idea made much sense.

We'd probably have figured out what to do by now.

Instead, she had no familiar mind to bounce ideas off of. She knew that this silence really wasn't Ann Marie's fault. It took years to cultivate the easy, productive rapport she shared with Bill.

But now...

Are Bill and I ever going to work together again? Riley wondered.

She fought down a surge of melancholy. Now was no time to give in to sadness. She had to think of something. And she had to get her young partner involved in whatever plan she came up with.

Riley was still trying to think of something to say to Ann Marie when her phone buzzed.

For a moment, she hoped the call was from Bill. Then her heart sank when she saw who was actually calling.

It was Sheriff Wightman. Had he somehow found out she and Ann Marie had stayed in town in spite of his dismissing them? Was he calling to give them hell about it? Worse, was he going to report their disobedience to her superiors?

The last thing she needed right now was for Walder to find out about some kind of confrontation on this job.

She was surprised at Wightman's subdued tone when she took the call.

"Agent Paige...I hope I'm not catching you at a bad time."

"Not at all," Riley said, switching the call to speakerphone so Ann Marie could hear. At the moment there weren't any other people close enough to overhear whatever might be said.

Wightman spoke haltingly, "I'm afraid...I was a bit short with you yesterday."

Riley felt an urge to say, *"Yes, you were."*

Instead she kept her mouth shut.

The sheriff said, "Look, I kept questioning Brad Cribbins long after you left the station, way on into the night. I went after him in every single way I could possibly think of. I'm pretty good at questioning reluctant suspects and..."

Wightman paused for a moment.

"And you were right," he said. "He's not our guy. I know it now. He would have cracked by now if he were. We can still hold him on the resisting arrest charges, but there's no way he's a viable suspect in the murders. His connection with Allison Hillis really *was* coincidental, just like you said."

Riley suddenly breathed much easier. She saw that Ann Marie reacted the same way.

Wightman added, "Look, I was just flat wrong, and I'm sorry. And to make matters worse, I've got Senator Danson calling every few hours to check on our progress with the case. I made the mistake yesterday of telling him I thought we had our man, and when he called this morning, I had to tell him otherwise. He's not happy. I understand it's personal for him, now that his niece's body has been found, but that kind of nagging doesn't help."

Riley's teeth clenched at the mention of Danson's name. She remembered how he'd glowered at her and Ann Marie the day before yesterday.

"How soon do you expect to catch this killer?" he asked, and he'd apparently expected a better answer than Riley could give him.

The fact that Danson personally knew Carl Walder also worried Riley. How long would it be before Danson contacted Walder to express his dissatisfaction with how the case was going?

Has he maybe talked to Walder already? she wondered.

If so, she could expect to hear from her surly superior at any moment.

And that was the very last thing she needed right now.

Wightman continued, "Anyway, I feel completely out of my depth, especially now that it's Halloween. We've got to expect the killer to strike again tonight. I hate to ask you and your partner to drive back here from Quantico but—"

Riley interrupted, "That's not a problem. Agent Esmer and I never left Winneway. We stayed here overnight. We're in the motel right now having breakfast."

Riley heard Wightman let out a sigh of relief.

"I'm glad to hear it," he said. "I'm hoping you've got some ideas about what to do next. We don't have a lot of time."

Riley gulped. So far this morning, ideas had been hard to come by.

Now would be a good time to have one, she thought.

She told Wightman, "I'm open to your thoughts."

"Well, I don't have *thoughts* so much as *questions.* You've worked on these kinds of cases more times than you can probably count. What are the biggest dangers we're facing right now?"

Riley felt a familiar tingle. This was exactly the sort of question she or Bill might ask if they were brainstorming together right now. And she had a pretty good idea of the answer.

"We might have one of two problems," she said. "One is, our killer has been successful at getting by with murder. We don't even know for how long. He might well be feeling confident, and with good reason. He's damned smart and he knows it. He might keep right on outwitting us for a long time. A lot more people might die."

"That sounds bad," Wightman said. "What's the other problem?"

Riley scratched her chin and said, "The other is, he'll get cold feet. He knows that the game is getting riskier. I'm pretty sure he'll kill again sooner or later. But there's also a strong chance that he might go dormant for a while. For years maybe. And that could make it a lot harder for us to catch him."

"That also sounds bad," Wightman said.

"It is," she replied. "We just don't know enough about this man to guess which way he might go. Even basic profiling measures don't narrow it down enough for us to close in on anybody without other indicators."

"So what can we do?"

That tingle of Riley's got sharper as an idea started to form in her mind.

She knew they had to accomplish two things.

One was to make sure the killer stuck with his schedule and tried to strike tonight.

The other was to goad him into too much self-confidence so that he got careless.

She said to Wightman, "The first thing I need is for you to call a news conference at the police station. Call it for this morning, as soon as possible. My partner and I will drive right over there, and we can talk everything through."

Wightman thanked her and ended the call.

Ann Marie's eyes had widened.

"So what are we going to do?" she asked.

Riley wasn't ready to say just yet. The idea was still gelling in her mind.

"Come on, let's head out to the car," she said.

Chapter Twenty Four

The man paced the floor with agitation.

Where is Pan? he wondered.

The god had gone silent yesterday evening, right around the time when the man had gotten word that a curfew would be in effect tonight. The man hadn't heard Pan's songs or words throughout the whole sleepless night. And now it was the morning of the Hallowed Eve.

Has Pan abandoned me?

Has he found a more able servant?

Or had Pan decided not to carry out his will, at least not tonight? Perhaps Pan had taken the curfew as a sign that the task would be too difficult. For one thing, a lack of trick-or-treaters would offer scarcer prey.

For another thing, things had changed a lot during the last couple of days. The police had found two bodies, just as Pan had intended. This surely meant that the police were more keenly alert now, and that they fully expected Pan to strike.

They might even be prepared for it.

Pan might have sensed too much danger in the air.

All the man knew was that he felt isolated and empty and perplexed.

What was he to do if Pan remained silent?

He had no idea, except that he couldn't act, couldn't abduct and kill, because he'd never done so by his own will, only by Pan's.

How could he even go on living without the purpose and meaning Pan brought to his empty life?

He cried out aloud, "Pan, you know I am your loyal and adoring servant! Please, please tell me what to do! I beg you!"

The silence that followed was deafening.

He didn't think he could take it for another minute.

He turned on the TV, just to have some noise in the room.

He was surprised to see Sheriff Wightman standing on the police station steps talking to a group of reporters. Standing beside him were two women, one around forty years old, the other a good bit younger. Wightman was introducing them to the reporters.

"I want to thank the FBI's Behavioral Analysis Unit for all their help," he said. "Specifically, I want to thank Agents Riley Paige and Ann Marie Esmer. We couldn't have solved this case so quickly without them."

The FBI was here!

The man felt a flash of satisfaction. The police were obviously beginning to grasp the seriousness of what he and Pan were doing. He was sure that Pan was going to be pleased.

But his satisfaction gave way to alarm.

"Solved this case"?

What on earth could the sheriff possibly mean by that?

Surely the foolish sheriff was just trying to put everyone at ease. Maybe Pan would actually like that. He loved catching mortals by surprise. He enjoyed feeling their shock when they realized what was happening to them.

Another reporter shouted a question, "How many murders have there been in all?"

"We know of two," the sheriff replied.

"But do you believe there were others?" the reporter persisted.

The sheriff quickly turned his attention to another questioner.

The man felt a sudden thrill.

He knows! he thought.

He knows there were earlier victims!

It was gratifying to know those killings had been noticed after all. But of course, Pan had planned it this way all along. Doubtless the god would soon dictate further messages leading the police to those bodies.

The reporter he'd called on asked, "So you're confident that you have the killer in custody?"

"I didn't say that," the sheriff said.

"But you're not denying that you have a viable suspect," the reporter said.

"We do have a suspect in custody," the sheriff said.

"But you won't release his name?" another reporter said.

The older BAU woman spoke up.

"Not yet. Just be patient, please. We'll make his identity known to the public soon, perhaps tomorrow."

The man noticed that the younger agent was looking at the older one with dismay. For some reason, she didn't seem to like what she was hearing.

The man certainly didn't like it either.

How can they be saying such a thing? he wondered.

The sheriff and the agents all ignored the clamor of reporters asking them why there had to be a delay in learning the suspect's name.

Shouting above the others, one reporter asked, "So does this mean that tonight's curfew has been canceled?"

"No, the curfew is still on," Wightman said. "The town's nerves are still on edge, and understandably so. Halloween tends to be chaotic in the best of times. We don't want any unnecessary confusion tonight."

Now the reporters were expressing public dissatisfaction with this decision.

Wightman smiled and said, "Now let's not make too much of such a small matter. Youngsters can still do their usual trick-or-treating. But I want everybody inside before dark. I'll have police on patrol to make sure of that."

With a slight chuckle Wightman added, "If I had my way, we'd have a curfew every Halloween. Believe me, it would save a lot of trouble in the way of vandalism and rowdy behavior. But I'm sure we'll be back to a normal schedule next year."

Wightman waved his hand as the cacophony of questions resumed.

"That will be all for now," he said. "Thank you for your time."

Wightman and the two BAU agents headed back into the station. A local TV anchor came onto the screen to restate for viewers what had just happened.

But what did *just happen?* the man wondered, aghast.

He turned off the TV and stood staring at the blank screen.

How could the police possibly believe they'd apprehended the killer?

I'm the killer—no, the soldier!

And I kill under orders from the god Pan himself!

Suddenly, he heard a shrill, sharp sound. He recognized it at once. It was Pan's sacred pipe. But the god wasn't playing music. Instead, he was letting out a sharp, piercing cry of fury.

The man felt his face redden and his pulse rising as he shared Pan's outrage.

Who was this anonymous individual who presumed to claim glory that rightfully belonged to Pan alone?

How could the police be so stupid as to believe him?

The discordant music grew louder.

Then Pan was singing again. His voice was harsh and grating, but the words were loud and clear.

The man welcomed the song with all of his heart. He felt the god rising within him.

This very night, the barriers between this feeble world and the mighty world of legend would fall.

Tonight we will prove them wrong.

Chapter Twenty Five

Ann Marie was seething as she followed Agent Paige and Sheriff Wightman back inside the police station. She kept reminding herself that what they'd said at the press conference shouldn't have come as a complete surprise. After all, her senior partner had hastily outlined her plan to both Ann Marie and the sheriff before they went out to face the eager reporters. But Agent Paige hadn't gone into a lot of detail beforehand and things had happened in an awful hurry. Ann Marie hadn't fully grasped the reality of what Agent Paige had in mind—not until everything had been said and the press conference was over.

Now she was embarrassed and upset. Her superiors had just misled the public. They knew that they didn't have the killer locked up. They knew that the public wasn't safe. Of course she'd had no real choice about keeping quiet. She was the rookie here and she certainly couldn't challenge her superiors in public.

As she followed her two colleagues along the police station hallway, Ann Marie was surprised at how angry she felt with her senior partner. When they reached the room where they intended to confer about what to do next, Wightman went inside, and Riley was right behind him

Ann Marie came to a stop outside the door. She just couldn't bring herself to go in with them.

Agent Paige turned back and saw her still standing outside.

"Aren't you going to join us?" her senior partner asked.

Ann Marie paced uneasily. She didn't yet know what to say.

Agent Paige politely told the sheriff that she and Ann Marie would be joining him in a moment. Then she stepped back into the hallway and shut the door behind her.

The senior agent crossed her arms and said, "Maybe there's something you'd like to get off your chest."

"Yeah, there kind of is," Ann Marie said in a tense voice.

"Spill it," Agent Paige said.

Ann Marie inhaled sharply and said, "We just lied to the public."

Agent Paige said, "We did nothing of the kind."

"But the sheriff didn't deny that we have a viable suspect in custody," Ann Marie said.

"We *do* have someone in custody," Riley said

"But not a *viable* suspect," Ann Marie said. "Do we have any business misleading people like this?"

Agent Paige squinted at her.

"We don't have a sworn duty to be honest with the public," she said. "Our job is to *protect* the public, and that means stopping killers. And that's what we're going to do."

"And you've done this kind of thing before?" Ann Marie asked.

"Sometimes," Agent Paige said. "When it's actually in the public interest."

"And who gets to decide when to lie?"

"It's my judgment call," Agent Paige snapped impatiently. "And I shouldn't have to explain it to you."

When Ann Marie just stared back wordlessly, her senior partner seemed to relent a little.

"With some luck," Agent Paige told her, "the killer already got the news that we think we've caught the killer. That should pique his ego and really piss him off. If it does, we're likely to accomplish two things. One, we'll make sure that he doesn't go dormant. The other is—"

"Yeah, yeah, I know," Ann Marie interrupted. "We'll shake him up, make him get careless, put him off his game."

"And you see something wrong with that?" Agent Paige said.

"We're playing games with a dangerous killer," Ann Marie said.

Agent Paige nodded. "Yes, that's *exactly* what we're doing. Whether you like it or not, this is a game—a deadly game—and the killer will keep right on playing it no matter what we do. We've got to play, and we've got to play to win. I'm using a tried-and-true tactic. If you can think of a better one, you'd better speak up."

Try as she might, Ann Marie couldn't think of an argument against what Agent Paige was saying. All she knew was that she really didn't like this plan of hers. It scared her, and it still offended her.

"We misled the public," she grumbled again.

Agent Paige scowled at her and said, "You're just a kid, Ann Marie. You've lived a sheltered life. You've been taught that honesty is always the best policy. You've been taught not to take risks. The trouble is, a lot of what you've been taught doesn't apply to this kind of work. This isn't the Girl Scouts. You'd better get used to that."

Ann Marie was stunned by Agent Paige's condescending tone.

"Are you saying I'm not adaptable?" Ann Marie said.

"I'm not saying anything about you," Agent Paige said. "I'm just telling you how things are in the real world of law enforcement. And if you don't like it, and if you're going to take criticism personally, you'd better look for another career."

Ann Marie's mouth hung open.

"Why don't you like me, Agent Paige?" she blurted.

She and her partner locked eyes for a moment.

"What makes you think I don't like you?" Agent Paige said.

Ann Marie shrugged with frustration.

Agent Paige added, "Being liked is really important to you, isn't it? I don't even understand that."

Ann Marie said, "Yeah, well, I never know what to expect from you. Sometimes you seem to be perfectly OK with me. Sometimes you're even nice to me, and you tell me I'm doing a good job. Other times you're downright mean, or you act like you wish I wasn't here."

Agent Paige seemed to be trying keep her temper in check.

"I'm sorry I make you feel that way," she said. "It's just that you've got some pretty big shoes to fill."

Agent Paige looked if she'd blurted out something she hadn't meant to say.

Suddenly, everything made much more sense to Ann Marie. She knew that Agent Paige was used to working with a highly experienced partner who was very nearly as brilliant as she herself was. Their partnership itself had been something of a legend at the academy.

"I'm not Agent Jeffreys," Ann Marie said.

Agent Paige winced sharply and looked away from Ann Marie.

Ann Marie said, "Look, I don't know why you're not working with Agent Jeffreys on this case. But it wasn't my idea, and you know it. And it wasn't my idea for you to get stuck with a rookie like me."

Agent Paige looked both hurt and angry now.

"This isn't going to work," Agent Paige murmured tensely. "We've both done our best, but we can't do this together. It will just slow everything down and there's no time for that."

"What are you saying?" Ann Marie asked.

Agent Paige was silent for a moment.

"I saw a car rental place just down the street," she said. "Did you notice it too?"

Ann Marie nodded.

Agent Paige said, "Then I think you should walk on over there and rent a car and drive back to Quantico."

Ann Marie could barely believe her ears.

"Do you really mean that?" she said with a gasp.

"Don't worry, you'll get a reimbursement from the Agency," Agent Paige added.

Their eyes locked again for a few seconds. Then, without another word, Ann Marie turned away had stormed back down the hallway. She could hear Agent Paige open the door to the conference room and then close it behind her as she joined the sheriff inside.

Ann Marie strode down the hall, her throat tight and her eyes stinging.

Don't cry, she told herself.

Don't cry until you get out of this building.

There would be plenty of time to cry during the drive back to Quantico.

As soon as Ann Marie walked away from her, Riley felt a pang of regret. She knew she'd said some things she shouldn't have said.

Why? she wondered.

What got into me? Why was I so hard on her?

She knew she'd been right about one thing. There was no time to work it out. She and the sheriff had set an audacious plan in motion and they had to stay on top of it. That was more urgent than a rookie's hurt feelings.

She hurried back into the conference room, where Wightman was seated and waiting at the table. He looked surprised to see that she was alone.

"Agent Esmer won't be joining us," Riley said.

Sheriff Wightman nodded uncertainly. To Riley's relief, he seemed to realize that she didn't want him to ask any questions about what had just happened.

Grateful that the man seemed able to read her expression and body language, she sat down with him at the conference table and they began to pore over their plans.

Wightman unfolded a map and they discussed how to deploy the local police throughout Winneway, especially the Aurora Groves neighborhood. Wightman drew lines on the map, sectioning the town into specific areas for small groups of cops to patrol.

At one point Wightman asked, "How sure do you feel about this? Are you really convinced that the Goatman maniac will show himself tonight?"

Riley nodded. She knew that her strategy was partially based on a profiler's basic training in criminal behavior. But it also came from her personal sense of the killer. This wasn't as strong an impression as she'd had in some cases, but she'd learned over many years that she could usually trust her intuition. Others on the case hadn't experienced anything like that personal ability of hers, and she usually didn't even try to explain it to them.

She just replied, "Quite sure. If we've played our cards right, he's gnashing at the bit right now. He'll defy the curfew, hoping to find someone else who is defying it too."

Wightman grunted and said, "Yeah, well, he can count on that. There are always a few smart asses out there who think it's cool to ignore my orders. I just hope the killer doesn't find any of those people before we find him."

I hope so too, Riley thought.

She couldn't deny that her plan had its risks.

Maybe that was one of the reasons she'd gotten mad at Ann Marie right now.

"We're playing games with a dangerous killer," Ann Marie had said.

And of course she'd been absolutely right. And of course it was the last thing Riley had wanted to hear.

Still, the more she and Wightman discussed the plan together, the more sense it made. Wightman had already told the media that he would have cops on patrol enforcing the curfew. But only a few cops in uniform would be doing that. Most of the force would be out in plainclothes, and they'd constitute the real dragnet. With some luck, the killer would never catch on that a dragnet had been set for him until he was actually captured.

If, as Riley suspected, the killer was flustered and was going to get uncharacteristically sloppy, they had a better than even chance of catching him.

When they finished making their plans, Wightman left the conference room to set up a conference with his cops. Riley found herself sitting alone, thinking again about her unpleasant altercation with Ann Marie. She wondered again just why she had been so harsh with the kid.

She remembered Ann Marie saying, *"Why don't you like me, Agent Paige?"*

Riley realized it was actually a pretty good question.

Ann Marie seemed to charm everybody else she met.

Maybe that's the problem, Riley thought.

As far as she was concerned, a BAU agent had no business trying to be likeable all the time. Every successful agent Riley had known had been rough around the edges at the very least, and sometimes downright disagreeable.

Most of all, they didn't have the luxury of *caring* about being liked.

I was right to send her packing, Riley thought.

Maybe it was for her own good.

And anyway, Riley felt better about the prospect of not having Ann Marie around to distract and annoy her. Something big was coming up tonight, and Riley knew that she had to be at the top of her game.

But I could also use a partner, she thought.

Her heart lightened as something occurred to her.

Why not ask Bill?

She picked up her phone and punched in his number.

When she got him on the phone she said, "Hey, how busy are you right now?"

She heard Bill sigh.

"I'm still office-bound, at Meredith's orders," he said. "I keep staring at my computer, searching through whatever records and information I can get my hands on. But the truth is, I don't even know what I'm looking for. I'm just spinning my wheels. But judging from the morning news, you might have the killer in custody. Is that for real, or is it a ruse?"

"It's a ruse," Riley said.

"I see," Bill said. "Well, it's a ruse we've used before. Sometimes it works and sometimes it doesn't. Good luck with it this time."

"Thanks, I'll probably need it," Riley said.

She took a sharp breath and added, "I could also use your help. As it happens, I'm between partners at the moment."

Bill let out a chuckle, "You and the sorority sister didn't see eye to eye, huh?"

Riley smiled. Bill obviously had a pretty good idea of why things hadn't worked out with Ann Marie.

"It's my fault as much as hers," she said. "I'm just a grouchy old woman fixed in her ways, and I don't get along with much of anybody except..."

Riley paused, expecting Bill to jump right in and tell her he'd be thrilled to join her.

Instead, he remained silent for a moment.

"Riley, I don't think so," he finally said.

"Why not?" Riley asked.

"I'd have to clear it with Meredith, and he might tell Walder we're working together, and..."

A longer silence fell.

Then Bill said, "Riley, I think Walder knows about us. How we feel about each other, I mean."

Riley's heart jumped up in her throat.

"How does he know?" she asked.

"The night before last, when we were talking on the phone, I'd left my office door open. When we finished talking, he was right there in the doorway. I'm pretty sure he was eavesdropping. And I'm pretty sure he knew I was talking to you. He didn't exactly say anything, but... he had that gloating look he gets when he knows he's got the best of somebody."

Riley's eyes widened with alarm. She knew that look of Walder's very well.

Bill went on, "I was stupid not to shut the damned door. But hardly anyone is around the building at that time of night. Least of all Walder. I thought we had some privacy. Believe me, it's shut tight right now. I'm sorry."

"It's OK," Riley said.

She almost asked, *"How much did he overhear?"*

But she quickly remembered one of the last things Bill said to her before they ended the call . . .

"I miss you more than I can say."

If Walder had overheard nothing but those words, he knew more than she and Bill wanted him to.

Bill said, "Anyway, I'm afraid he's just waiting for the best opportunity to screw us over. If I come out there to work with you now . . ."

"I understand," Riley said with a sigh. "As it happens, there may be other Walder issues brewing."

She told Bill about Senator Walker Danson—how impatient he was about solving the case of his niece's murder, and how he and Walder seemed to know each other, and how she thought he might complain directly to Walder.

Bill let out a grunt of dismay.

"It sounds like a perfect storm is brewing," he said. "I'd better let you get back to work."

"Yeah, I guess," Riley said. "I miss you. I wish you were here."

"I do too."

They ended the call, and Riley sat staring at her phone.

Walder's going to make problems for us, she thought.

She didn't know how or when, but she knew it was going to happen, and probably soon.

But she also knew she couldn't think about that right now. She had to work with Sheriff Wightman to prepare for tonight's ambush.

She was all but sure the killer was going to show himself this very night.

And we can't let him slip through our hands.

Chapter Twenty Six

Riley rubbed her tired eyes. She was feeling worn out and frustrated and anxious after being cooped up most of the day, working alone in Sheriff Wightman's office.

I've got to get out of here or I'll scream, she thought.

She'd decided that she needed to stay somewhere out of sight to support the story they'd told the public at the news conference this morning. If she were seen still investigating, people might get the idea that the case hadn't been solved after all. Having a few police out and about could seem natural, but an FBI agent would surely arouse the media's interest.

But it had been a long and dull day so far, just poring over records and information she'd already looked at dozens of times. Worse, her work had produced no helpful results. She glanced at her watch and saw that it was just a few minutes before dusk, when the curfew was set to take effect. She figured it would be all right to slip outside then and do her own part in helping the police to track down the killer.

Meanwhile, she found it hard to focus. For one thing, she kept thinking about Ann Marie, who had surely gotten back to Quantico by now. What had she done when she'd gotten there? Had she gone straight to Meredith and Walder and reported how Riley had treated her?

You're getting paranoid, Riley told herself.

But she remembered what Bill had told her about Walder overhearing their phone call. There was also the fact that the sheriff was being pestered for news on the case by a politician who knew Walder. She could almost hear Bill's words again…

"It sounds like a perfect storm is brewing."

He was probably right. She only hoped that Walder wasn't going to make trouble before she managed to solve this case.

But Riley also couldn't help worrying about the way she and Ann Marie parted. She knew she had been hard on the young agent. Whether she wanted to or not, she must have hurt the rookie's feelings. Surely Riley could have handled the situation more gracefully.

Should she call Ann Marie and try to make things better?

No, this was no time for that.

Keep your head in the game, she told herself. *Lives are at stake here.*

She pushed the files away for a moment to give her eyes a rest. It occurred to her that she hadn't talked to April and Jilly since yesterday morning, when they'd been having another fight. She did need to find out how things were going. Maybe this would be a good time to check in with them. She only hoped she wasn't going to step into another family crisis.

She got out her cell phone and quickly got Jilly on the line.

"Hey, Mom. Are you on your way home yet?"

Riley was surprised at the question.

She said, "Um, no. Why do you ask?"

"Well, April and Gabriela and I saw on the news that you have a suspect in custody. We figured you'd wrap things up and drive straight back."

Riley stifled down a sigh. With luck, she might get home tomorrow. But tonight was really out of the question.

"Jilly, I'm afraid—"

Jilly interrupted good-naturedly, "Don't tell me. Things are complicated."

Riley smiled. Her daughter was definitely catching on to the way things went in her line of work.

"Yeah, like always," she said. "I'm hoping for a break tonight, though."

Jilly said, "Good luck, Mom. April and Gabriela and I pulling for you."

"Thanks," Riley said. "Are you and your sister ready to go trick-or-treating?"

"Yeah, we're just now heading out. I'm already in my zombie costume. You ought to see it, Mom. It would scare even you."

Riley chuckled. "It just might. So what did you decide about April wearing a costume?"

"Huh?" Jilly said, as if she didn't understand the question.

Riley said, "Well, yesterday the two of you were fighting about whether she should wear a costume or not."

Riley heard Jilly scoff.

"Well, that would be dumb, wouldn't it?" Jilly said. "She's sixteen years old, Mom. She'd look pretty silly wearing a costume."

Riley was momentarily dumbstruck. It seemed as if Jilly remembered nothing of yesterday's altercation. In fact, she was fully sympathetic with April on the matter.

Kids, Riley thought.

They were utterly unpredictable, probably even to themselves. Nothing about raising them seemed simple or straightforward. Sometimes she thought it was easier to make sense of serial killers than ordinary teenagers.

"You two have fun," Riley said to Jilly. "But be careful. Halloween can be dangerous, you know."

"Yeah, we know," Jilly said. "But April and I can take care of ourselves. We had a good teacher."

Riley smiled at the compliment and said goodbye. As she ended the call, she fought down a pang of worry. She'd meant it when she'd said that Halloween could be dangerous. And right now, that seemed truer even than usual. She thought she'd feel better if her daughters simply skipped trick-or-treating altogether this year, and perhaps for good. At least she was glad that they were in Fredericksburg, Virginia. That should be well out of reach of the so-called "Goatman" here in Maryland.

Riley looked at her watch. She had time to take one last pass through some of these records on the desk. She opened up the folder for Yvonne Swenson. As she glanced through it, a detail stood out to her that so far hadn't seemed very meaningful. It was a fact that Sheriff Wightman had mentioned.

She was a widow.

Riley felt an odd tingle. She wasn't sure just why. From what she was reading, it appeared that Yvonne's husband, Russell Swenson, had died three years before her disappearance. But why did that matter? What could that possibly have to do with what had eventually happened to Yvonne?

Riley didn't know. But she got on Sheriff Wightman's computer and searched for the man's obituary. She saw that he'd died rather young in a motorcycle accident. The obituary included a few innocuous details about his life, and also information about the upcoming funeral and memorial service.

But what struck Riley most was his birthdate.

He was born on October 31.

He was born on Halloween!

It seemed like a weird detail. Riley wondered if it had any significance.

The obituary also gave the date and time for his burial, which was to take place in Gracefield Cemetery.

Gracefield Cemetery . . .

The name rang a bell with Riley.

She unfolded a map of Winneway and Aurora Groves and quickly found Gracefield Cemetery. It was in Aurora Groves, and it adjoined an area called Garfield Park.

Riley felt a surge of interest as she recognized the location of Garfield Park.

It was the park she had explored the night before last. Garfield Park was where she'd gotten her strongest sense of the killer's presence—and of how he'd ambushed and killed Allison Hillis.

Riley put her finger down on the spot where she'd entered the park. Then she traced her way along a trail that led through the park. The cemetery was at the end of that trail, less than a mile away from where Riley had been when she got that sense of the killer.

She quickly got back on the sheriff's computer and searched for a map of the cemetery. She used it to locate Russell Swenson's grave, which was right at the edge of the cemetery bordering on Garfield Park.

A jumble of thoughts began to come together in Riley's mind.

Yvonne's husband was born on Halloween.

His grave is only a short distance away from where Allison Hillis was killed.

Riley felt a shiver of excitement.

She wasn't yet sure what this discovery might signify. But at least she knew where she could go next. Maybe she could use these odd clues to pick up more about the killer.

She looked at her watch again. Sheriff Wightman's curfew was now in effect.

She got up from Wightman's desk and headed out of his office. Her hopes began to rise as she continued down the hallway and out of the building.

If she was lucky—very lucky—she just might find her way to the killer.

Chapter Twenty Seven

Sheriff Wightman slowed his car when he spotted the group clustered under a streetlight. Officer Tyrone Baldry seemed to be in heated conversation with three teenaged boys. Like the other cops involved in the dragnet, Baldry was in plainclothes, but he was showing the boys his badge.

Wightman pulled to a stop along the curb and rolled down his window in order to hear what Baldry and the boys were arguing about.

Baldry's voice was rising as he warned them, "And I'm telling you for the last time—"

"Yeah, yeah, yeah," one of the youths replied with a sneer. "There's a curfew. We're not supposed to be out. We get it."

"Good. Now go home."

A second boy added, "It's Halloween, Officer. This is a holiday. A once-a-year kind of party."

Another argued, "What's the point of the curfew, anyway? You've caught the killer, right?"

"We've just got a suspect," Baldry said. "We don't know for sure he's the killer."

"The sheriff sounded pretty sure on TV," the second boy said. "And what are you doing out of uniform, anyway?"

The first boy demanded, "What are you going to do, arrest us?"

Obviously flustered, Baldry stammered incoherently.

Sheriff Wightman leaned out his window and called out to the group.

"What's going on here, boys?"

Baldry and the boys all turned and looked at him. None of them seemed to have noticed his arrival until just now. The boys seemed a bit chastened to see the sheriff. Baldry looked relieved.

Baldry said, "Just dealing with some ornery kids who are out and around when they're not supposed to be."

"Is that right?" Wightman said with a smile. "Maybe they got lost. Maybe they don't know their way back to their houses. They don't look awfully bright to me. Hey, guys, there's room for three more in my car. I can give you a lift somewhere."

Then with a chuckle he added, "If you don't know your way home, I'd be happy to drive you down to the station. We've got some nice clean cells where you can spend the night. You'll be perfectly comfortable."

The boys shuffled their feet and grumbled.

"It's OK," one said. "We'll head on home."

As the boys walked away, Baldry came over to the sheriff's open window.

He said, "What do you want to bet I run into them again before the night is over?"

"I wouldn't doubt it," Wightman said with a sigh.

He'd been patrolling ever since the curfew had gone into effect, and he'd seen kids of all ages wandering about—little kids in cute costumes, and mischievous teenagers just out to make trouble. Maybe there weren't as many as he'd have expected without a curfew, but way too many for his liking.

He'd also seen his cops trying frantically to get them off the streets.

"Some curfew," Wightman said.

"Yeah, and some dragnet," Baldry said. "Not working out quite like you planned, is it? Me and the guys are supposed to be watching out for the killer. But now we're spending the whole evening watching out for stragglers and trying to round them up and send them home."

"Any other news?" Wightman asked.

"Yeah, a couple of the kids I talked to mentioned the 'Goatman' in joking kind of way. So I guess the word is out about the killer's supposed identity."

Wightman stifled a growl of dismay. He'd known all along that the public was going to get wind of the "Goatman" angle sooner or later. It had only been a matter of time.

But I'd sure like to get my hands on whoever leaked it.

Wightman felt like apologizing to Baldry for how things were turning out. But admitting his own role in what was starting to seem like a huge miscalculation would hardly boost anyone's morale.

Instead he shook his head and said, "Just keep doing your best, you and the rest of the guys."

"We'll do that, sir," Baldry said.

Wightman rolled his window back up and watched as Baldry started to walk away. But the younger cop didn't get very far before he ran into a group of five costumed kids. None of them looked more than ten years old. Wightman growled under his breath. As far as he was concerned, that bunch was too little to be out this late without any parents even on an ordinary Halloween.

And this is no ordinary Halloween.

If Agent Paige was right, a killer was also prowling the streets right now and everyone else out here could be in danger. This Goatman character didn't seem to be after a specific type and he hadn't struck in any consistent location. They had no idea how he chose his marks.

Wightman watched as Baldry successfully herded the new group of youngsters away—toward their homes, he hoped. He thought he might as well continue on his way, but as he reached out to put his car in gear, his cell phone buzzed. He saw that the call was from Agent Paige.

She said, "I just wanted you to know I'm following a hunch that will take me out to the Gracefield Cemetery."

Wightman suppressed a sigh.

"I hope you're not going to ask me to send any more cops there. Because I don't have anybody to spare."

"No, it might be just as well if you don't," Agent Paige said. "I want to stay as inconspicuous as possible."

"Good luck," Wightman said.

As soon as the call ended, he was surprised to get another call—this one from Agent Ann Marie Esmer.

What the hell…?

The last time he had seen Esmer was earlier that day at the police station, the moment before she had oddly disappeared.

Wightman remembered Agent Paige's cryptic comment when she'd come into the conference room alone.

"Agent Esmer won't be joining us."

Because of the expression on Paige's face, he hadn't asked any questions. He'd assumed right then and there that Riley and her young partner had had some kind of falling out, which had made him distinctly uneasy. He'd also figured that whatever was going on between them was none of his business.

But he hadn't actually expected to see Agent Esmer still on the case. Why was she calling him right now?

He took the call and said, "What's going on, Agent Esmer?"

Esmer's voice sounded agitated.

"I'm parked outside Pater High School. I see that the gymnasium is all lighted up. Do you realize there's a party going on there?"

Wightman stifled a sigh. He'd talked all this over with Principal Cody earlier today.

He said to Esmer, "Yeah, but the party was supposed to end at curfew."

"Well, it's still going on," Esmer said. "I can see through the windows. Most of the kids seem to have left, but a bunch are still there. I see Principal Cody in there too. What do you want me to do?"

Wightman thought for a moment.

Then he said, "I'll give Principal Cody a call. It will help if you can stay put and keep an eye on things at the school. That will give my guys one less location to worry about. Watch who comes and goes. Make sure the kids stay safe. If you see anyone suspicious hanging around, call me for backup right away."

"I'll do that," Esmer said.

Wightman ended the call and sat staring ahead.

He wasn't happy with what he'd just heard about what was going on at the school. But he wasn't surprised either. Neither Principal Cody nor anyone in his current administration were real disciplinarians. That job had belonged to Vice Principal Yvonne Swenson, who'd had a reputation for being tough as nails with the students when she'd still been alive. Nobody had been able to fill her shoes in that department during the two years since her death. Wightman thought that the school had suffered in many ways from her loss.

He guessed that the kids at the party had probably begged to keep the party going, and Cody had caved to their wishes. But since they had all been there this long, maybe keeping the party going was the best thing to do. At least the kids were in the gymnasium and not out on the street.

Wightman tapped Cody's phone number into his cell phone, planning to talk things over with the principal.

Meanwhile, Wightman felt uneasy that Agent Esmer wasn't with Agent Paige. The two BAU agents didn't seem to be coordinating their efforts.

That seemed odd to him—and it certainly didn't make him feel any more confident that this tactic was going to help them catch the Goatman.

Everything seemed to be going wrong. At this point, he could only hope that Paige's odd plan to draw out a killer wasn't going to go terribly wrong too.

Chapter Twenty Eight

After the end of the phone call with Sheriff Wightman, Ann Marie sat in her rental car staring at Pater High School. It was dark outside now and the school itself was an enormous silhouette. Through a row of large windows, she could see activity in the brightly lit gym. The glimpse of costumed kids dancing and frolicking among crepe paper decorations was a rather surreal sight, but there certainly didn't seem to be anything sinister going on.

She sighed as she remembered what the sheriff had said to her just now.

"It will help if you can stay put and keep an eye on things at the school."

He didn't sound like he thought the party was a very serious problem. Worse, he sounded as though he was just giving Ann Marie something to keep her occupied while he and his cops and Agent Paige went about their more urgent business.

Ann Marie really didn't like how that made her feel. She'd already had a bad day and wasn't feeling great anyhow. But she wasn't in any position to complain, since she wasn't even supposed to be here in Winneway. Fortunately, the sheriff apparently didn't even know that Agent Paige had sent her back to Quantico. She wondered why Agent Paige hadn't told him.

Of course, Agent Paige had no idea that Ann Marie was back in town.

Maybe I should call her and tell her.

But no, Ann Marie couldn't see any point in doing that. Agent Paige would just get mad and tell her to leave all over again. Well, she was here now and she was going to contribute to this case in some way, even if it was just keeping watch while nothing at all happened.

After a few more minutes, Ann Marie thought she'd go crazy just sitting in the car. Surely she could be more effective patrolling the area on foot. She got out of the car and walked across the street.

As she continued along the sidewalk in front of the school, she was met by a man with four costumed little kids, obviously out trick-or-treating.

She took out her badge and waved it at them.

"FBI," she said. "You're not supposed to be out here. There's a curfew, you know."

The man looked a bit ashamed of himself.

"I just thought... well, since you've got a suspect... everything would be safe and..."

Ann Marie grumbled, "Yeah, well, there's a curfew anyway. You should know that. Head on home."

"We'll do that," the man promised.

Ann Marie watched as the man hurried away with the children. But they were barely out of sight when she spotted another group of trick-or-treaters farther down the street.

Some curfew, she thought. None of these people seemed to realize they were possible targets.

It's like we rang the dinner bell, she thought.

We're just telling the killer, "Come and get it."

Somewhat guiltily, she couldn't help feeling vindicated for having objected to this plan from the start. She'd felt in her gut that giving the public the impression that the killer had already been caught was a big mistake.

As she'd said to Agent Paige, *"We're playing games with a dangerous killer."*

But Agent Paige hadn't listened. Ann Marie wondered—did her senior partner wish she'd listened now? Did she realize she'd made a mistake? If so, might all be forgiven if she called to tell Riley she was back?

No, she decided. *That woman just plain doesn't like me.*

And she knew that bothered her a lot more than it ought to. Agent Paige had been right in what she'd said about her earlier.

"Being liked is really important to you, isn't it?"

Yes, it was, Ann Marie had to admit. Wanting to be liked had always seemed perfectly normal to her. Why wouldn't anybody want to be liked?

But, she realized now, she might need to give that question some thought. If wanting to be liked drove her behavior, could it become a problem?

After her altercation with Agent Paige, she'd done as she was told and driven all the way back to Quantico. But after she'd parked and walked toward the BAU building, she simply couldn't force herself to go inside. Instead, she'd gotten back into the car and returned here.

Why was that? At the time she'd told herself that she hated leaving in the middle of a case, that she really wanted to finish the job she'd started. She'd convinced herself that returning was the right thing to do.

Now she realized that she'd just been too chicken to go into the building and report to Agent Meredith, telling him the truth about why Agent Paige had sent her back. That would have meant admitting that she had failed her first test as a new agent. It probably would have meant facing her inevitable termination as an agent.

Worse, it would have meant feeling that nobody liked her.

Ann Marie was catching on that this was maybe her fatal weakness—not just in trying to be an FBI agent, but in anything else she might try to do with her life. She thought that maybe she still had a lot of growing up to do. She needed some time to think about all that...

Suddenly a shrieking scream tore at her nerves.

She spun around to see a mechanical ghost hanging on one of the porches. She'd set off its recorded, motion-activated scream by walking near it.

She could see that this was a very different neighborhood from the much more upscale Aurora Groves, and the Halloween decorations on the lawns and weren't as high tech and expensive.

But they were definitely louder. A ghost that screeched this noisily wouldn't be tolerated in the more muted streets of Aurora Groves, where relatively subdued cackles were more the rule. People here had also put a lot more effort and creativity into their Halloween displays. The pumpkins were much more elaborately carved, and many of the porch monsters were carefully handcrafted.

She took a few deep breaths as she settled her nerves.

Focus on your job, she told herself. *Think later.*

Then she kept a sharp eye out for trouble as she kept walking along.

As she turned the corner and began to walk alongside the school, she heard footsteps hurrying behind her. She didn't let herself get scared again. Instead, she stopped walking and calmly turned around.

She found herself facing a kid wearing a werewolf mask.

No, too big for a kid, she realized as the guy stopped and just stood there looking at her.

He was tall and muscular—and obviously way too old to be trick-or-treating. He was dressed in perfectly ordinary clothes and was carrying a leather satchel slung over his shoulder.

Annoyed, Ann Marie took out her badge again. This time she spoke more sharply than she had to the man and his kids.

"FBI," she said. "Don't you know there's a curfew?"

The guy wearing the mask didn't reply.

"I could arrest you, you know," she said. "And I will if I see you again. Just get on out of here. Go home. Get off the streets."

Without a word, the masked man turned and hurried away from her, heading across the street and disappearing into the adjoining neighborhood.

The least he could do is growl or something.

After all, he was obviously out here for no reason except to scare people—especially little kids. Even though he wasn't succeeding at being scary, he really pissed Ann Marie off.

Maybe I should have arrested him, she thought.

But then she would have had to call Sheriff Wightman to come and pick the guy up, which would be a waste of everybody's time and energy. Besides, she reminded herself that she'd been ordered to keep watch over the school. And making sure that the kids inside were safe was certainly a more urgent task than dealing with some adult with an infantile sense of humor.

She continued walking around the building until she could see into the gym windows again. She could see that Principal Cody and a couple of teachers were now rounding up the costumed kids and escorting them out of the gym.

She remembered the sheriff telling her he was going to give the principal a call.

I guess that call did the trick, she thought.

She continued on her way until the school's front entrance came into view.

Sure enough, kids were now coming out in a steady stream. Some of them were headed toward their cars. She couldn't help but worry about the ones who might be walking home, but they all seemed to be traveling in groups, which should be safe for them.

The best thing she could do was to hang around the school building and make sure that everybody got out safely.

And that's just what I'll do, she thought. It felt good to be part of the team even if so few people even knew she was here.

Chapter Twenty Nine

April had decided that this was as far as she would go. Mom had insisted that April had to be out here tonight, and she was doing exactly as she'd been told. But she wasn't going up to front doors with these kids again.

I'm through with that, she thought.

She'd refused to put on a costume, and now she was finished with joining the younger kids as they and badgered adults for treats. She'd actually gone up to a couple of houses with them when they'd first started out, but she'd felt so silly and awkward that she was determined not to do it anymore. She was just fine waiting for them here on the sidewalk.

But why do I have to be here at all? April wondered.

She'd been asking herself that question over and over again. Surely Jilly was old enough to watch out for herself. For that matter, so were her smaller friends, whose parents had sent them out unchaperoned. This neighborhood was about as safe as it could be, and the people who had greeted them were all friendly and welcoming to the trick-or-treaters. Even some of those adults had been wearing costumes.

The kids returned from the house and showed April the added loot in their already-overloaded tote bags. One thing April didn't miss from her trick-or-treating days was how bad she'd felt after eating insane amounts of candy. She smiled again as it occurred to her that a massive stomachache was one rite of passage Jilly was due for soon.

As the group headed toward another house to trick-or-treat, Jilly turned toward her big sister and asked in a wistful voice, "Won't you come too?"

April shook her head no and sighed.

She wanted to reply, *"Are you going to ask me that at every house?"*

With a glum expression, Jilly followed her friends away.

April realized that Jilly probably wasn't having such a great time herself. She was at least a year older than any of her companions—the only one of them who was already in high school. She had been looking forward to trick-or-treating for the first time in her life, but it might not be turning out to be as much fun as she'd expected.

Even so, April smiled yet again at the sight of her sister's costume. She had to admit, Jilly looked a lot cooler than her younger friends. Bruce was dressed up as Captain America, Dina was wearing a Peter Pan outfit, and Lynn was dressed as a winged fairy. The sisters Nicole and Janice were pretending to be M&Ms, one clad entirely in blue and the other in red, both in tutus and puffy sweatshirts with big M's on them.

By comparison, Jilly's zombie outfit really was impressive. Her latex mask convincingly showed a face with one eyeball hanging out and the flesh all in shreds showing parts of the skull beneath. Her wig flung itself in all directions, looking grimy and wild. Best of all were her clothes, which dangled off her body in tatters that really looked rotten and moldy. The front of her jacket exposed what appeared to be human ribs.

April's own bygone Halloween costumes—witches, vampires, ghosts, and such—paled by comparison.

April also admired how well Jilly was playing the part, lurching and limping along with her arms wildly twisted, growling hoarsely and fiercely at passersby and the people who answered doors. She really did look and act as though she'd just dug herself out of a grave.

She's really trying to make the best of things, April thought. She was sorry that it might be turning out to be a disappointment.

Watching from the sidewalk, April saw a smiling middle-aged woman answer the doorbell and squeal with feigned delight to see the costumed children. She noticed that Jilly was standing back from the others, no longer going through her zombie act. She seemed to be just waiting for it all to be over.

The poor kid, April thought. *We should talk about this later.*

April liked playing the role of the emotionally supportive big sister, offering sympathy and understanding based on her own experiences as a kid. But with a pang, she realized that conversation wasn't likely to happen tonight. Or maybe ever again.

Her little sister was growing up. Most of the time, Jilly made a show of being independent and self-sufficient—too grown up for her big sister's help. April was starting to miss the days when Jilly had first joined the family.

I guess this is what it feels like to get older, April thought sadly.

She turned at the sound of voices and saw three kids her own age walking along the other side of the street. They weren't wearing costumes, and she shuddered as she recognized them from her own school.

Oh, no, she thought as she realized they'd spotted her.

How much teasing was she going to have to take for getting stuck with this babysitting job?

"Hey, April, what's up?" called Ted Kirkland as the group came toward her.

April forced a smile.

"Not much," she said. "Just helping my sister survive trick-or-treating."

Ted smiled a rakish smile that April had long admired.

He practically owns cute, she thought.

Ted was a track athlete and student council president, and he even fronted his own band—a high school star in every possible way. He was so cool that April hadn't really dared even have a crush on him. She couldn't remember him ever walking up to her and talking to her like this. April hadn't imagined that she'd ever registered on his social radar.

With him was his gawky, chinless sidekick Ian Black, as well as Andrea Fife and Lily Berry, each of whom was gazing at Ted with adolescent longing.

Ted said to April, "We're heading on over to Scarlet Gray's party. You'll be there too, right?"

April fought down a moan of despair.

I should have known, she thought.

Ted and his companions were on their way to the very party that Mom had told her not to attend.

Ian added with a note of awe in his reedy voice, "It's really going to be a big deal. Scarlet's got a *huge* rec room, and absolutely everyone is going to be there."

April gulped hard and said, "I can't. As you can see, I'm kind of occupied this evening."

April shuddered again as Andrea and Lily giggled and whispered to each other, obviously amused by her current plight.

Ted shrugged and said, "Bring your sister along."

April tried to keep her jaw from dropping. The possibility hadn't occurred to her.

"I can't," she said. "That's going to be really late and we don't have a ride home."

"No problem," Ted said. "I live really close to Scarlet. When you're ready to go home, I'll walk you over to my house, and then I can drive you both home in my dad's car."

April felt a little dizzy.

Ted Kirkland is offering to drive us home, she thought.

It felt like a once-in-a-lifetime opportunity.

But she remembered what her mother had said the day before yesterday.

"You're not going to any party. You're still grounded."

Feeling almost ready to cry, she said, "Sorry, I just can't."

Ted seemed about to protest, but Andrea and Lily were tugging at him to get moving.

"Hope you change your mind," Ted called back as he headed off with his companions.

They quickly disappeared down the street.

April felt so frustrated, she thought she might explode.

This is just unacceptable, she thought.

But what was she going to do about it?

Chapter Thirty

As she drove back into the Aurora Groves neighborhood, Riley was worried by what she saw. She wasn't bothered by the brightly lit jack-o'-lanterns and other Halloween images that decorated so many houses and lawns. The swaying ghosts and glowing skeletons were innocent enough. It was the number of young people out on the streets that bothered her. She sympathized with the plainclothes cops she saw trying to herd them up and send them home.

It was obvious that Sheriff Wightman's curfew wasn't having much effect. And now she wondered—had it been such a good idea to give the public the impression that the killer had been caught? She hadn't realized how casually they would decide to defy the sheriff's curfew. At least in this neighborhood, people didn't seem to be used to taking these sorts of orders.

As things were turning out, she thought that Ann Marie had probably been right to criticize her scheme. Maybe Riley should have listened to her instead of sending her away. Not that there was much to be done about that now. Ann Marie had surely long since gotten back to Quantico. Riley was definitely working without a partner tonight.

Following the curving streets of Aurora Groves, she soon arrived at the location she was looking for. She parked her car and got out, then stood looking over the grassy, sparsely wooded area of Garfield Park where she'd been two nights ago. If she was right, the Goatman killer might well be choosing his targets from this very piece of public land.

The last time she'd been here at night, the park had been empty of people, but tonight there was a lot of activity out there beneath the trees. She headed toward the movement to see what was happening.

She tensed up when she heard a child's voice squeal.

But the next thing she heard was laughter.

Kids playing, she realized.

But of course, on Halloween night the park was practically a magnet for kids. There weren't many of them now, but she was worried. If the theory that was shaping in her mind was correct, the killer was also out here somewhere. She didn't want to leave those kids in the park alone.

Then she heard an adult male voice calling out in a scolding tone. When she got closer to the activity, she saw that a bunch of kids had been TP'ing a tree with toilet paper. A couple of cops were chewing them out about it and taking down their names and telling them to get back home.

She breathed a little easier.

All the same, the police had blown their cover by producing their badges. Had they also scared away Riley's prey?

She somehow doubted it.

She was sure that the so-called "Goatman" was nothing if not determined and audacious. If he considered this his territory, he would surely be somewhere around here tonight.

She began to retrace the same steps she had followed the night before last, returning to the bushes where she'd gotten her keenest feeling of the killer's presence. Again, she sensed the possibility that he had crouched here watching the street. When he'd spotted the skeleton-costumed Allison Hillis, he'd somehow lured her to the spot where he'd been waiting.

But how did he lure her? she wondered.

Again, the possibility that he'd sung or whistled some sort of "goat song" crossed her mind. But as she had the night before last, Riley decided against that. The sound of singing or whistling from this bush would only have freaked Allison out and sent her on her way.

So what had he done, then? How could the killer have caught the girl's attention and draw her directly to him?

A cry for help, she quickly realized.

Maybe he'd cried out in a way that provoked her sympathy and concern. Maybe he'd imitated a lost or frightened child.

Riley felt a tingle of near-certainty.

Yes, it must have been something like that.

The realization brought back an eerie sense of closeness with the killer. She felt that he was cunning, with an exalted sense of himself and his own importance—or at least of what he was trying to do. Bill's research had suggested that the killer felt a supernatural, almost religious sense of purpose, a dark connection to the roots of myth and tragedy.

Riley breathed long and slowly, trying to hold onto the sense of connection while at the same time mulling over her evolving theory. Could all of the links she had discovered back at the police station have been purely imaginary? Allison Hillis had been taken and killed near one end of this park. Could it be a coincidence that Yvonne Swenson's husband was buried not far from here in a graveyard at the far end of the property—and that her husband's birthday had been on Halloween?

She knew very well that some apparent connections truly were accidental and meaningless. But she really had to follow up these leads and see where they took her.

A walking trail led from this area to the other end of the park and that graveyard. She left the area where Allison was killed and began to follow that trail. It certainly felt to her that she might be following a route that the killer had taken. A possible scenario continued to develop in Riley's mind as she made her way through the park

When she arrived at the edge of the cemetery, she looked out over the graves that stretched eerily before her in the moonlight. It was an older cemetery, with a variety of types of headstones, ranging from simple low markers to stately columns. A few areas were in rows but others seemed to be random groupings. Some statues among the graves almost looked like they could come to life on a night like this. She saw one drooping angel that appeared about to lift her wings.

Riley heard a sound and sank back farther among the trees to avoid being seen. Then she saw a figure walking among the tombstones. It was a young woman, her eyes cast downward to see where she was going. Riley was about to warn her that she shouldn't be out here when she saw another figure following behind the woman. The second figure was wearing a demonic mask, a red devil face with projecting horns. He was definitely closing in on the woman.

It could be the killer after a new victim.

Riley put her hand on her gun, about to step forward and confront him. But even as she did, the young woman turned and saw her stalker.

"Ralphie," she giggled. "You devil."

The second figure pushed back his mask and the two kissed passionately. For a moment Riley thought they were going to make love right there among the tombstones. Fortunately the man said, "C'mon, let's go somewhere more comfortable," and they ran off hand-in-hand.

Riley relaxed, glad she hadn't confronted the lovers at gunpoint and spoiled their rendezvous. The graveyard seemed empty of living beings again now, so she turned her attention back to her reason for being here. Remembering the chart she had studied, she soon located the grave she was looking for. Rather than walk out into the open where she would be visible to anyone nearby, she worked her way closer to it by edging her way along the trees that bordered the cemetery. From where she stood, she could see that the spot had a stately double gravestone. She could even read the large carved letters:

TOGETHER FOREVER

But only one side of the double-wide stone was engraved with smaller letters. She knew that must be for Russell Swenson, and that it must be engraved with the dates of his birth and death. The space beside it was blank.

Riley understood it perfectly. Like many devoted couples, Yvonne and Russell had intended to be buried together. The empty gravesite and marker was reserved for Yvonne Swenson. In fact, sometime during the next few days, Yvonne's mangled corpse would be buried right here alongside her husband's—a sad, ironic consolation for the horror of her own demise.

Riley got a different feeling now—less a sense of the killer than of poor Yvonne.

In fact, she could almost feel Yvonne's presence right now.

When Yvonne Swenson had been alive, Riley guessed that she'd always visited her husband's grave on his birthday—Halloween. Perhaps the killer had found her at his grave, then abducted and killed her.

That would have been two years ago. Maybe since then the killer had treated that grave as a sort of shrine.

If so . . .

Maybe he'd come here again exactly a year ago on Halloween night, with the purpose of meditating at this grave before striking again.

But would he come here again tonight?

Riley didn't know.

But again, she started to slip into his mind as she pictured him standing there looking down at the double gravestone. She could imagine him feeling a weird, occult charge from knowing that someday Yvonne's body would be discovered, and she would be brought here for her final rest. The visit had a profound effect on the killer.

He felt very powerful.

And he felt ready for a new victim.

When he'd turned away from the gravestone, Riley thought he'd gone back through the park the way Riley herself had come, retracing his own steps. When he'd come within view of the street, he'd ducked behind the bush where Riley had just been.

And then . . .

Riley felt sure of what had happened then.

He'd lured Allison off the street and killed her.

Riley's sense of connection to the killer broke at a rustling sound behind her.

She turned around, and her heart jumped up into her throat at what she saw. This was no simple devilish costume.

It was a weird creature with a snout, two horns, and hairy legs.

The Goatman!

She drew her weapon.

Chapter Thirty One

Riley leveled her weapon at the weird, animal-like figure. He was heavy and tall, with horns extending from a massive head. She didn't want to tangle with him physically if she could avoid it.

"FBI!" she barked. "Put your hands up!"

The figure obediently stopped in his tracks and raised his arms. His voice sounded genuinely scared as he stammered a high-pitched reply:

"I—I don't understand."

Before Riley could explain, a group of costumed children came dashing into the graveyard. They ran around the grotesque character shouting with mock terror.

"Eee! Eee! The Goatman! The Goatman! The Goatman!"

Suddenly the whole situation seemed weirdly unreal to Riley.

What on earth is going on? she wondered.

One of the children pointed at Riley and squealed out, "Look!"

The other children turned and let out shrieks of terror at the sight of Riley with her weapon aimed at the goat figure. Several of them ran away. The smallest kid, dressed up as a one-eyed pirate, grabbed the man by one of his hairy legs.

"Don't shoot my brother!" he screamed at Riley. "Please don't shoot him!"

Riley's spirits sank as she began to realize she'd made a big mistake. She'd let her imagination run away with her at the sight of such a vivid costume.

"Take off your mask," she commanded the costumed figure.

He obeyed and lifted the entire goat-like head up and off of his own. Riley saw that the unmasked "Goatman" looked like a teenaged boy. A rather large boy, but probably not a dangerous one. He stared at her with his mouth hanging open and his eyes wide with terror.

"I—I didn't do anything! I promise."

Riley herself stammered now, "Why—why are you dressed like that?"

The boy shrugged. "It's Halloween. I dress up like this every year. I made the head myself out of papier mâché. But I'm not the only kid who wears this kind of costume. Lots of others do. Haven't you ever heard of the Goatman?"

With a discouraged sigh, Riley lowered her weapon and put it back in her holster. She reminded herself that the Goatman was a Maryland urban legend. It wasn't surprising that some kids around here dressed up as the creature every Halloween. It was probably a common costume.

I should have expected this, she told herself.

The boy lowered his hands and peered at Riley.

"Wait a minute," he said. "You're not FBI. What is this, some kind of Halloween prank?"

Riley stared back at him, unsure what he meant.

He added, "I heard the cops have got the Goatman in custody. So you're not really after the killer. Sure, local cops are always out on Halloween, but the FBI's got no business here, not now. So who are you really? Is that even a real gun?"

Riley rolled her eyes wearily.

There's no way to explain, she thought.

"I'm really FBI," she said. "Look closer at this badge if you don't believe me. Or—go ahead, don't believe me. It doesn't matter. You're not supposed to be out here. There's a curfew, and you know it, and the cops out here tonight mean business. So get on home. Don't make this harder than it has to be."

The boy grumbled under his breath. Then he looked down at the little pirate, who was still clinging to his leg. "It's okay," he said. "Where are the other kids?"

The child let go and pointed to the others, who were clustered behind one of the larger grave markers. With a final skeptical glance at Riley, the teenager led the children away.

As Riley leaned against a tree and tried to gather her wits, she remembered what the boy had just said.

"I heard the cops have got the Goatman in custody. So you're not really after the killer."

She knew that meant the killer's apparent alter ego had finally been leaked to the public. She'd known all along that it was only a matter of time. And now that she'd blown her own cover, word would soon get around that the FBI was still in the area for some reason. How soon would the public figure out that the supposed arrest was only a ruse, and that the killer was still at large?

Not long, she figured.

And that wasn't going to make things any easier for her or for Sheriff Wightman and his team.

Meanwhile, she wondered what to do next.

Everything was very still and quiet in the graveyard now. She saw no sign of anyone. It was getting late—too late even for boisterous young people, especially with cops on patrol.

But what about the killer?

Might he show up here even yet?

For all Riley knew, he might have been lurking unseen around here for a while now. If he'd witnessed her encounter with the costumed boy and the smaller children, would he sneak away and go into hiding, and possibly not try to kill until next Halloween? That had been one of her principal worries to begin with.

But as Riley tried to tap into her sense of the killer, she thought otherwise. If she was right and this grave was a kind of shrine for him, he wouldn't let himself get scared away from it too easily.

He's too determined for that, she thought.

In fact, if he was somewhere nearby right now, maybe even watching her, he might be thrilled by the presence of an FBI agent. He might consider it some sort of challenge. If so, his overconfidence might yet prove to be his undoing. He might even get careless and show himself. If nobody else came along, perhaps he'd even try to come after Riley herself. A female FBI agent might prove to be irresistible bait to the kind of killer Riley sensed him to be.

She went back to the spot where she'd been lying in wait and disappeared back into the shadows.

I'll just have to wait some more, she thought.

She crouched, watching keenly in all directions.

She was sure the killer would be out tonight. He would try to take someone and murder them. She had no way to guess who that might be.

Or where it might be.

If the Goatman killer wasn't going to turn up here, then where could he be?

⚜ ⚜ ⚜

April's frustration grew as she waited for Jilly and the costumed kids to visit yet another house. She kept thinking of Ted calling out to her as he and his three friends walked away.

"Hope you change your mind."

She growled under her breath.

If only it were up to me, she thought.

But then again, she considered, maybe it *was* up to her. Ted had said that Jilly would also be welcome at the party. What would be the harm of taking her? She knew the kind of kids who were likely to be there. She didn't expect any drugs or drinking—nothing that her little sister needed to be protected from. What would be the harm...?

When Jilly and her friends came back, April pulled her sister aside. She saw that Jilly's purple tote bag with a picture of a ghost on it was bulging.

April smiled at her sister and said, "Quite a bit of loot you've got there, huh?"

She could hear Jilly sigh behind her zombie mask.

"I guess."

"How much more do you want to get?"

"I don't know."

Again, April realized that Jilly really wasn't having the great time she'd hoped to have trick-or-treating. She hoped that maybe Jilly was ready to call it quits.

"Hey, how would you like to go somewhere else?" April asked.

"Where?" Jilly muttered, without any sign of enthusiasm.

"To a party?" April said.

"What kind of party?" Jilly asked.

April said cautiously, "It's the one... well, you know. The one I mentioned a couple of days ago."

"You mean the one Mom said you're not supposed to go to?"

April nodded nervously. Then she heard Jilly gasp behind her mask.

"You mean an honest-to-God high school party, with seniors and juniors and everything? I'm in!"

Unable to keep a note of guilt out of her voice, April added, "OK, but you know I'm supposed to be grounded, so ... we can't tell Mom about this."

"I won't say a word," Jilly said. "But ..."

"But what?" April said, worried about what Jilly was about to say.

"What about Gabriela? She'll be expecting us at home."

April fought down a discouraged sigh. How could she have forgotten about Gabriela?

April said, "Um, I guess I'll call her and ..."

"And what? Tell her we're going to a party Mom said not to go to?"

"Not exactly," April said.

"What, then?"

April didn't reply. Instead, she took out her cell phone and called home.

When Gabriela answered, April gathered up her courage and said, "Hey, Gabriela, Jilly and I might be out longer than we'd expected."

A deafening silence followed. April could positively feel Gabriela frowning at her.

"How much longer?" Gabriela finally said.

April felt flustered.

"Oh ... we don't know exactly, it's just ..."

"Are you still trick-or-treating?" Gabriela interrupted.

"Yes," April said.

As soon as the word was out, April more than half-wished she could take it back. Of course, it wasn't completely untrue. She and Jilly were technically still trick-or-treating at this very moment. At least they weren't on their way to the party just yet. Nevertheless, April always found it hard to be less than completely honest with Gabriela—actually a lot harder than it was with Mom.

And she doubted very much that Gabriela believed her.

Another silence fell. Then Gabriela said firmly, "I expect you home in an hour."

April gulped down a gasp.

An hour?

That would give them hardly any time at the party at all. But she knew she was in no position to negotiate.

"OK," she said. "Bye."

Gabriela said nothing, which made it really awkward for April to end the call.

As April put her phone away, Jilly asked, "So what did she say?"

"We've got to be home in an hour," April said.

"An hour!" Jilly moaned with dismay. "We'll get there just in time to leave."

April shrugged and said, "Hey, don't gripe at me about it. Do you want to call Gabriela back and get her to change her mind?"

Jilly shook her head and looked down at the ground.

She looks like one discouraged zombie, thought April.

Then April said, "Look, it's not much more than a ten-minute walk from here. We can get there in time to have some fun."

"So where is this party exactly?" Jilly asked.

When April told her the address, Jilly seemed to perk up again.

"Hey, we can make it there in less than ten minutes," Jilly said, pointing down the street. "All we've got to do is cut through that park."

April looked where Jilly was pointing. She knew the park well, and it appeared to be reasonably well-lighted. Even so, she felt uneasy about this shortcut. She wasn't even sure how much time it would save them.

"Jilly, I don't know . . ." she said.

Jilly was jumping from one foot to another with agitation.

"Come on, April. I was just starting to take you for a really cool big sister. Don't disillusion me now."

April swallowed down her anxiety.

"OK," she said. "But let's get a move on. It's only a shortcut if we hurry."

April took off toward the park at a trot while Jilly skipped along beside her, somehow managing not to spill any of her candy in her haste and excitement.

As they followed the paved path, April realized that their route was going to be quite a bit darker than she'd expected. A couple of lamps up ahead had gone out. Feeling a bit nervous, she began to walk faster.

Apparently noticing the same thing, Jilly slowed down and fell a little bit behind.

April looked back and said, "Come on, let's keep going. We'll be all right if we just go really fast."

With that, they both broke into a run.

Then they both stopped dead in their tracks.

A large, shadowy figure had stepped in front of them, seemingly from out of nowhere.

"Who's there?" April demanded.

The figure didn't reply, but April could see it more clearly now. It was a tall, muscular man entirely clad in black. Even his face was concealed by a plain black mask.

This is no trick-or-treater, April thought, fighting down a wave of panic.

Chapter Thirty Two

April stood frozen in her tracks, staring at the sinister figure. He just stood there without replying. He wasn't moving out of their way either.

April tried to sound braver than she felt…

"Whoever you are, this isn't very funny."

There was still no reply, but she could feel his eyes staring at her.

She heard Jilly say in a shaky voice, "Maybe this wasn't such a good idea."

"Maybe you're right," April whispered back. "Let's get out of here."

She and Jilly turned around, ready to run, but the same dark figure seemed to be standing in front of them again.

How is that possible? April wondered.

Then she turned back and saw the first figure standing where he'd been before. She began to feel dizzy with panic.

Was this some kind of monster who could be in two places at once?

No, there are two of them! she realized, forcing herself to calm down.

Her mind flashed to the gun her mother had bought for her and was now sitting unused in its case in Mom's closet. She wished she had it in her hand. But if she did, would she know what to do with it?

It doesn't matter now, she thought.

April felt a rush of adrenaline. Whatever else happened, she was determined that no harm would come to her little sister. It was her own fault they were in this situation.

She leaned toward Jilly and whispered, "You get out of here. Run like crazy. Run every which way you can. Head off into the bushes. Just get clear of these guys."

Jilly asked, "But what are you going to do?"

"Whatever I have to do," April said.

Her gaze still locked on the first figure, April heard Jilly scurrying away behind her. During the scant seconds that followed, everything seemed to stand still as April's mind clicked away—trying to gauge whatever was about to happen, wondering whether she or the man in front of her was going to make next move, flashing back to self-defense tips she'd gotten from her mother.

But before she could go into action, she heard sharp cry of pain behind her.

April spun around and saw the second black-clad man falling to his knees. Her little sister was buzzing around him like a hornet, swinging her candy-laden tote bag by its handles, smashing it at him again and again.

April realized that Jilly must have landed her first blow in a sensitive place that had incapacitated the man—his groin, most likely. April began to move toward them to join the fray. But she felt as though she were moving in slow motion while her little sister seemed to be striking with supernatural speed. Candy was tumbling out of the tote bag, but there was still enough weight to it so that Jilly could smash the disabled man in the mask and send him sprawling backward.

Jilly didn't let up even then. She kept kicking and pounding as he curled up in a writhing, pathetic fetal position. It was a weird and almost comical sight—a miniature zombie beating the hell out of a big, powerful-looking, black-clad man.

"Get off me!" the man was screaming desperately. "Get off me!"

April quickly realized that Jilly didn't need her help after all. She spun around to face the first black-clad man, only to be surprised that he'd taken off his mask and was looking dumbfounded. And she knew him.

"Eno?" she yelled. "Eno Bishop?"

He was a big, stupid bully who was always making trouble at her high school. And now April recognized the other guy's voice. Jilly was beating up Fritz Ollinger, Eno's best buddy.

Furious with both of the bullies, April took a menacing step toward Eno.

Looking past April, he backed away. The expression on his face was one of sheer terror.

April turned and saw that Jilly had finished beating up Fritz, who was groaning and twisting on the sidewalk. Jilly was now charging toward Eno.

"Keep that crazy kid off me!" Eno yelled. "I mean it, don't let her near me! She's like some kind of wild animal. She's out of her mind!"

April knew they weren't in any danger now. She put out her hand and blocked her sister's way.

Jilly flayed her arms and yelled, "Let me go! Let me at him!"

"That's enough," April told her. "Enough! We're OK now."

Jilly stopped and stood beside her, still looking fierce.

Then April turned back toward the unmasked bully.

"What the hell did the two of you think you were doing?" she snapped.

"Fritz and me were just playing a joke," Eno said. "We just thought it would be fun to scare somebody."

"Some joke," April said.

Making a wide berth around the girls, Eno went to his friend and helped him to his feet. Together they lurched away as fast as they could.

Meanwhile, Jilly had taken off her mask and was picking up pieces of the scattered candy.

She yelled after the guys, "Come back here and help me pick this up!"

"Leave them alone," April said. "They've learned their lesson. I'll help you."

As April joined Jilly in putting candy back into her bag, she asked, "Where did you learn to fight like that, anyway?"

Jilly scoffed.

"You're kidding, right?" she said. "Where I grew up, I had to be a tough kid just to survive."

April suddenly understood. She'd heard about Jilly's rough Arizona childhood from Mom and from Jilly herself. She remembered Mom describing how she'd first found Jilly in a truck cab trying to sell her own body in order to get away from her brutal father. Before that, Jilly had spent the whole night hiding in a drainpipe.

It's no wonder she can fight, April realized.

Jilly stopped putting candy into the bag before it was even a quarter full again.

"Even then, I almost didn't survive," she admitted with a sigh.

April could see that Jilly was shaking a little now. She put an arm around her sister.

"Well," April told her, "I might have been in real trouble tonight if you hadn't been here."

Jilly looked at her and then grinned. "That's enough candy," she said brightly. "I don't want to eat that much anyway. Let's head on home."

April smiled. She wasn't in the mood for a party now, not even one with Ted Kirkland and seniors and juniors and everything. She glad to hear that Jilly was no longer interested in it either. Besides, she knew that Gabriela would be glad to see them home earlier than she'd promised.

As they headed out of the park, Jilly chuckled a little and danced a few steps.

She said, "You know, trick-or-treating turned out to be a lot more fun than I expected."

Chapter Thirty Three

The man watched through the leaves and branches of a tall hedge as the young woman kept walking around Pater High School and students continued to pour out of the building. He could barely contain his elation.

Pan is so wise, he thought.

And Pan is so audacious.

When the man had come to this school at Pan's command, he'd had no idea of what the goat-god had in mind. After all, he'd taken a woman from this area before and later buried her beneath the maple sapling. That had been after a Halloween party at the school, and he'd thought that tonight would present someone similar. Or perhaps this time Pan's choice would be one of the partying teenagers he could see through the gym windows. But which of them had Pan chosen for his next victim? And how was the man supposed to carry out the murder?

He hadn't known then.

But now he did know.

None of the teenagers were his target. Neither were any of the adults at the school party.

It was the young blonde woman he'd encountered just now.

He felt a renewed thrill at how he'd felt when she raised her badge and spoke to him.

"FBI," she'd said. *"You're not supposed to be out here."*

How wrong she'd been! He was exactly where fate intended him to be. For right then and there, he'd heard Pan's flute-like voice loud and clear.

"There she is!" Pan had said.

The wide-eyed blonde woman was Pan's chosen sacrifice for this All Hallows' Eve.

He'd almost lunged for her right then and there, but Pan had held him back.

"Wait," Pan had said. *"The moment hasn't come."*

Again the man realized that Pan was right. He shouldn't take the new sacrifice while partygoers were still leaving the school across the street. They might try to interfere.

So the man was waiting, just as Pan commanded.

He was in an ecstasy of suspense now, wondering exactly when that moment was going to come, and what kind of opportunity Pan had in store for him.

He knew he must be patient.

But that was hard to do.

After all, Pan had chosen no ordinary prey.

An FBI agent! he thought.

She was nothing like the unwitting, defenseless, and unsuspecting victims he'd grown used to. In fact, he was sure that she regarded the man himself as her prey. She was searching for him, although she had no idea who or where he was.

She might even be armed. In any case, she was hardly helpless and defenseless. This was to be a formidable challenge, and the man felt honored and proud about that.

Pan believes in me.

At last he fully believes in me.

He felt humbled, too—and daunted, in spite of himself.

He reached into the satchel and fingered the tools he'd brought with him—the wooden hooves, the mallet for hammering hoofmarks into the victim's body, and the cord he'd always used for strangulation.

There was so much he didn't yet know.

For example, what was he supposed to do with the body tonight? He hadn't packed a shovel in his van for a burial because he was going to take her to his freezer as he'd done before. He had no idea how long it would be before he buried her or before he revealed the whereabouts of the body. But so far, he had no specific orders.

Seeming to hear his unspoken question, Pan spoke to him in his soft, whistling voice.

"No. No freezer. No burial. No messages to the foolish police. Not tonight. Tonight will be different. Tonight my true reign shall begin."

The man felt his nerves and sinews surging with power and excitement. That's why Pan had chosen this special victim, an FBI agent, a woman whose death would be known beyond this mere community. This death would strike fear into the wider world.

"Then tonight is the night?" he murmured aloud to Pan. "The night when it comes to pass—your apocalyptic panic?"

"Yes. My name will circle the globe. I shall be 'all' indeed."

The man almost wept tears of joy. But he knew that, somehow, he mustn't let his passion get the best of him. That wouldn't be easy, for he'd yearned for this special night ever since he'd been a child—ever since the only time he'd ever met Pan face to face.

He'd been lost for two days in the woods when his friends had abandoned him there one Halloween after filling his mind with "Goatman" stories. His canteen soon ran dry, and for two whole days and nights he'd had no food, the nights had gotten cold, and he'd gotten no sleep. He'd given up hope and settled against a tree to wait for his death until…

Pan had appeared!

The lost boy had seen the goat-god standing right in front of him, with his impish face and curving horns and hairy legs that ended in cloven feet. Pan had played him a happy melody on his pipe—a melody that filled him with the courage to live.

"Fear not," Pan had told him. *"You are to be the servant of my will."*

Soon after that the search and rescue team had arrived. It had taken him weeks to get back his health and strength. He had never told a single soul about his meeting with the god. He would never have thought of it.

After all, it was a sacred secret. He'd known ever since then that a special destiny was in store for him. His was to be a lonely but noble fate.

And tonight that fate would be fully realized!

Tonight he would see Pan again and stand at his right hand!

The man kept watching the young woman, who was herself watching the departing students.

She doesn't know, he thought wistfully.

She doesn't know the role she will play in the Panic of All.

It seemed sad that she would never live to know it.

The partygoers were almost gone. The moment was almost here.

Chapter Thirty Four

The gymnasium lights finally went out. Ann Marie stood watching from the sidewalk as Principal Cody followed the last of the students out of the building. She waited until the remaining cars in the school parking lot drove away. The big building was soon silently silhouetted against the moonlit autumn sky.

Ann Marie sighed deeply. Everybody had left, and there had been no sign of the man she was watching for. Even the streets around the school were quiet now. The stray trick-or-treaters must have given up and gone home. She knew she ought to feel relieved that all the kids seemed to be safely on their way home, but she was struggling with a sense of futility.

It's over, she thought. *I waited out here for nothing.*

Even so, she decided to take one more foot patrol around the building just to be sure that all the activity had ended.

As she left the sidewalk and headed across the parking lot, Ann Marie wondered if she should have stationed herself somewhere else tonight. She'd come to Pater High School on her own, and when Sheriff Wainwright had asked her to stay, that's what she'd done. Now it seemed extremely unlikely that she would play any kind of a part in the killer's capture—if he even *was* going to be captured tonight

She doubted that he would be. So far, there had been no news of any arrest or even dangerous activity, nothing more than the ordinary Halloween pranks.

Ironically, it was as though the curfew was finally in effect.

Agent Paige's plan struck her as less and less sound the more she thought about it. Was Ann Marie's senior right in thinking that the news of the killer's capture would provoke the real killer into action—and maybe sloppiness?

Ann Marie knew all about Agent Paige's celebrated instincts. But she had taken her share of psychology courses at the academy, and based on what she'd learned, she questioned her senior partner's theory. She thought it more likely that the killer would breathe a sigh of relief at the law's mistake and lie low for a while, maybe even until next year.

But what do I know?

For all she knew, the killer had been caught already but no announcement had been made. If so, how would she even find out about it? Agent Paige probably didn't even know she was back in Winneway—unless Sheriff Wightman had told her. And if Agent Paige *did* find out about her return, of course she'd be furious.

Maybe even with good reason, Ann Marie thought.

What did she think she was doing, anyway? When she'd called Sheriff Wightman, she'd probably distracted him from whatever he'd been doing at the time, and Agent Paige would certainly be distracted if she found out she was here.

Distractions were the last things the team needed right now.

They really needed to focus.

Face facts, kid, she told herself. *It's time to get out of everyone's way.*

Should she maybe check back into the motel where she and Agent Paige had been staying and get a good night's sleep before driving back to Quantico? No, that might mean running into Agent Paige in the morning. And that was about the last thing Ann Marie wanted.

The best thing to do was drive back tonight.

But as she came around the side of the building, something caught her peripheral vision.

She turned quickly to look.

All she saw was the building still standing there in stern, stony silence, looking darker by the moment.

I'm sure I saw something, she told herself.

She stared some more until she glimpsed a fleck of light through the gym windows. From where she stood, it looked like a firefly wafting about inside, popping into view and then out again.

It looked too small and weak to be a regular flashlight.

Was it maybe the little flashlight from someone's cell phone?

If so, who was in there, and why?

She stood there staring until her eyes felt strained, but she didn't see the moving light again. She began to doubt her own eyes.

Probably just a trick of the light, she thought.

Maybe it was just a reflection from a nearby streetlamp.

Still, it made Ann Marie distinctly uneasy.

As she continued on her way around the building, she took out her own pocket flashlight and shined it ahead of her. Everything was quiet, but when she came near a side entrance something looked odd about one of those doors. When she checked, she saw that one of the doors was propped slightly open. A book had been placed there, preventing the door from completely closing.

Her heart beat faster.

Someone seemed to have deliberately kept the door from shutting and locking.

Did that mean someone was in the building—someone who wasn't supposed to be in there?

Ann Marie thought about maybe calling Agent Paige or Sheriff Wightman.

But what if they sent backup over what turned out to be nothing at all, wasting precious time and manpower? Did she really want to face Agent Paige's wrath over such a distraction? Worse, did she want to *cause* another distraction when so much was at stake?

She pushed the door open and stepped inside. Everything seemed quiet. Not wanting to make any noise, she let the door close softly against the book and stood there for a moment, listening. She could hear no one moving about inside. She didn't want to call out and ask whether anyone was there.

She realized that the hallway in front of her was dimly lit by a pale overhead light, so she turned off her little flashlight and pocketed it. Even in the weak light, she could see that this hallway connected with another and there were probably plenty of places to hide. Announcing her presence would give whoever might be here a chance to do that, and Ann Marie would surely never find him.

Glad to be wearing soft-soled shoes, Ann Marie managed to walk so quietly that she could barely hear her own footsteps. As she approached a spot where the hallway branched into a T, she thought she heard something odd. She stopped in her tracks and watched and listened. There seemed to be a faint glow, as if from a stronger flashlight, from around the left corner.

Then she definitely heard a peculiar, unsettling sound. It was some kind of hissing.

Someone was right around that corner, doing something weird.

Now would be a good time to call out and ask who's there, she realized.

But she hadn't known until just this moment just how scared she'd gotten.

Her breath was coming in short, shallow gasps, and she was shaking all over.

If she tried to say anything now, it would come out in some sort of weak-sounding croak.

That wouldn't be good, she decided.

Instead she drew her weapon, struggling to control how it shook in her hands. Then she stepped past the hallway corner, pointed her weapon, and called out in a voice so strong and firm it surprised her.

"FBI! Let me see your hands!"

She heard a clatter of metal fall to the floor.

It took a moment for her to absorb what she was looking at.

One teenaged boy had been spraying graffiti on a row of lockers, while another had been holding a flashlight so he could see what he was doing. At Ann Marie's appearance, they'd dropped both the spray can and the flashlight, and now they stood with their hands high and their eyes wide and their mouths hanging open.

"Holy shit!" one of the boys said.

"What are you doing here?" the other said.

Ann Marie breathed deeply, at once disappointed and relieved.

"You're the ones who'd better answer that question," she said.

Holstering her weapon, she shone her flashlight on the lockers, which were scrawled with seemingly random patterns of spray paint.

"We didn't mean any harm," one of the boys said.

Ann Marie said, "You mean, no harm except to vandalize public property."

One of the boys smirked and replied, "Hey, it's Halloween."

He sounded as though that explained and justified everything. The other one didn't look nearly so cocky.

Ann Marie quickly assessed the kinds of kids she was dealing with. One was a real smart-ass who thought he was tough and cool, while the other was his sheep-like follower.

"Tell me how this happened," Ann Marie said.

The smart-ass kid shrugged, looking rather proud of himself.

"I hid in my gym locker until the party was over," he said. "Then I came out and stuck a book in the side door so Saul here could get into the school too."

The kid named Saul said nervously, "This whole thing was Barry's idea."

Ann Marie stifled a groan of annoyance.

"And what if Barry's idea was to jump off a cliff?" she said.

Saul looked embarrassed by the question.

"Please don't arrest us," he said in a pathetic voice.

Ann Marie replied with a silent scowl.

Saul said, "You're not *going* to arrest us, are you?"

Barry kept smirking like he thought it might be cool to spend a night in jail. Ann Marie doubted he'd enjoy it much if it happened for real.

She had a good mind to march both of these guys out of the school to her car and drive them straight to the police station. She only had one set of handcuffs, but she could slap those on smart-ass Barry, and she was sure Saul would come along quietly.

But she felt like that would be a waste of time right now. And besides, she didn't need to arrest the kids to make sure they didn't get away with this.

"Let me see some ID, guys," she said.

The kids showed her their school ID cards. Saul's last name was Blessing, and Barry's last name was Forster. Ann Marie made a mental note of those names and handed the cards back to the kids.

"I'm telling Sheriff Wightman about this," she said. "He can figure out what he wants to do about it. Now get out of here before I change my mind about arresting you."

The two kids scurried away toward the door they'd come in by.

Ann Marie leaned against a row of lockers, trying to decide what to do next. All she knew at the moment was that she was glad she hadn't arrested the kids. She didn't want her first-ever solo arrest for the BAU to be a couple of teenaged punks spraying graffiti.

Meanwhile, she figured she might as well have a look around to see if anyone else was in the building. She drew her gun again and continued on down the hallway, but soon realized that the school complex spread in all directions and it wouldn't be possible to check the whole building. The halls were silent now, and Ann Marie felt truly alone in the dark maze. The creepiness of the place was really getting to her, and she felt more than ready to get out of there. She went back the way she'd come in until she got to the side door.

To her annoyance, she saw that the book was still there holding the door cracked open. The kids had obviously left without stopping to pick it up, so the door hadn't closed and locked.

"Kids," Ann Marie muttered with disgust.

She reached down to move the book out of the opening, but before she could touch it, the door flew open. Someone rammed into her, throwing her sprawling on the floor and sending the gun flying out of her hands.

Before Ann Marie could recover, a large and strong person was upon her, gripping her by the throat.

She heard a voice murmur, "Pan is waiting."

It's him! she realized.

The junior agent's academy training kicked in, overcoming even her terror. She struck out, twisted violently, and managed to get out from under her attacker.

As she struggled to her feet, she glimpsed his large, dark form as he stood up to block the doorway.

With no way out in front of her, Ann Marie whirled and ran madly into the dim maze of school hallways.

Chapter Thirty Five

Riley kept staring into the surrounding darkness of the cemetery until her eyes were tired. The truth was finally dawning on her.

My hunch was wrong.

The proximity of the gravestone to where Allison Hillis had been abducted was purely a coincidence. The killer probably didn't even know where the marker was. Her notion that he'd come to it as a shrine had been way off.

It's time to report in to Wightman, she thought.

She took out her cell phone and got the sheriff on the line.

"There's nothing at the cemetery," she told him. "Please tell me that you and your cops have had better luck."

"I wish I could," Wightman replied. "My guys are too busy getting civilians off the street to seriously look for the killer—if he's really out tonight, which I doubt. I'm afraid we're not going to get him, at least not tonight. What do you want to do next?"

Riley stifled a sigh.

She said, "It's getting near time to call it a night. Give your team another hour. Then call them all back to the station, and we'll send them home."

"OK," Wightman said. "I talked to your partner a little while ago. Do you want me to contact her, or do you want to do it yourself?"

Riley squinted with surprise.

"My partner?" she asked.

"Yeah. The last time I talked to her, she was over at the high school. There was a party going on there, and she was keeping watch to make sure everybody there stayed safe. Do you want to call her, or should I?"

Riley stammered, "Uh . . . I'll do it."

They end the call and Riley stood staring at her cell phone.

Ann Marie is still in Winneway.

With a burst of sheer animal terror, Ann Marie fled down the hallway.

Don't panic, she told herself.

But she'd lost her gun and a madman was chasing her. She didn't dare look back to see how close he was. She couldn't even hear his footsteps over the sound of her own.

She just had to keep moving.

I've got to get a grip on myself. I've got to think.

What was there to think about? What sort of plan could she come up with? What was there to do except run and try to stay away from her pursuer?

The hallway seemed to stretch longer in front of her, and she thought she was moving much too slowly.

She knew he could see her. The dim, intermittent ceiling lights gave her enough light to run by—but also enough light for the killer to see her by. The throb of her pulse felt like both her head and her chest were about to explode.

Her soft soles skidded and she almost lost her balance as she whirled and turned at the first hallway corner she came to.

Had he seen her make that last turn?

Surely he must have.

But she still didn't dare slow down to look behind her.

She ran until she came to another corner and turned again. It dawned on her that she was running blind. She didn't know the layout of the school, and in this maze of hallways, the killer could be either in front of her or behind her. Tearing through the hallways like this was pointless. For all she knew, she might be running directly into his clutches.

Ann Marie slowed to a walk and struggled to bring her breathing under control, listening as well as she could. If he was anywhere nearby, she couldn't see or hear him.

She fumbled in her pocket for her cell phone, hoping she could call for backup, or at least punch 911 for help. But then she felt a new jolt of panic as a gleeful voice echoed around her.

"Why are you running? There's no need to run."

She flattened herself against the row of lockers along the wall as the voice spoke again. Where was he? What could she do?

"Pan just wants to be friendly," the voice said.

The eerie voice seemed to be both everywhere and nowhere. Try as she might, Ann Marie simply couldn't tell which direction it was coming from.

"You dropped something. A gun, I believe. Pan and I just want to give it back."

Ann Marie stifled a moan of despair.

My gun, she thought. *He's got my gun.*

And who on earth did he mean by "Pan"?

Did he have someone else with him—an accomplice of some sort? Suddenly the stakes in this chase seemed much more dire than even before. She had some vague recollection of a mythological figure with that name, but she couldn't pin it down.

"You can trust me," her pursuer said. "I would never shoot you. That isn't Pan's style."

His words were obviously meant in a mocking way.

No, he wouldn't shoot me.

Her pursuer surely had a much crueler death in mind. And since he'd killed at least four other people, she knew better than to underestimate either his prowess or his viciousness. He knew how to hunt as well as how to kill.

Staying tight against the wall, she crept around another corner.

She felt a surge of hope at the sight of an EXIT sign at the far end of this hallway.

A way out! she thought.

She broke into a run again. But this time, she heard a clanging sound and a masked figure leapt in her way. It was the very man she'd been fleeing.

Where had he come from?

Then she saw a large locker door hanging open, and she remembered the kid named Saul mentioning that he'd hidden in a locker.

That was exactly what her pursuer had done. As she'd feared, he'd circled around to get ahead of her and waited there for her. He obviously knew these hallways well.

She stood frozen in place, staring at him. Now that she got a good look at him, she recognized his werewolf mask, and also the leather satchel slung over his shoulder. It was the man she'd confronted a little while ago outside the school.

I should have known, she thought. *I should have been aware that he was dangerous even back then.*

A voice from behind the mask demanded, "What are you going to do now, little girl?"

Ann Marie was sure there was a sneer behind that mask, and she heard a note of challenge in that voice.

He considers it my move, she realized.

He was standing squarely in front of her, just waiting for her to do something. But Ann Marie was paralyzed with indecisiveness. The EXIT sign at the end of the hallway suddenly looked much farther away than it had before. She almost turned around to break into another mad dash away from him.

But then she felt a surge of resolve.

She remembered how she'd taken down Brad Cribbins yesterday. Even Agent Paige had admitted that Ann Marie had pretty good fighting skills. Those Krav Maga classes she'd taken in high school had really paid off.

Eyeing the EXIT sign, Ann Marie decided that she wasn't going to run away from the killer.

I'll run right through him.

She broke into a run again, toward her tormenter this time. Everything seemed to slow down as she got closer. With her every step, he looked bigger and stronger and more dangerous. Then everything lurched to a halt as she smashed into him.

It was like running into a brick wall.

Staggering backward, she flashed back to one of the main rules of Krav Maga.

Use any object you can get your hands on.

She knew that the leather satchel was hanging by a strap from the man's soldier. With a swift, deft move, she snatched it away from off his arm. When he lunged to take it back, she ducked down low and slung the strap between his feet, then scrambled crablike around him. When he tried to take another couple of steps, his feet became entangled with the strap and he stumbled badly.

Ann Marie gave him a sharp kick to the chest, and this time he toppled backward. She briefly considered leaping on him and trying to pummel him. But now that she had an idea of his size and strength, she didn't dare.

Instead, she turned and ran again. But she realized she was moving away from the exit she had spotted, rather than toward it.

And now the familiar ugly voice rang through the hallway behind her.

"Really, now. All this violence isn't necessary. Pan is quite put off by it."

Pan again, she thought, as she fled around yet another corner.

I've got to hide.

She glanced to her left and saw that she was standing next to a classroom door. She grabbed the doorknob and turned it and yanked it. She was hardly surprised that the door was locked. She hurried to the next classroom door and found it was locked as well. Then she rushed to a third door, expecting the same results.

But this time the door came open.

She could hardly believe her luck.

At that very moment, she heard his voice behind her.

"I see you!"

She charged through the door and shut it behind her. Leaning against the inside of the door, she fumbled for a lock, but she didn't find anything she could turn with her fingers. Her mind raced, trying to sort some kind of logic to offset her fear. She was pretty sure now that the man had come here alone. So who the hell was Pan? His imaginary friend?

Something from her psychology classes dawned on her...

Yes. That's exactly what Pan is.

She was dealing with a psychotic who experienced hallucinations. And like many psychotics, this one had serious delusions of self-importance—and possibly supernatural power. He was even more dangerous than she had imagined.

I've got to keep him from coming in here, she thought.

She grabbed a chair and shoved the back of it under the doorknob, but before she could get it braced in place, the door flew open and the chair went flying. Her pursuer came hurtling into the room with her.

Ann Marie turned to flee, but she was stunned to find herself face to face with a grinning face... a human skull.

It took her a fraction of a second to realize where she was.

A science classroom.

The skull was part of a complete human skeleton that was hanging from a stand.

She grabbed the skeleton and slung it toward the man as she dashed around to the other side of a big lab table. Glancing back, she caught a glimpse of him colliding with the strange figure, looking almost comical as he wrestled with the rattling bundle of bones.

But she knew the skeleton wasn't going to slow him down. She grabbed beakers and test tubes and hurled them at him wildly. He raised his hands to protect his eyes, and she made a rush toward the door, pushing a large desk between her and her pursuer as she fled the way she'd come.

In an instant, Ann Marie was careening through the maze of hallways again. She'd long since lost any sense of direction and had no idea where she was. As she turned down one hallway, she saw an open doorway at its end. When she ran through it, she found herself on the stage of a school auditorium.

She felt relieved at the sight of the rows and rows of seats extending beyond the stage. Perhaps she could disappear among them and stay hidden until he gave up searching for her.

Like that's going to happen, she thought with a groan.

Then she heard his voice from behind her again.

"A stage-struck little girl, are we?"

She spun around and saw him standing in the doorway through which she'd just come. She knew it was no good trying to hide among the auditorium seats now that he could see her. She whirled and saw another door, yanked it open, and dashed into total darkness.

Ann Marie found herself suddenly tangled and tumbling in some sort of soft, chaotic mass of material. Before she could work herself free, a light snapped on, momentarily blinding her.

Then she saw that she was in the school's theater storage room, full of costumes and props and even masks. She'd tumbled into a rack of costumes and was now struggling on the floor trying to pull herself loose from them.

The man was standing in the doorway now. He'd flicked on the light switch, and he'd lifted his mask to reveal an insanely grinning, wild-eyed face that seemed scarcely more real than the mask itself.

He let out a laugh and said, "Pan has chosen the perfect spot."

Ann Marie was too tangled to pull herself loose. And in a flash, the man was upon her, and he had looped a cord around her neck and she couldn't breathe.

As he ruthlessly tightened the cord, he spoke in a gleeful whisper.

"Pan's will be done."

Ann Marie felt the whole world disappearing around her.

Chapter Thirty Six

It only took Riley Paige a moment to realize that her junior partner was in terrible danger—if she wasn't dead already. With a yell of fury, she rushed up behind the crouching man and threw her arm around his neck, yanking him fiercely backward away from his intended victim.

As they staggered together, she realized that he was startlingly large and bulky and not as affected by her charge as she had expected. He was regaining his balance and she was struggling with her own. Riley knew she had a desperate fight on her hands, and there was no time to properly assess the situation.

A glance to the side told her that Ann Marie was still lying motionless in a pile of colorful costume clothing and broken stage props, her face bluish from the man's attempt to strangle her.

Am I too late? Riley wondered fearfully.

Her fleeting inattention to her target was costly. She found herself reeling from a sudden crack to the right side of her head. The man had punched her, and although it had been a glancing blow, she was momentarily dizzy and disoriented. His grinning, wild-eyed face seemed to be swimming in front of her.

"Oh, Pan is generous tonight!" he said. "He already gave me one life to take, and now he has honored me with another!"

Pan? Riley wondered as she recovered her wits.

And was Ann Marie already dead?

She launched a punch at him, but he intercepted it and clutched her wrist in a vise-like grip.

He's strong, she thought. *Too strong.*

She twisted her elbow sharply inward, and the man lost his grip on her wrist. He threw another punch at her, but she ducked low, then rushed into what seemed like a jungle of props and clothes hanging from racks.

She quickly realized she was tangled up in fabric and had no idea where she was. But as the man kept trying to punch her, the clothing served as a buffer to keep any of his blows from landing. Still engulfed by a whirl of costumes, she somehow managed to wade clear of his punches. At least the blows had stopped coming.

She managed to disentangle herself until she was standing between two costume racks. She realized that she wasn't going to be able to take this one in by simple physical force. She might not even be able to take him in alive.

Riley drew her weapon.

But where is he?

As if in reply, she heard his voice call out, "It's no use trying to defy the power of Pan."

She flashed back to what she had long ago read about mythology.

Of course, she thought. *Pan is the goat-god.*

Then he burst through the clothing at her, a fair distance away from her. Riley raised her weapon and fired, hitting him in the shoulder. He looked vaguely surprised, then let out of a roar of fury. He staggered toward her again, and she fired again, hitting him in the thigh this time.

Even though one foot was dragging badly now, he barely seemed to even notice.

He was limping toward her.

Reluctantly, Riley raised her gun higher and fired directly into his rib cage.

With a look of shock on his face, he toppled to his knees.

Groaning with pain, he cried, "Help me, Pan. Don't forsake me. I won't fail you. I'm always faithful to you. Just… stay faithful to *me*. Don't let me go down in defeat."

Then he tumbled over onto his face.

Riley looked around among the heaps of costumes lying everywhere until she spotted Ann Marie again. She was coughing, and the color was returning to her face.

She's alive, Riley thought with relief, holstering her weapon.

⚜ ⚜ ⚜

In a matter of minutes, paramedics arrived at the auditorium in response to Riley's emergency call. Riley watched as they lifted the killer up from the costume-strewn floor and loaded him onto a gurney.

Meanwhile, one of the paramedics was checking out Ann Marie, who was seated nearby. The younger agent looked somewhat shaken up but not at all badly hurt.

Riley asked the medic, "Is my partner going to be all right?"

He nodded at Riley. "She's going to be fine. I'd recommend that she come along with us to the hospital for some observation—"

Ann Marie interrupted sharply, "I'm fine. I'm not going anywhere."

The medic shrugged.

"Have it your way," he said. "We've got our hands full with this other guy."

The medic joined his colleagues in tending to the killer, who had taken three wounds from Riley's handgun. Riley was amazed that he was still alive.

Riley walked over to Ann Marie and put her hand on her shoulder.

"You probably ought to go to the hospital," Riley said. "One of these days you're going to learn to respect authority."

"I guess I ought to do that," Ann Marie said.

Then she squinted at Riley and said, "You just called me your partner."

Riley chuckled. "I guess I did at that."

"Wow," Ann Marie said. Then the rookie shuddered. "I guess I'd be dead now if you hadn't shown up."

"Probably," Riley said.

"How did you know where I was?"

Riley stifled a sigh. She didn't feel like getting into details about how she'd wound up here. For one thing, she felt rather embarrassed about her long stay in the cemetery.

She explained to Ann Marie, "I called the sheriff. He told me you were here. Then I tried to call you, and when you didn't answer, I got worried and drove over here. I didn't see you anywhere outside. I walked around the school until I found a door that was propped open by a book. I came inside and heard a ruckus somewhere inside the building."

Riley shrugged and added, "It wasn't hard to find where all that noise was coming from."

Riley heard voices nearby. Then Sheriff Wightman and several of his cops came into the costume and prop storage room. The paramedics were getting ready to roll the killer out on a gurney. Riley saw Wightman's eyes widen with alarm and worry as he saw the man's face.

He leaned over the gurney and said, "Taylor! What happened to you? Are you all right?"

In a hoarse voice the killer replied, "Pan will be revenged."

"Pan?" Wightman said.

Before the killer could make any effort to reply, one of the medics put an oxygen mask over his face, then wheeled him out of the room. Wightman stared after the gurney with his mouth hanging open.

Riley said to Wightman, "Do you know that guy?"

"Yeah, I've known him for years," Wightman said. "That's Taylor Voigts. What happened to him? What was he talking about 'Pan' for?"

"He's the killer," Riley said. "I had to shoot him in order to stop him from killing Agent Esmer."

Wightman stared at Riley wide-eyed.

"My God," he said.

"How do you happen to know him?" Riley said.

"He owns the Calico Deli. My cops and I eat lunch there a lot. He's lived in this town all his life. Went to this very high school."

A deli, Riley thought.

That probably explained the frozen bodies. A deli owner might well own more than one large freezer chest. Perhaps he kept one of those chests away from public view—in the deli basement, maybe.

Riley said, "Did you have any idea there was anything wrong with him?"

Wightman scratched his head. "Well, he's always been kind of odd. He runs a nice business, and he's never seemed like a bad sort, but he's always been awfully nervous and kind of cranky. I seem to remember hearing that he went through some kind of trauma as a kid that maybe he didn't get over."

"I'm sure he'll tell us more now that he's in custody," Riley said.

Looking somewhat dazed, Wightman followed after the paramedics, leaving Riley and Ann Marie alone in the cluttered room.

Ann Marie hung her head and said, "I guess I really screwed up, huh?"

Riley let out a chuckle. "Well, I guess that depends on how you look at it. You're the one who said it was a bad idea to try to taunt the killer. You were right, and I was wrong. Don't let it go to your head, though. And I'm not wild about how you snuck back here without telling me. You almost got yourself killed. But…"

Riley shrugged and said, "It worked out OK. The killer came after you instead of someone else. And now we've got him. All told, I'd say you did a pretty good job for a rookie. We're not a bad team."

Ann Marie beamed proudly. She tried to get up from the chair, but still seemed a little wobbly.

That's no surprise, Riley thought.

Riley helped her get up and said, "Come on, let's get out of here. We could both use a snack and a good night's sleep."

CHAPTER THIRTY SEVEN

A while later, Riley realized that her younger partner could barely keep her eyes open. Ann Marie's eyelids were drooping and her head was nodding. They were sitting in a diner where they'd ordered sandwiches and coffee. Riley was hungry, and she had eaten her own sandwich eagerly, but Ann Marie seemed to have little appetite and only nibbled at hers.

"I don't remember ever being this tired," Ann Marie mumbled.

Riley smiled at how she sounded almost like she was talking in her sleep.

"I'll bet," Riley said. "You've had one hell of a night. Come on, let's get back to our rooms. You need to get some sleep."

Ann Marie had already returned her rented car, and Riley drove them to the motel in the FBI vehicle they'd been using all along. She escorted her exhausted partner into her room and watched as she flopped down on her bed and went straight to sleep.

Riley went back to her own room, but she'd just gotten inside when her phone buzzed.

She saw that the call was from Sheriff Wightman.

"I hope I'm not calling too late," he said.

"No, it's fine," Riley said, eager to hear whatever news he might want to share.

"I'm at the hospital with Taylor Voigts. You'd never believe he'd been shot three times."

An image flashed through Riley's mind of the big man lurching relentlessly toward her, even when he'd been shot twice and was dragging one foot. She'd seldom faced that kind of manic persistence.

The sheriff continued, "He's been talking nonstop all this time, saying the craziest things you can imagine."

"I'll bet," Riley said.

"He says that Goatman is really the god Pan, and that he's Pan's servant, and that this is just some temporary setback. Pan will prevail, he says, and some kind of apocalyptic 'panic' is still on its way. He also told us where he'd buried Henry Studdard and Deena McHugh. My guys and I will check out those locations tomorrow."

"I'm sure you'll find the bodies there," Riley said.

She heard the sheriff take a long, slow breath. She knew he wasn't looking forward to that grim task.

"He's also told us about that childhood trauma I mentioned," Wightman said. "One Halloween, he went out on a camping trip with some older pals. They decided to play a prank on him. They told him a lot of scary Goatman stories, then left him alone in the woods in the dark. It was just supposed to be some kind of initiation thing. But Taylor got lost, and it took two whole days before a search team could find him. He never seemed to quite get over it..."

Wightman's voice faded away.

Then he added, "I guess that explains the whole thing, huh?"

Riley's mind boggled at how such an experience could traumatize a child, probably for life.

"It's a start, anyway," Riley said.

Then Wightman said, "I can't thank you and your partner enough for how you've taken care of this. If it weren't for you two, someone else would probably be dead by now. God knows how long it would have taken to stop this guy."

Riley smiled and said, "I think my partner deserves your thanks more than I do. I made my share of mistakes this time out. She's the one who finally located the killer."

Even if she almost got herself killed in the process, she thought.

"Well, let her know I'm grateful," Wightman said. "You two have a safe drive back to Quantico tomorrow."

"We'll do that," Riley said.

She ended the call and found herself thinking about Taylor Voigts, the ordinary town businessman who'd turned out to be a serial killer. She remembered the madness in his eyes when they'd struggled earlier tonight. She was sure that his lawyer would plead not guilty on the basis of insanity.

Riley normally hated insanity defenses. But in this case, she couldn't disagree. Taylor Voigts was hopelessly insane. All that mattered to Riley was that he be put away for a very long time. He would probably spend the rest of his life in some kind of mental institution. He'd never be a threat to the public again.

Riley took a long, hot shower and put on her pajamas. She came out of the bathroom and sent a text message home to tell April, Jilly, and Gabriela that the case was finished and she'd be driving back home tomorrow morning.

Then she opened her laptop computer and to her FBI email account for one last time tonight. Among a routine batch of company memos, she saw an email from an unknown address with a cryptic subject line.

To RP from JR

She realized with a start what the initials "JR" might stand for.

Jenn Roston!

Her hands were shaking as she opened the email, which was written in all caps in a peculiar, telegraph-like style.

RILEY. I NEVER MEANT TO GET BACK IN TOUCH WITH YOU. I KNEW IT MIGHT BE COMPROMISING TO YOU. BUT NOW I FEEL THAT I MUST, IF ONLY OUT OF GRATITUDE FOR EVERYTHING YOU DID FOR ME. I KNOW YOU THINK I HAVE GONE BACK TO A.C. AND HER CRIME NETWORK. I DID NOT. I GOT CLEAR OF HER FOREVER. THANKS TO YOU, I FEEL THAT I CAN START LIFE ALL OVER AGAIN. IT WILL BE WITH A NEW NAME IN A NEW PLACE. YOU WILL NEVER FIND ME. BUT PLEASE KNOW THAT I AM ALL RIGHT.

J.R.

Riley immediately knew what the initials "A.C." stood for.

Aunt Cora.

Riley felt a lump of emotion rise in her throat as she reread another sentence.

YOU WILL NEVER FIND ME.

Her eyes stinging with tears, Riley climbed into bed.

"It's over," she murmured aloud, wiping her eyes with a tissue. "I'll never see Jenn again."

But just as she started to fall asleep, another sentence echoed through her head.

THANKS TO YOU, I FEEL THAT I CAN START LIFE ALL OVER AGAIN.

"She's going to be OK," Riley whispered aloud, then fell asleep.

Chapter Thirty Eight

The next morning, Riley felt a strange mix of emotions as she parked in front of her townhouse in Fredericksburg. For a few moments, she just sat in her car staring at her house, thinking about a lot of things. She was glad to be home, of course. But her home life was very different from her life as a BAU agent, and it always required some readjustment. Was she ready to start being a mother again right here and now, when just yesterday she'd shot a madman three times?

She'd had no time to unwind—and no real time to herself—since the killer had been caught. The drive back from Winneway had seemed much longer than it really was, and she'd been grateful to finally drop Ann Marie off at her apartment in Quantico. Her junior partner had obviously gotten a better night's sleep than Riley had, and this morning she'd been her usual perky, talkative self. She'd chattered away about an indiscriminate range of subjects, including the case they'd just solved, crime fighting techniques, the latest fashions, celebrity gossip, and popular music.

Again Riley had found herself wondering whether she could really keep working with this young woman. She had to admit that the girl had done excellent work on the case—better than Riley's own efforts in some ways. At least Ann Marie hadn't made any huge mistakes, like risking the public's safety by misleading them about having the killer in custody. In fact, Ann Marie had rightly called Riley out on that tactic.

All the same, Riley wondered whether she and Ann Marie could ever feel the chemistry she'd had with Bill, or with her two other young protégés, Lucy Vargas and Jenn Roston

With a sudden surge of emotion, Riley spoke the two names aloud.

"Lucy and Jenn."

She'd shared a lot with them, had been proud of their work and their promising talents, and had developed deep nearly-parental feelings for them…

And now they're both gone.

What might become of Ann Marie if Riley kept working with her?

All Riley knew right now was that she missed working with Bill terribly. But was that partnership even going to be possible now that their relationship was evolving into—what, exactly?

Riley also found herself brooding about her pointless vigil in the cemetery. She felt embarrassed about that mistake—embarrassed and worried.

Were her well-known instincts, her keenly honed gut feelings, starting to fail from age and overuse?

Maybe it's time to do something different, she thought.

She finally got out of her car and walked up to her front door. When she reached her front stoop, the door flew open.

Riley felt a wild rush of horror.

The figure in front of her appeared to be a walking corpse, its face falling apart from decay, and naked ribs showing through its tattered jacket.

For several seconds, Riley believed she was caught in one of her awful nightmares.

Then the corpse spoke in a familiar voice.

"Cool costume, isn't it, Mom?"

The mask came off, and Riley saw Jilly's happy face.

Jilly said, "It's what I wore last night trick-or-treating. I put it back on this morning, just for you. It was April's idea. She thought you'd get a kick out of seeing it."

Riley felt a burst of relief.

"Yeah, it's… uh… cool," she stammered. "I'm—I'm really impressed."

"Come on inside," Jilly said. "April has breakfast all ready."

"April?" Riley asked. "Is Gabriela all right?"

"Sure," Jilly replied with a giggle. "But April wanted to do it."

The delicious smell of bacon wafted through the house, and Riley realized that she actually was hungry. As she followed Jilly into the kitchen, Riley thought about how she'd reacted at the sight of her daughter's costume just now. Her moment of shock had been silly, but she knew it was partly the result of having seen two corpses in much the same condition during the last few days. But surely she wouldn't have let herself be startled this way back when she'd been at the peak of her abilities.

An odd sort of silence fell as Riley and her family—Jilly, April, and Gabriela—sat down together and started eating.

Finally, April said cautiously, "Mom, I think there's something you should know."

Riley's heart beat faster with apprehension.

Then April confessed that she'd tried to go the party Riley had forbidden her to attend. Worse, she had taken Jilly with her. Before they'd gotten to the party, they'd been threatened by a couple of bullies.

"But you should have seen Jilly, Mom," April added. "She really beat the crap out of one of the guys. They both ran away, scared out their minds."

Riley couldn't help but smile at the image of her small daughter in a zombie suit fending off a couple of obnoxious guys.

She said to Jilly, "It sounds like you handled it well."

Then she added to April, "And I'm glad you told me what happened. Telling me was the right thing to do. It was a brave thing to do."

April smiled broadly.

"Does this mean I'm not grounded anymore?"

Riley mulled that over. April had been honest but she had broken the rules, or been about to. She was about to say "still grounded for a little while" when her phone buzzed. Seeing that the call was from Brent Meredith, she left the kitchen before answering.

Meredith said sharply, "Agent Paige, you need to get over here right now."

"What's the matter?" Riley asked.

"Walder's what's the matter," Meredith said. "He's furious with you about something. He wants to see you in the conference room right now. Right this minute. Whatever is wrong, it's serious, Agent Paige."

Meredith ended the call without saying another word.

Riley stared at the silent phone for a moment as though it could tell her what turn her life was taking now, then went back into the kitchen to tell her family that she had to go.

⚜ ⚜ ⚜

When Riley walked into the spacious conference room to meet with Special Agent in Charge Carl Walder, she found her baby-faced superior on his feet and pacing the floor.

Riley gulped hard.

This really is *serious,* she thought.

"I'll get right to the point, Agent Paige," Walder said, waving a piece of paper that he held in his hand. "I want to know who this 'A.C.' is."

Riley squinted with surprise.

A.C.? she wondered.

Then she flashed back to the message she'd received last night.

Aunt Cora.

Could that possibly be who Walder was talking about?

She said cautiously, "I'm not sure what you mean, sir."

"Oh, I believe you do, Agent Paige," Walder said, pointing to the paper in his hand. "And you also know who 'JR' is. And so do I. It's Special Agent Jenn Roston. And now I know for a fact that you've been concealing information concerning Roston's disappearance."

Riley felt a flash of anger as she realized what was on the printout he was holding.

She said, "You had no business reading that email."

Walder smirked smugly.

"You received it on your FBI account," he said. "Those emails are company property. That makes it my business."

"But why were you reading my emails in the first place?" Riley demanded. She was tired and already having trouble sounding appropriately respectful to the head of BAU.

"I've got my reasons," Walder replied with a smirk.

Reasons? Riley wondered.

Then she remembered the taciturn Senator Danson, who apparently knew Carl Walder. She'd been worried all along that Danson was just another politician who would take any opportunity to contact Walder to complain about progress on the case.

"Has Senator Danson been in touch with you?" Riley asked.

Walder raised an eyebrow with a look of apparently genuine surprise.

"As a matter of fact, he has," Walder said. "He called early this morning to tell me how pleased he was with you. I regretted having to tell him that I didn't share his high regard for you—and that you were about to suffer the consequences of your behavior."

Riley felt swept by confusion now. She hadn't imagined that Danson would call Walder to *compliment* her on her work. But now that she'd thought about it, he'd never actually criticized her to her face. He'd only wanted to know how the case was progressing. And now that it had been solved without a new Halloween murder, he had every reason to think well of her.

Walder continued, "But Danson has nothing to do with the matter at hand. And he has nothing to do with why I felt compelled to monitor your communications."

"So why did you...?"

Riley's voice trailed off as she remembered what Bill had told her yesterday. Walder had eavesdropped on Bill's end of an especially intimate phone conversation.

Suddenly her predicament made much more sense.

Walder had obviously gone poking through her emails hoping to find details of her relationship with Bill. Instead, he'd found the message from Jenn.

Walder began to pace again. He looked at the printout in his hand and read aloud.

"Roston writes, 'You think I have gone back to A.C. and her crime network.' I demand to know who 'A.C.' is, and the nature of your connection with her."

He folded the paper and held Riley's gaze.

"Agent Paige, it's no secret that you've consorted with criminals in the past. Shane Hatcher comes to mind."

Riley bristled at the mention of Hatcher's name. Her relationship with that master criminal had begun as a purely professional matter when Hatcher had offered his expertise to help her with a case. But their relationship had turned into a sinister entanglement that had finally come to a violent end last spring. Walder had never learned all the details of that relationship, but Riley knew he'd been suspicious about it—and not without good reason.

She said, "My relationship with Shane Hatcher has been over for some time now."

"I know. Now you've got a new criminal crony—a certain 'A.C.' And I'm sure your dealings with this person are unsavory, to say the least. And I think you should come clean about it right here and now."

Riley's anger was mounting by the moment.

"I've got nothing to explain to you, sir," she said.

Walder chuckled sardonically.

"No? Well, there's no hurry. You'll have plenty of time to decide how to explain yourself while you're waiting in a holding cell."

Riley gasped aloud.

"Are you saying I'm under arrest?"

Before Walder could reply, his secretary came into the conference room door and spoke to him.

"Sir, I'm sorry to interrupt, but Director Gavin Milner is on the phone. He wants to talk with you."

At the sound of the FBI director's name, Walder's pale, freckled face turned a shade paler.

"Did he say what this is about?" Walder asked.

His secretary said, "No, but he insists on speaking with you right this minute."

"I'll be there in just a moment," Walder said.

Walder turned toward Riley again.

"I'll be back soon," Walder said to her. "This conversation we're having isn't over. Meanwhile, I think you should put your badge and your gun on the table. I'll be taking them shortly."

Walder followed his secretary out of the room.

Riley was completely stunned now. She obediently took out her badge and gun and put them on the table. They had been taken from her before, but always soon returned. Would they be gone for good this time? Even worse, did Walder have any basis for pressing criminal charges against her?

She doubted it. Aside from a single phone call some time back, she'd never had any direct communication with the mysterious Aunt Cora, much less any criminal dealings with her. While it was true that Riley had concealed the truth about Jenn's disappearance, that probably wasn't illegal.

But Walder had been Riley's adversary for years now. She had to admit her sometimes-insubordinate behavior had given him some justification. This time, she had no doubt that he'd succeed.

Riley sat there at the table, just staring at her gun and her badge. As she waited for Walder's return, her whole FBI career seemed to pass in front of her.

She couldn't count the murderous minds she'd thwarted over the years. She remembered one killer who had dressed dead women up like dolls, a young man obsessed with chains, a health worker who poisoned her own patients, a high school coach and his wife who murdered teenaged girls together... and many others. She'd also faced danger and personal trauma, especially when a psychopath named Peterson had caged her like an animal and tortured her with fire. She had struggled with PTSD for a long time after that, but with the help of a psychiatrist friend, she had managed to get back to work.

And she was good at that work. Riley knew she had an outstanding record of success in her cases, even if she had also stirred up some complaints. In just a few years, she could retire from the FBI with a full pension, but if her career ended early at the whims of a petty bureaucrat, she'd face some pressing problems. Her two daughters would be headed for college soon. She had depended on her ex to help with those expenses, but in his debauchery Ryan had lost everything. She'd thought about taking on less field work at the BAU but never considered quitting altogether.

And now...

Her future seemed desperately uncertain.

Chapter Thirty Nine

Riley heard Bill whisper in her ear.

"What are you thinking about?"

Riley snapped out of her reverie and remembered where she was—sitting in a high school auditorium with Bill at her left and Jilly and Gabriela on her right.

This was April's graduation ceremony. Right now someone was giving a speech that Riley hadn't been paying attention to.

She chuckled and whispered back, "I was just thinking of Walder's untimely demise."

Bill chuckled as well.

"I'm glad you were thinking happy thoughts," he said.

Riley had to admit to herself, revenge was sweet.

A year and a half ago, Walder had grilled her in the BAU conference room, threatening to fire her and even to jail her. Riley had long ago learned why he'd been suddenly called away for that phone call from Director Milner—and also the true nature of his relationship with then–State Senator Walker Danson.

It had turned out that Danson and Walder had been enemies for many years, ever since they'd been students at Yale together. Danson had kept close tabs on Walder's career during all the years since then, knowing that he was dishonest and hoping for a chance to trip him up.

Danson's private investigations had revealed that Walder harbored more than his own share of "unsavory" secrets. One of them was a serious gambling problem. Danson had finally found proof that Walder had skimmed off enormous amounts of BAU funds to pay off vicious loan sharks. He'd already reported his discoveries to FBI Director Milner. They'd both been watching Walder closely for several months, to see what else might turn up.

When Danson had called Walder that day to praise Riley for her work, he'd been infuriated to hear that his longtime nemesis planned to fire her. As soon as he'd hung up, Danson had contacted Director Milner to urge him to close in on Walder right away, before he could do further damage to the Quantico office.

Walder had been arrested, and Riley had been reinstated.

Now Walker Danson was in the U.S. Senate, and Brent Meredith was Special Agent in Charge at the BAU.

And Carl Walder was in prison.

Happy thoughts indeed, Riley thought with a smile.

With Walder out of the way, Riley now had true job security at long last. She'd chosen to spend most of her time lecturing and teaching at Quantico instead of working in the field. Whenever she did accept a field assignment, she always insisted upon having Ann Marie Esmer as a partner. They had developed a fine rapport, with Riley serving as Ann Marie's mentor. More than that, they had become great friends.

Just like me and Jake Crivaro, Riley thought.

But Riley's field assignments were few and far between. To her surprise, she hadn't missed the excitement of field work. She'd soon realized she'd put in quite enough time in conflict with crazed minds.

Instead, she had really enjoyed the added time she was able to spend with her girls. They were doing very well. April was headed for Georgetown University this fall, and she had substantial scholarship help for college. She was planning to pursue a psychology degree.

Typically for a girl her age, Jilly was still trying to find her passion in life. But she was doing well enough in school that Riley felt confident that she, too, would get her share of financial help when she headed off to college.

The principal called April's name, and Riley's oldest daughter crossed the stage to pick up her high school diploma.

Riley cheered and applauded, and Bill, Jilly, and Gabriela cheered even louder. Then Riley took hold of Bill's hand and squeezed. She leaned over and kissed him on the cheek.

It was no longer a mystery where things were going between them. Their relationship had deepened and grown over the last year and a half. The addition of a romantic sex life to their strong friendship had bonded them in ways that neither of them had ever imagined. In about another year they would both retire, still in their forties, and then decide what they were going to do with the rest of their lives together.

All in all, Riley Paige felt happier than she'd ever been. She'd had a long and successful career, and the years to come were sure to be even richer and more rewarding.

Life is good, she thought, squeezing Bill's hand again.

A New Series!
Now Available for Pre-Order!

LEFT TO DIE
(An Adele Sharp Mystery–Book One)

"When you think that life cannot get better, Blake Pierce comes up with another masterpiece of thriller and mystery! This book is full of twists and the end brings a surprising revelation. I strongly recommend this book to the permanent library of any reader that enjoys a very well written thriller."

—Books and Movie Reviews, Roberto Mattos (re Almost Gone)

LEFT TO DIE is book #1 in a new FBI thriller series by USA Today bestselling author Blake Pierce, whose #1 bestseller Once Gone (Book #1) (a free download) has received over 1,000 five star reviews.

FBI special agent Adele Sharp is a German-and-French raised American with triple citizenship—and an invaluable asset in bringing criminals to justice as they cross American and European borders.

When a serial killer case spanning three U.S. states goes cold, Adele returns to San Francisco and to the man she hopes to marry. But after a shocking twist, a new lead surfaces and Adele is dispatched to Paris, to lead an international manhunt.

Adele returns to the Europe of her childhood, where familiar Parisian streets, old friends from the DGSI and her estranged father reignite her dormant obsession with solving her own mother's murder. All the while she must hunt down the diabolical killer, must enter the dark canals of his psychotic mind to know where he will strike next—and save the next victim before it's too late.

An action-packed mystery series of international intrigue and riveting suspense, LEFT TO DIE will have you turning pages late into the night.

Books #2 and #3 in the series – LEFT TO RUN and LEFT TO HIDE – are also available for preorder!

LEFT TO DIE
(An Adele Sharp Mystery–Book One)

Made in the USA
Monee, IL
28 May 2022